I0733703

THE HAND OF DESTINY

ANGELO THOMAS CRAPANZANO

ISBN: 978-1-961017-14-6 (sc)
ISBN: 978-1-961017-15-3 (e)

Rev. date: 04/27/2023

DEDICATION

This book is dedicated to all of my brothers and sisters in Christ at West Hill Baptist church.

CONTENTS

CHAPTER ONE

Out of the Blue

On Sunday, Tom went to church as he had done since he and his wife moved to Fairlawn from Cleveland. He went and sat at the seat in the area where he and his wife Rita always sat. Even though Rita had passed away three years ago, Tom still missed her siting besides him. He felt alone sitting there by himself. After the service he walked out into the lobby where he met John Winton.

"Hi John," said Tom, "How are you doing?"

"I'm doing fine," said John. "How are you doing?"

"I'm surviving," said Tom with a smile on his face.

"What are you doing this afternoon?" asked John. "Do you have any plans?"

"No," said Tom. "I will just go home make myself a sandwich and watch a movie."

"Why don't you come with me," said John. "We can use the help and it will give you the feeling of doing something for the community."

"What are you talking about?" asked Tom not being aware of what John was involved with.

I'm sorry," said John, "I though you knew about my charity work. We have a large house on Hametown road in Montrose. We help people who are in trouble. Most are homeless people who are begging for food on the roads. We help them find a job and give them a room to stay in until our help is successful."

"I'm sorry," said Tom. "I don't see how I could help anyone"

"Come on," said John. "What can you lose? Come and meet Mrs. Crawford. If you can't find some way you could help, you can just go home. Perhaps all you can do is to donate something to the charity."

"What is it that you do most of the time after you find a needy person?" asked Tom.

"Most of the times we assign a needy person to a volunteer like you who then try to help them, maybe just to make them feel better. If one is available we will assign him or her to you to see if you could help"

"Ok," said Tom. "You talked me into it. What can I lose? Let me go home and have a quick lunch and I will meet you there. Give me the address." John gave him the address and they said goodbye. At about one in the afternoon Tom went to the address John gave him. He walked inside the main room, that looked like they had taken down the wall between the dining room and the living room and made a large room. The room had several small tables. Some of the tables had two people sitting at them. Some were two men, some were two woman and some were mixed. He saw John by one of the tables talking to the ones sitting there. At the end of the room was a desk and an elderly woman was sitting there. John saw Tom and started to walk toward him.

"Hi Tom," said John, "glad to see you. I was afraid you would not come."

"I said I would," said Tom. "However I think I'm sorry I said it."

"Come with me," said John. "I want you to meet Mrs. Crawford." As they walked up to Mrs. Crawford, she got up to go to the next room.

"Mrs. Crawford," said John stopping her from leaving the area. "I want you to meet a new volunteer."

"Of course John," said Mrs. Crawford. "We can always use extra help."

"This is Tom Corely," said John. "He just retired and has nothing to do."

"Well we can find something for him to help us with," said Mrs.

Crawford. "Unfortunately all the people that need help are already assigned to a volunteer. "I'm sure we will get one soon. Give me your name, address and phone number and I will call you when we have someone that needs help." He gave her the information and she left for the other room. Fortunately Tom hung around talking to John about the other things the charity did, when he heard his name called out. It was Mrs. Crawford.

"I'm glad you are still here," she said. "We just got a homeless woman that the police brought in. Come in and I will introduce her to you. If it is alright with you I would like to assign her to you."

"Let's go see her," said Tom not wanting to accept the assignment yet. As they walked into the other room two policemen were writing down the information they needed to release her to the charity. The woman was standing there telling the officer what he wanted to know. As they walked in Mrs. Crawford addressed the officer taking the information.

"If you have all the information you need I will take her into the main room," said Mrs. Crawford. As the woman turned to see who it was she froze when she looked at Tom. She looked at Tom and her face became like a mask not showing any emotion or life at all.

"This is Tom Corely," said Mrs. Crawford to the woman.

"Hi" the woman said very softly and without any facial activity.

"Hi," said Tom and as he looked at her he felt something he had never felt before. He had no idea what it was that he was feeling. He figured that it was probably the fact that he was now responsible for a person's life. "What is your name?" asked Tom snapping out of his thoughts.

"Name," whispered the woman softly.

"Her name is Victoria Grafton," said Mrs. Crawford. She then led them into the other room and to an empty table. Tom and Victoria sat down on opposite sides of the table. "You two get to know each other." She said, and went back to talk with the police.

"I know Victoria, that this is awkward," said Tom. "But please relax. I am here to help you. Think of me as an old friend that you haven't seen for a long time."

"Please call me Vicki. Why are you doing this?" she asked.

"I just retired," answered Tom. "I am bored having nothing to do. I was a detective for the Fairlawn police department. They allow us to retire after we have served twenty five years. While I was working I was always thinking about getting evidence and solving cases. Besides, I also owe this to God. God has been so good to me my whole life. I have two wonderful Children and I had a very loving wife who God has taken home with him, but I still thank him for her. I am a Born again Christian and a servant of Jesus. I think he sent me here to be with you."

"I'm so sorry that you lost your wife," said Vicki. "I also lost my husband."

"There is one thing I would like to know," said Tom. "You have acted so strange since we met. I know that you have a problem or we would not be here, but it seems more than that."

"Look at me," said Vicki now beginning to act like a woman. I must look like an animal that came out of a mud hole. Also, I haven't had anything to eat in three days. I need a shower and something to eat." She didn't want to tell him that her strange reaction was because she was very attracted to him.

"I completely understand now," said Tom, "what showed up is your pride. I can take care of that. Come, you are coming with me." As they got up to leave, Mrs. Crawford walked up to them.

"I'm sorry," she said. "I don't have a place for Vitoria to stay tonight at this time. There is only one bed available and it is in a room with a man in the other bed. Will you try to find a place for her to stay tonight?"

"That is alright Mrs. Crawford," said Tom. "I will take complete responsibility for her. I will see she gets all that she needs."

"I'm sure you will," said Mrs. Crawford, "God be with you." Tom and Vicki left and got into Tom's car.

"Why are you doing this?" Vicki asked again.

"I explained it all to you before," said Tom.

"Yes but this is different," said Vicki. "Now you have to find a place for me to sleep tonight and maybe longer."

"I have a house with five bedrooms. Although, I have one converted into a TV room two are empty. You can have one of the rooms as long as you want. We don't have to go back to the charity house. I have no interior motives believe me."

"Oh I trust you," said Vicki. "I am a Christian also although I have not been a good one. I have not been going to church as often as I should have. I was too busy taking care of my husband." After they got to Tom's house and he brought Vicki inside he started to talk to her.

"Let's sit at the table," said Tom, "where you can tell me the story of your life and what is your main problem."

"Oh Tommy," said Vicki looking very tired. "Can we hold off on that for a while? I am so tired. I have not had anything to eat in three days and I have not had more than a couple of hour sleep."

I'm so sorry," said Tom. "I'm so thoughtless. Let me make you some chicken soap. Since you haven't eaten in three days, I don't think you can handle anything heavier." Tom got a can of chicken soap and quickly warmed it up. When it was warm he gave it to Vicki. You could tell by the way she ate it that she had not eaten for a while. After she had finish he took her up stairs to the bed rooms. He took her to the last room off the hall way.

"This will be your room as long as you need it," said Tom. "I will show you the rest of the house after you had a good night's sleep." He then left her there and went into the room opposite the one she was in. He brought out a pair of pajamas' that had been his wife's. "I think these will fit you. Next door to you is the bathroom. Go in take a shower and go and take a nap."

"Thank you so much," said Vicki as she took the pajamas and went into the bathroom. Tom went down stairs and made himself a hot dog for dinner.

The next morning, Tom got up at eight and started to make breakfast. He decided that some Mother's Oats would be best for Vicki. He had the Mother's Oars on the stove when Vicki came down from the bedroom area. She was dressed in a nice dress.

"Wow," said Tom. "I can't believe you are the same girl I brought home yesterday."

"I hope you don't mind my using you wife's cloths," said Vicki.

"That's fine," said Tom. "My wife will not need them anymore. However, I wonder why you didn't use your clothes. You have a pretty large suitcase that I carried in for you."

"The clothes in the suitcase are dirtier than the clothes I was wearing yesterday," said Vicki. "I will wear them after I wash them, if it is alright with you and if you let me use your washing machine."

"You can use anything in this house," said Tom. "After we eat and have a little talk I will take you through the house so that you will know where everything is." Tom then set a dish of Mother's Oats for her and himself. He set a cup of coffee and cream for each also. Then before they ate, Tom said a prayer. After they finished eating Tom took everything to the sink. He was surprised that Vicki helped him. Tom washed the dishes and Vicki took on the job of drying them. When they finished they sat at the table with another cup of coffee.

"Thank you so much for all that you are doing for me," said Vicki.

"You are welcome," said Tom. "Now please tell me your story. Start from the beginning."

"I was born and raised in Columbus Ohio," said Vicki. "I went to school at Ohio State University. I got my degree in Nursing. Later I went back for my master's degree. I am a Nurse Practitioner. I also learned about Lab testing and evaluations. I learned to use all the lab equipment like the X-ray and other patient test equipment. I also learned how to perform blood tests. At the end of the tests I provided the results of the tests to the doctor who ordered them. My first job was with Doctor Grafen. I was his surgical assistant. When Doctor Grafen left I was assiged to the lab. It was there that I met Walter. He was the hospital maintenance manager. He was responsible for all the hospital equipment and the head of the janitorial service. To make this short, my husband got cancer. I took him to our doctor. He couldn't help him so he had me taken him to the Columbus hospital. After much testing they recommended I take him to a

Cancer Research Center. The closest one was in Chicago. I took him there. My insurance company would not cover much of the cost. We had a bad insurance. So I closed my bank account and put the down payment required before they would accept him in the center. After much testing and examinations they said he would need several surgeries. First he needed a kidney transplant. Then if that worked he would need a surgery to remove cancer tumors that had grown in several locations. To make the story short he died a year later on his last surgery. I had to sell my house, to have enough for his surgery. I spent all the money I had for his surgeries, his burial, and the cost of the hotel room I stayed in during all of that time. I had enough gas to drive to Montrose Ohio. There I had a distant relative, Aunt Nicolina. She was one of my husband's relatives. It was his father's brother's wife. For an unknown reason they were not close. Anyway, I had no choice. She accepted me with joy. She was glad to have someone stay with her. I ended up taking care of her. To pay some of the depths I still had in Chicago I had to sell my car. It ended up that all I had was a suitcase of cloths. However Aunt Nicolina and I were happy. I had started to look for a job with no success. After I sold my car I had no way to go looking for a job. Unfortunately Aunt Nicolina passed away. She was ninety two years old. Her son Mathew, who lived in Arizona, came to her funeral. He arranged to sell all the furniture and the house. I was left in the street with a suitcase of old dirty clothes. There were some nice people that gave me a slice of bread ever once in a while. I found that one of the families on the street has a nice swing on their front porch. That is where I got a few hours' sleep. The owners were on vacation so no one objected. However, the owners soon came home late one evening and found me and called the police. That was when you found me."

"Wow that is quite a story for you to tell your kids," said Tom. "Do you have any of your family in Columbus that we could contact?"

"No," said Vicki. "My father died when I was a young woman in college. My mother passed away about four years ago. My husband's mother and father were not very close to us. They were angry that he didn't take over the store they had. They were angry with me for taking his side."

"Didn't you contact them when your husband died," asked Tom.

"I sent them a letter telling them about everything that had taken place. I even told them that I was staying with aunt Nicolina, but they never answered. So you see I have nothing. I don't even have a car to go looking for a job. Where do we go from here? You can't keep taking care of me the rest of my life."

"I will if I have to," said Tom. "However, I have a plan. First we have to find you a job. I'm retired so I have the time. I will drive you back and forth to work until you have enough money to buy a small car. Then we will find a place for you to rent. I will take care of you till that all happens.

"You were sent by God," said Vicki with tears in her eyes.

"God did give me a great life. I have a great retirement income and a good income from my investments. I didn't earn it. It was given to me by God. It is his money. I am only spending it as he leads me."

"Are you an angel pretending to be a human man?" asked Vicki in awe of his statement.

"Very funny," said Tom. "I am just a good Christian." After they finished their coffee, Tom got out his phone book. After he looked at it for a while he changed his mind. He felt it was not smart to just call. "I think it would be smarter to go and get an interview personally," said Tom. "You feel like taking a little trip to the closest medical centers?"

"I'm all dressed up," said Vicki. "Let's go."

"Let's first go to the Akron City Wellness Center," said Tom. "It and the Cristal Clinic are just ten minutes away." It was just about ten minutes later that they got to the Wellness Center. After parking the car they entered the building and walked up to the front desk.

"Hello," said the woman at the desk. "How can I help you?"

"My name is Victoria Graton. I am a Nurse Practitioner. I am looking for a job."

"Look," interrupted Tom. "I am going to sit in the waiting area. I don't need to be with you for your interview." With that said he went to a chair to the right of the desk and sat down. From there he could see Vicki at the front desk. Vicki apparently got directions of where to go and left heading for the elevator. It was almost two hours later that Vicki came back down to the area where Tom was sitting.

"Let's go," said Vicki. "I have had three interviews. One with the, what do you call it, the reception department. Next I was interviewed by the head of the health department, which was mostly checking after the exercise period and finally the emergency department. That was the worse. The only opening was the third shift spot."

"I'm sure the Crystal Clinic will be better," said Tom. "It is just around the corner. But before we go there let's take a lunch break." They found a small restaurant on Market Street and had a light lunch. After they ate Tom drove to the Crystal Clinic. Tom stopped at the first building. Tom sat in the waiting area watching television that was provided for patients that had to wait. Vicki went to the desk and talked to the girl there. Soon she disappeared as she had done at the Wellness Center. About an hour later she came out.

"They recommend that we go on to the next building," said Vicki. "They feel that my knowledge and experience would be better fit in the next building where major surgery takes place. This building is mostly doctor's offices and light surgery, like hand and feet." Tom then took her to the next building. Tom and Vicki did the same as they had done in the first building. Vicki's interview took about an hour as it had done in the first building.

"Let's go home," said Vicki. "I left them your phone number and they said that they will call me as soon as an opening occurs."

"So there was no luck here?" asked Tom.

"They seemed impressed," said Vicki, "but they didn't have an opening at this time. They did promise that they will talk to all the doctors about my credentials." Tom then drove home. It was almost six o'clock. They sat down in the family room to rest for a while. They went over all that Vicki learned about the job possibilities. Just then they heard the front door open. Tom's young daughter Ellie walked in.

"Hi dad," she said.

"Have you come home for good?" asked Tom. "Did you complete what you had to do in Lexington?"

"Yes," said Elli. "As you know I got the job at the Universal Hospital here in Fairlawn. I start this Monday"

"I'm sorry," said Tom as he turned to Vicki. "This is my daughter Elaine." Then turning to Ellie he said, "This is Victoria. We all call her Vicki. She is in trouble and needs our help. We have to help her find a job"

"What kind of help do you need," asked Ellie.

"Why don't you girls get to know each other," said Tom. "I will go up and prepare dinner. I took out some Tilapia. There is enough for three." He then went upstairs to prepare dinner.

"Before I tell you my long story about my problem," said Vicki, "tell you something about your life."

"I graduated from Kentucky State University," started Ellie. "After a small job here, I went back for my master's degree. While going to school I got a job at a Lexington hospital. I worked at the entrance window. I accepted all new patients' information and did all the financial work. When I got my master's degree I came home for a vacation. While here I looked for a job. I didn't like being so far from home. I found one at the Universal Hospital here in Fairlawn. They offered me the job as financial director. It's the job my boss had in Lexington. I went back to Lexington to give up my rented apartment, to sell all my furniture and possessions and here I am. Now it is your turn. What is your background and what is your problem?"

"My name is Victoria Grafton," started Vicki. "Most of my friends call me Vicki. I was born and raised in Columbus Ohio." Vicki then told Ellie the whole story of her life as she had told to Tom.

"Wow," said Ellie, "that would make a fantastic novel."

"Girls," said Tom from the kitchen. "Dinner is ready" Ellie and Vicki went up the eight steps to the kitchen. They all ate a delicious dinner.

"You know Dad," said Ellie when they had finished their dinner.

"I think we have a very talented lady here. I think we can use her at the University Hospital right here in Fairlawn."

"I believe that building," said Tom, "only has doctor's offices and a Lab. Do you think that lab would have an opening for Vicki?"

"Dad where have you been?" said Ellie. "Haven't you heard? The building is renovating. They are making it a full hospital. They are adding about fifty hospital beds, several operating rooms and a small cafeteria in the place that was behind the elevators. There is a hallway there now. The elevators are on the south side of the hallway and the cafeteria's entrance is on the north side of the hallway. At the other end of the building where the lab is they are adding the emergence entrance and a patient admissions office. That is going to be part of my job. I will be responsible for that area. I understand that they are ready to start performing surgery."

"I had heard that it would happen someday," said Tom. "I had no idea that it is going on now."

"You know," said Ellie being deep in thought. "I don't officially start until Monday, even though this is Wednesday, there is no reason that I can't go, look around, and ask questions. What do you say Vicki, do you want to go tomorrow and see if there is a possibility for you to get a job there?"

I'm for it," said Vicki. "What can we lose except a little time and I have a lot of that."

The next morning Ellie and Vicki got up early, ate breakfast and were at the Hospital at nine. Ellie knew where to go. When she arrived at the manager's office she walked up to the secretary.

"My name is Elaine Corely. I would like to speak with Mrs. Donavon." The secretary got on the phone and called her boss.

"Mrs. Donavon, There is a young lady here named Elaine Corely that want to see you." She hardly ended her sentence when Mrs. Donavon came running out of her office.

"Hello Elaine," said Mrs. Donavon. "You were not supposed to be here until Monday. But I am thrilled that you are here."

"I came here because my friend needs a job," said Ellie. "I was hoping that you would find time to interview her."

"You don't understand," said Mrs. Donavon. "I am so glad that you are here. I need you so badly. I didn't know if you had come back from Kentucky. If you are available I could use you right now."

"I am available," said Ellie, "but first I want you to meet Vitoria Graton. She is a Nurse practitioner."

"Will miracles never end," said Mrs. Donavon. "I may have just the job for her to fill both problems I have. However I need to get you going first. The company has opened the Emergency and Outpatient Departments. Since it is finished they decided to open it to new patients. It is about a month before we had planned for it. We now have a couple of patients waiting to be admitted, but we have no one at the office. I need you to go there right now. I have a doctor and a nurse at the emergency room but I have no one at the outpatient entrance office. Once you get it taken care of please come back. I need you to do the administrative accounting. I understand you have a BA in accounting. You also will be the personnel Manager as well as the financial manager."

"I have my friend Vicki to take home," said Ellie.

"Don't worry about her," said Julia Donavon. "I will take care of her even if I have to drive her home myself. However I think I may find a job for her." Ellie Quickly went down to the first floor lobby. From there she went to the outpatient office. She found that a nurse was just coming down. They talked for a while and then Ellie got the information from the patients and the nurse led them to doctor's office. About an hour later she returned with another nurse who was told she was to take over the office. After a short talk Ellie headed for the emergence room. Since she was responsible for all the incoming areas, she wanted to know how things were going. Every one she met knew that Ellie was their boss. Finally Ellie felt like she had set everything up as well as she could. She set everything like she had it in Kentucky. It needed a lot of work to get it running smoothly. However she now was encouraged that she could handle it all. It was late in the afternoon when she went up to the second floor to her office. She had a lot of work to get her office the way she had in Kentucky.

Back at Mrs. Donavon office, Vicki was being interrogated.

"What is your experience with Heart surgery?" asked Mrs. Donavon.

"Well Mrs. Donavon," started Vicki, "At first I assisted Dr. Grafen for about eleven years. Most of that was heart surgery. I also supported the doctor in other types of surgery. After Dr. Grafen left I was assigned to the lab where I spent nine years."

"I don't want to hear any more," said Mrs. Donavon. "I need to take you to see Dr. Wilson right away. Also by the way call me Julia, and I will call you Ellie." She then took Ellie to the surgery area and into Dr. Wilson's office. As she got to the office Dr. Wilson was just leaving.

"Dr. Wilson," said Julia.

"I'm sorry'" said Dr. Wilson. "I don't have time to talk now. I have a patient in the surgery room that will die if I don't perform surgery right away."

"Did you find a surgical assistant?" asked Julia.

No I have to do it all myself," said the doctor as he started to walk away.

"Well," said Julia. "This is Vicki Graton. She has spent eleven years as a heart surgeon's assistant." The doctor then grabbed Vicki by the arm

"Come with me," he said. "I don't need to know more about you right now. I need you in the surgery room." He then led her into the surgical preparation room. He provided her with a surgical garment, a mask, and gloves and led her into the surgery room. Vicki tried to do the best job she had ever done. She tried to predict every move the doctor made and was there when he needed her the most. About three hours later they came out of the surgery room and went back to the preparation room. They took off their garments washed their hands.

"You know," said Dr. Wilson. "It is almost twelve thirty. Let's go down to the restaurant and have lunch. It is on me. There we can talk."

"Lead the way," said Vicki. As they proceeded down to the

restaurant Vicki commented her feelings. "I don't know about you but I need a rest. That was a very tough job. In all my years as a surgeon's assistant, I never assisted in a five bypass heart surgery.

"That was my first too," said the doctor. "That is why I was in such a hurry." When they got to the restaurant they were seated and they placed their order with the waitress that was there as they sat down. After the waitress left Dr. Wilson turned to Vicki.

"I don't know if I should say this," he started, "but I will take the chance. I think you did a fantastic job in there. I thought I had four hands. I have just moved here from Cleveland. The hospital there provided whoever nurse was available when I had a surgery scheduled. I didn't like that. I want an assistant that works for me. Here they allow that. So I would like you to work for me and be my personal assistant."

"I will need more information," said Vicki. "What will my other duties be, and what would my income include?"

"Of course," said the doctor. "We will go over that after we eat. We will go upstairs to do that. I just wanted to know if you are at all interested."

"Yes," Said Vicki. "I would like to work here." After they ate they went back to the doctor's office.

"Please just wait here," said the doctor. "I will go and get the information you need and what I need to hire you." He was gone for about ten minutes.

"That didn't take long," said Vicki.

"No," said the doctor. "I just had to go to Mrs. Donavon's office to get her approval and the documents I need. Anyway, here is the document that explains all the information you will need about the rules of employment. Please review them quickly." Vicki read the main part of the document. It was easy because at the end after the details they had the important items listed in a row.

"I can live with this," said Vicki.

"Great," said the doctor. "Now this sheet is your employment agreement. If you check on the bottom you will see your monthly salary." Vicki looked at the salary. What she saw stunted her. She was surprise at the amount. It was almost double what she expected. It was more than fifty percent more than what she was getting in Columbus. The doctor thought that she hesitated because it was too little.

"I want you to understand that you will be rewarded with any over time you may be required to do. They will give a monthly bonus for excellent work."

"It is acceptable," said Vicki as she signed the agreement. "When do I start?"

"You already started this morning with the bypass surgery," said the doctor. "What I would like you to do now, is check the progress of the patients in the hospital rooms." Vicki did just that for the rest of the afternoon.

Ellie was checking her computer when Julia Donavon came into Ellie's office.

"I see that you got some departments set up," said Julia. "How much have you done and how did you make out?"

"I'm sorry," said Ellie. "I only did two. I completely reorganized them. I know I should have talked with you first, but I couldn't leave the department until I got someone to run them."

"What is this reorganizing all about?" asked Julia.

"When I was studying at the Kentucky state U, I was given a part time job at the Lexington Hospital. There I worked in their reception desk most of the time. After I graduated with my financial degree I decided to go back for my Master's degree. It was a two year course. After the first year I stayed there and worked in the hospital during the summer. One of the things I was assigned to was to see how the hospital could increase its income. It was barely making it. I then reviewed all the departments operations. I found that the way they were operating the departments was obsolete. They were not using the latest equipment like the computer. So I reorganized all the departments. It was new to me so I had to come up with the software and new procedures. It saved anyway from 30 to 40 percent on the cost of running the departments. Unfortunately it also eliminated several jobs. Now I reorganized two of your department so far. The reorganization saved 25 percent on one and 42 percent on the other. Fortunately it did not cost any jobs because you have not hired to many department operators."

"Wow," said Julia. "I think God did send you. You continue doing what you are doing. You have my approval. I will not interfere with what you are doing." With that said she started to leave.

"Julia," said Ellie, "before you leave what is the story about my friend Vicki?"

"I'm sorry," said Julia. "Haven't you heard?" she has been hired by Dr. Wilson. She has already assisted the doctor in a heart bypass surgery"

"That is fantastic news," said Ellie. "I'm so glad to hear it." Ellie then went back to her job of reorganizing the hospital organizations. At about four thirty Vicki went to Ellie's office. She had to ask several people before she found it. The door was open but she knocked on the door anyway.

"Come in Vicki," said Ellie. "I hear that you have good news. So we both got a job here. We can drive together. However today I have too much work to do. So I will drive you home and come back."

"Nonsense," said Vicki. "I can keep busy here in the hospital. There is an older woman who is here for possible heart surgery. She is so sweet. She has no one to be with her. I will go and keep her company until you are ready to go home. I'll call your father and give the news of our employments and tell him that we were going to come home late. As a matter of fact I was wondering that if we went home how I could come back. I would like to spend time with Margie."

"It could be a couple of hours," said Ellie.

"Great," said Vicki. "The room Margie is in is room 312 on the third floor. See you then." Vicki then went back to her office. She immediately called Tom.

"Hi said Tom when he answered the phone. "How can I help you?"

"Hi" said Vicki. "This is Vicki. I am calling to tell you that I got a job here at University Hospital. Ellie and I will both be working here.

As a matter of fact I aided in a surgery this morning and got hired by the doctor right after the surgery."

"That is great," said Tom. "But why are you calling to tell me over the phone. Couldn't you tell me over dinner?"

"That is the other reason I am calling you," said Vicki. "Since we are new we have a lot of work getting settled in our new jobs. I'm calling you to let you know that Ellie and I will not be home for dinner. We will be working late. We are going to have a sandwich here at the hospital cafeteria."

"Thanks for calling," said Tom. "Take care of yourselves." Vicki then went up to the third floor with the plan to visit some of the patients. When she got there she ran into Dr. Wilson.

"Hi Vicki," said the doctor. "I see that you are still here."

"Yes," said Vicki. "I thought I would visit some of your patients."

I would like you to visit Margarita Mellio," said the doctor. "She is in a very depressed condition. She had a heart attack and I am waiting for test information to come from the lab. She had no family and no friends to visit her. Try to cheer her up a little."

"I will do my best," said Vicki. "That is where I was going anyway."

"Thank you," said the doctor. "Good night." With that he left the hospital. Vicki went directly to Margareta's room.

"Hi Mrs. Mellio," said Vicki. "How are you feeling?"

"I am not feeling too well," said Margie. "Who are you? Are you my night nurse?"

"No," said Vicki. "I am Doctor Wilson's assistant. I am a Nurse Practitioner. I am a little higher than a nurse but a little lower than a doctor. I am Doctor Wilson's surgical assistant."

"So why are you here?" asked Margie "Am I ready for surgery?"

"No I'm here to check up on how you are doing and to cheer you up a little. The doctor told me that you were a little depressed."

"I have no family, no friends, no one to care what happens to me," said Margie. "Why do I even want to continue living?"

"Oh Margarita," said Vicki. "You have to have some faith."

"What should I have faith in?" asked Marge. "By the way please call me Margie. I don't like Margarita. It is too Italian. And why do you care?"

"You have to have faith in the Lord," said Vicki. "He is in control; of everything."

"Why is this so important to you?" said Margie. "What will you get out of this?"

"You don't understand," said Vicki. "I want to help you. I know exactly how you feel."

"How in the world could you come any way close to know how I feel?"

"It's because we have something in common," said Vicki. "That is why I know exactly what you are experiencing."

"What ever could we have in common?" said Margie with a sad and unbelieving expression. "You have a wonderful job and probably have a sweet and wonderful family."

"I have no family and only just recently got two friends," said Vicki. "I was an assisted to a doctor in Columbus. I met my husband and was very happy for about twenty years. Then my husband got cancer. The x-rays showed that there were several small growths all over his body. They tried with radiation but it didn't work. They then recommended that I take him to a Cancer Center. I took him to Chicago Cancer Research Center. It was the closest one." Vicki then described what she went through for the next eighteen months. How she had to go back to Columbus to close her bank account, sell all her furniture, and sell her house to pay for the many surgeries and new advanced procedures her husband had.

"After all that my husband died anyway," continued Vicki. "I then left Chicago for Ohio. I only had enough gas to get to Ohio where I had Aunt Nicolina where I stayed for a while. I had to sell my car to finish paying all the bills I had incurred one of which was my rent while I was in Chicago. However she lived for only six months while I was there. I was then in the street, with no car and no money. I had to beg for food. I found a porch near the house my aunt had that had a swing on the front porch I stayed there until the owners came home from a trip and call the police. They took me to the

Charity house. I was then rescued by a generous man named Tom. He and his daughter helped me get back on my feet."

"Wow," said Margie. "That is a lot more then I have ever had. I at least still have a house and a car."

"So you see," said Vicki. "If I could recover so could you. I would like to be your friend and help you get back on your feet."

"I feel better already," said Margie. "I at least have one friend."

"I will see that you have at least two more," said Vicki. Just then Ellie walked in.

"Hi girls," said Ellie. "I'm all finished for today. I'm too hungry and too tired to do more today."

"My goodness," said Vicki. "It is almost eight. Where did the time go? I'm hungry too, but before we leave I want you to meet Margie Mellio."

"HI Margie," said Ellie. "I am Elaine Corelli. We are Paeseano as the Italians call it. That makes us closer than friends. At the hospital I go with the name Ellie Corely. My father changed the name when he became a police officer. Aren't they going to bring Margie any food," asked Ellie of Vicki.

"I think Dr. Wilson is thinking of doing surgery tomorrow so he doesn't want food in her belly," said Vicki.

"Let's go then," said Ellie. "See you tomorrow Margie."

"Good night, Margie," said Vicki. "See you early tomorrow. Have a good night sleep and have faith. I will help you." That said Vicki and Ellie left. On the way home both Ellie and Vicki thought about their new jobs and wandered what the future would bring.

CHAPTER TWO

A Look at the Future

When Ellie and Vicki got home Tom met them at the door.

"I bet you girls have had nothing to eat for super," said Tom.

"No," responded Ellie, "we were just too busy. We intended to go down to the hospital cafeteria but it was closed when we got there. So we decided to come home and have a small sandwich."

"Well, you will not have a sandwich," said Tom. "I saved you girls some Sausage casserole. You just have to heat it in the microwave and eat.

"Thanks dad," said Ellie. Vicki also thanked him and they sat down and ate. After eating Tom, asked them what their day as like.

"As soon as I got there, my boss sent me down to the emergence room to get things started. She was overwhelmed with all the help that she suddenly needed. She was so glad to see me. If you remember I was supposed to start on Monday."

"How about you Vicki," asked Tom, "Did you have trouble getting a job there like you did in the other places we tried?"

"No," said Vicki. "As a matter of fact as soon as the doctor heard that I had experience as a surgeon's assistant he grabbed me by the arm and took me in the surgical preparation room. He gave me all that I needed such as apron, mask, and gloves and I soon was assisting in the heart operation. After the surgery he hired me on the spot. He said that with me in there he felt like he had four hands."

"I'm so glad for you," said Tom. "You are back to your normal self."

"Not really," said Vicki. "I have changed in one way. I am more sensitive, more attached to the patients. I have feeling for their recovery. As an example we have a patient that may need surgery tomorrow. She is an older woman who has no family or friends. I want to help her. I want to be more than her nurse. I want to be her friend."

"I think you kind of see yourself when you think of her problem," said Tom. "I think that is you anyway. I don't think it is a change. I think it is a way you could finally be yourself."

"Thank you Tom," said Vicki. "I feel I have a long way before I feel like I was on solid ground. I need a car, a house and a good bank account before I will have confidence in myself."

"I think that is just around the corner," said Ellie.

The next morning Ellie and Vicki were at the hospital a quarter to eight. Ellie went to her office and Vicki went directly to Margie's hospital bedroom.

"How are you doing today Margie?" asked Vicki. "I see that you are wide awake."

"I am wide awake and very hungry," said Margie.

"That sounds great," said Vicki. "It sounds like you are better." Vicki went and sat next to the bed. She reached out and held Margie's hand. It was about fifteen minutes after eight that the doctor walked into the room.

"How are you girls doing this morning?" asked the doctor.

"I hope you will tell me," said Margie with a smile on her face.

"I see that you are in a better mood today," said the doctor. "That is good to see."

"How are you Doctor Wilson?" asked Vicki. "I hope you have good news for us."

"Well let me examine Margie and I will tell you," said the doctor. Then he did a thorough exam of Margie. When he got through, he turned to the girls.

"First I see from the heart monitor that her heart is beating normally. That is a change for the good. As you can see we have the heart equipment that helps pump the blood which relieves the pressure from the heart. The heart beat shows that it is working and the heart is in recovery. Next I got all the test results from the lab. The tests show that two blood vessels are blocked. That results in the heart having to work muck harder than normal. It also shows that the heart is week and sort of worn out. What we need to do is take the pressure off the heart. I was hoping that they were just narrow arteries, so that we could have used two stints, but they are too blocked. We will need to do bypass surgery. Since you are doing so much better let's schedule for surgery this afternoon. Vicki, let's do it right after lunch. Please be ready at say one o'clock"

"I will have everything ready," said Vicki"

"Good," said Margie, "Then I could have something to eat. I'm staved."

That afternoon Vicki had everything ready. She had Margie in the surgery room and she was all prepared for the surgery. The doctor came in at about ten after one and they proceeded with the bypass surgery. The surgery took two and a half hours. All indications were that it was a success. They brought her to the recovery room and the doctor hooked her up with the heart equipment as she had been before the surgery.

"Stay with her and keep tract of her vital signs, for at least an hour. I have given her a shot to keep her asleep until tomorrow" said the doctor to Vicki.

The next morning Vicki was there a few minutes before eight. Margie was still asleep. Just as Margie was waking up Dr. Wilson walked in.

"How is our favorite patient doing?" he asked.

"I feel like I was run over by a six wheel truck." said Margie still half a sleep. The doctor checked all of the instruments that were attached to her.

"I think you are doing fine," said the doctor. "You are better than I thought you would be. I will give you another shot to relieve your pain. I will have a floor nurse come and look at you every few minutes. If you have any problem just ring the nurse."

"Can't Vicki stay with me for a little while?" asked Margie.

"I'm sorry," said the doctor. "Right now I need her to help me with a surgery. We got an emergence call. They are bringing her up to the surgery room."

"What is her problem?" asked Vicky as they started to walk out

"She was shot in the chest," said the doctor. "I don't know if we will be able to save her."

"I will be in to see you as soon as we deal with this emergence," said Vicki to Margie as they left.

The surgery took almost two hours. The bullet just scrapped the heart and punctured several arteries. They had to make sure they would not leak blood. When they were finished she was taken to the recovery room. As the doctor requested Vicki stayed with her till noon. Vicki left the floor nurse in charge and went down and had lunch. After lunch she went back to the woman who had been shot to make sure she was on the way to recovering. After checking her vital, she went to be with Margie.

"Hi Margie," said Vicki as she entered the room. "How are you feeling?"

"I'm a lot better," said Margie. "I seem to be able to breathe easier. So tell me about the surgery that you did this morning"

"The woman was shot in the chest," said Vicki, "The bullet just grazed her heart. An inch more and she would have been dead."

"Wow," said Margie. "You lead an interesting life, never a dull moment."

"I'm glad you understand," said Vicki, "because I can only stay a little while. I am going to have an early lunch and then I have to go and check on the woman we just did the surgery on. I have to make sure she is recovering as expected." Vicki then left and went to the cafeteria. After lunch she went in and stayed with the new patient. As she walked in she asked the nurse on duty to get all the information of the new patient she could get. About an hour later the nurse walked in.

"I checked the emergence room that brought her in," said Christa the nurse. "They had the police report. They got information from a neighbor who was the one that called them when she heard the gun shots. She said that the people next door where James and Tania Siden. She also said that the young boy they found there was their son Ron. You know that the man and the young boy were both shot and didn't make it. The woman was the only survivor. "

"Thank you Christa," said Vicki. "It is nice to know who the patient is." Vicki stayed with Tania until later in the afternoon when Vicki heard moaning from Tania. She was slowly waking up. She was in a semi-awaken state. It wasn't until eight fifteen when she became fully awake. Vicki was about to leave for home.

"Where am I?" was the first words that came out of her mouth.

"You are at the Universal Hospital," said Vicki. "You have been shot in the chest. We removed the bullet in surgery this morning."

"Yes," said Tania. "I remember this guy coming into our house shooting his gun at us. Are my husband and son OK?"

"I'm sorry," said Vicki. "I don't know how to tell you this, but they are not OK."

"Are they both gone?" said Tania starting to cry out loud. Fortunately Vicki was still there to comfort her. Five minutes later she would have been on her way home. She did what she could to comfort her. After about an hour she settled down.

"Do you need anything," said Vicki. "Do you want a glass of water?"

"What I want you to do is to call my attorney," she said getting some of her strength back.

"I don't know who to call," said Vicki. "Do you have a name and phone number?"

"Look in the closet where they hung up my cloths," said Tania. "My purse should be there. It was hung on my neck when I was shot. I was ready to go out when it all happened." Vicki went into the closet. Sure enough the purse was hanging along with the cloths. Vicki took the purse down and took it to Tania. "Here is your purse," said Vicki, as he handed it to her. Tania was too weak to raise her hand to look through the purse so she asked Vicki to do it.

"Open up the purse and find the wallet. Inside the wallet you will find the attorney's card." Vicki did what Tania asked. She found the card and called the number on the card.

"Hello," said a woman's voice. "How can I help you?"

"I would like to talk to Attorney James Flesner," said Vicki.

"Who may I ask is calling," asked the woman.

"This is Victoria Graton. I am a nurse at the Universal hospital. I am calling for Tania Siden."

"Yes," said James, taking over the phone. "I have been trying to contact her. Is she alright?"

"Yes," said Vicki. "She was shot in the chest. She just came out of surgery. She will be alright although at this time she can hardly move. She asked me to call you. She is concern for her husband and son. We understand that they did not make it."

"I'm afraid that they did not make it," said James. "Tell Tania that I am following the instruction I was given from them. The police have done an investigation and released them to the investigating doctor. The doctor has done a complete check on them and has released them to me. I had them shipped to the funeral home."

"Will Tania be able to see them or go to the funeral?" asked Vicki.

"I don't see how," said James. "Unless she could come out today she will not be able to see them. Tomorrow, after a prayer and blessing by your church pastor, they will be cremated as directed in their instruction. Their ashes will be distributed in Wyoga Lake where I believe they met."

"Thank you very much," said Vicki. "I will pass all the information to Tania." After hanging up Vicki told Tania all the information that her attorney James told her.

"I'm glad that is taken care," said Tania.

"Is there anything else I could do for you before I go home and leave you in the care of the attending nurse?"

"Yes," said Tania. "I would like you to get me a detective to find out who did this to me."

"I have the exact man that will do a great job for you," said Vicki. She then called Tom.

"Tom," she said after he answered his cell phone. "I have a job for you if you are available and willing to help a patient of mine."

"What is the problem?" asked Tom.

"I have a patient that was shot in the chest," said Vicki. "She needs a detective to find out who shot her. Could you come here tomorrow morning?"

"Yes I know of that case," said Tom. "I cannot make it tomorrow morning. Chief Richard called me and wants to see me tomorrow morning. I still have my credentials so I think I can get in even if it is after eight o'clock. So perhaps I could come over right now. Is that alright?"

"That will be great," said Vicki. "I was ready to go home, but I will wait for you." Tom arrived at the hospital about eight forty-five. Showing his credentials he went right up to the third floor. There he met the nurse.

"Hi," said Tom. "I am detective Tom Corely. "I came to see Tania Siden. Is Nurse Vicki here?"

Not right now," said the nurse. "I am the only nurse on duty at this time on this floor. Mrs. Siden is in the last room down the hall on your left." Tom went directly to the room. As he entered the room he saw a person dressed with a nurse's apron and a face mask pressing a needle into the patient feeding tube. Remembering that the nurse said she was the only nurse on the floor at that time Tom realized that this was not right. Tom grabbed the fellow to stop him. The person twisted himself free and ran out of the room. Tom wanted to chase him but decided that it was more important to save the patient's life. He then removed the tube from the patients arm and twisted the end so that the fluid would not spill out. Just as he was ready to call Vicki, Vicki came into the room.

"What is going on?" asked Vicki seeing that Tom had removed the feeding tube.

"When I got here there was a fellow that was injecting a needle into the feeding tube," said Tom. "I tried to stop him but he got away. Instead of chasing him I decided to save the patient instead. You had nine years of experience in the lab so will you take this down to the lab and check to see if there is some kind of poison in the fluid. I don't think you will have trouble getting in the lab. If you have trouble call Ellie. She will find a way to get inside." Vicki grabbed the feeding equipment and started down to the lab. On the way she called and informed Ellie of all that was going on. Tom then decided to call the police chief Captain Richard to inform him of what was going on and ask for police protect for the patient. He called the captain's cell phone.

"Hi Captain," said Tom. "This is Tom Corely. I am at the University Hospital. I was asked by Tina Siden, the woman who was shot in the chest, to be her private detective to investigate who shot her and murdered her family."

"We had a meeting scheduled for tomorrow morning," said the Captain.

"I intend to keep that meeting," said Tom.

"Well," said the Captain, "It may not be necessary. The reason I wanted to meet with you is to have you come back as a part time Police detective. I still have you listed as an on call police officer. It will be just like the other times since you retired that I assigned you to a part time job. The interesting thing is that I am assigning you to the investigation of the shooting of the Siden family.

"That will be great," said Tom. "I accept the assignment. But isn't this Bill's job?"

"Bill is out of town and will not be back for weeks. So you are the only one I have with the necessary skills for this job. Anyway I want you to understand that you will be paid as an employee of this police department. You cannot be paid by her."

"I understand," said Tom. "I will be a city detective investigating a crime"

"By the way," asked the Captain, "why did you call me?"

"When I first got here," said Tom, "as I walked into Tania's hospital room I saw a young man injecting something into the Tania's feeding tube. I tried to stop him but he got away from me. Instead of chasing him I decided that Tina's life was more important. So I pulled the feeding tube out of Tania's arm and closed the end so that the fluid would not spill. I then sent the nurse down to the lab to check it for possible poison. I was sure that he was trying to poison her." Just as he finished talking Vicki, Ellie and a young man came running into the room. The young man ran directly to Tania. The girls stopped to talk to Tom.

"It was poison alright," said Vicki. "Doctor Brian recognized the poison and is injecting Tania with a drug that will neutralize the poison."

"Captain," said Tom. "It was poison and the emergency doctor is injecting her with a drug that will neutralize the poison. Anyway that is why I called you in the first place. I was sure that it was poison, therefore I thing we need an officer here day and night to protect the patient."

"I will take care of it right away," said the Captain. "Please don't leave until a police officer gets there." With that said he hung up.

"I'm sorry that I didn't stop to speak with you," said Doctor Christopher Brian. "I had to inject the patient before the poison got too far into her body."

"I'm detective Corely," said Tom. "I'm so glad that you did that. I'm also glad to meet you."

"I'm glad to meet you too," said the doctor. With that said the doctor left.

"You girls did a great job," said Tom. "Your quick action probably saved Tania's live."

"That is our job," said Vicki.

"I have to stay here until the police officer comes to protect Tania from other intruders," said Tom, "but you girls don't have to stay here with me."

"We can stay and keep you company," said Ellie.

"I think it is a better idea if we leave and go home. We can cook a nice dinner for your father," said Vicki.

"Great Idea," said Ellie. "I didn't think about that," said Ellie. "I think we are all very hungry."

"I have some Lamb Chops in the refrigerator," said Tom. "If you like to cook them and make a simple salad, I would love that. I won't be long. I'll come home as soon as the officer gets here. He is on his way now." The girls left, feeling honored to be able to cook for Him. It was only about fifteen miutes later when the police officer arrived.

"Hi Tom," said Officer Samuel Becket when he got there. "How are you? Back at being a detective for our department are you?"

"Hi Sammy," said Tom, "Looks like I can't get away from you guys,"

"Are there any instructions you want to give me before you leave?" asked Sammy.

"I would like you to introduce your replacement to the nurse on duty," said Tom. "I also would like you to have the nurse introduce the new nurse to the officer that in on duty when she leaves. I want to make sure no one enters the room that is not on duty at the time. I don't even want a doctor to come in without the nurse on duty."

"I understand," said Sammy. "I will make sure it is carried on with all replacements." Tom then left for home. When he got home the girls had a wonderful dinner waiting for him. They ate dinner and after eating they discussed all that had happened that day and soon all went to bed

The next morning, after they had breakfast, they all went to the hospital. Tom drove by himself not knowing how long he would be there. After talking with the nurse on duty Tom went into Tania's room. Tania was just waking up. She was still kind of drowsy when Tom walked in. She looked at him as if she kind of recognized him.

"Do I know you?" she said almost to herself. Then thinking it over she added, "You are the one who removed my feeding tube when the nurse was injecting something in it."

"That is right," said Tom. "The fellow was not a nurse. He was trying to poison you. I arrived just in time. We checked the fluid in the tube and found that it was poison. By the way I am Detective Thomas Corely. I was assigned to find out who is trying to kill you."

Are you the detective that the nurse Vicki said she would call for me?"

"Yes," said Tom, "she is a very good friend of mine. Can you think of any one that would like to kill you?"

"I cannot think of anyone who would want to harm us detective Corely," said Tania. "We were so happy. We just moved here not too long ago. We didn't have an enemy in the world."

"Please call me Tom," said Tom. "You had an enemy somewhere."

"What reason would someone want to harm us?" asked Tania.

"There are two common reasons," said Tom. "One that is the most common is to get an inheritance. The other is if you have knowledge that they would not want to be known. Tell me who are in your family that would be in line for your inheritance?"

"I have a sister Sophia that lives in Arizona," said Tina. "Her husband's name is Carl Marks. They have a daughter that is named Gloria. But we love each other very much."

"What about your husband?" asked Tom. "Does he have relatives nearby?"

Jim was the only son and his parents died in an auto accident. He has no other relatives."

"That is enough for me to go on for now," said Tom. "I'm sure that your family would have no reason to hurt you. However let me get them out of the way before I try somewhere else." Tom then left and spent all afternoon to investigate Tina's family. He found out that both Tina's sister and brother-in-law were at work. Their daughter was in college located in California. That evening he contacted Tina's sister by phone. They had not heard that her husband and son were killed and that she was hurt. Tom asked her if she knew anyone who would want to harm them. She said that they were such loving people that hurting them had to be a mistake. Have you asked her best friend Sara Brent? She would know more about her life then I would. She lives in Cleveland. That satisfied Tom. He decided that he had to look elsewhere. That evening he had dinner with Vicki and Ellie. They had all kind of questions that Tom could not yet answer.

The next morning Tom went directly to Tina's room. There was a police officer watching the room. Since he knew Tom he let him in the room. Tina was awake.

"Good morning Tina," said Tom. "How are you today?"

"I am a little better, thank you," said Tina. "What have you found out?" She asked getting right to the point. By the look on her face Tom was aware that she was still suffering the loss of her husband and son.

"I have investigated all possibility and have come up with nothing. I have contacted all of your family and found them all innocent of anything to do with your problem. In fact they were very saddened to hear of what has happened to you. By the way, your sister told me that you have your best friend living just a few miles away in East Cleveland. She said that her name is Sara. Why haven't you told me about her? Perhaps she may have an idea of who would want to harm you."

"I haven't seen Sara for a very long time," said Tina. "She would not know anything about my problem. I don't want to bother her with my problem. Please leave her alone"

"Tell me," said Tom. "How did you meet Sara?"

"We went to school together in Arizona. We were both born there in Phoenix. I moved up here to Ohio when my husband got a job here. Sara traveled all over the country with her job. She just moved here a little while ago when she changed jobs."

"Ok then," said Tom. "I had better go if I'm going to find out who did this to you. Goodbye for now." Tom left the hospital and went directly to Tina's house. It was still in a very disorderly condition. He searched in the office and found what he wanted. He found Tina's personal phone book. The police had searched it for all the family information but had not recorded the two numbers that were not family numbers. He found what he wanted. It was Sara Brent's phone number and address. When he got home he called the number. No one answered. After searching for other information he started to cook supper for the girls. They both showed up about five. They were both very hungry. They loved the Lamb chops Tom had cooked. After spending the evening discussing all that went on during the day they watch a nice movie on TV and after the movie ended they all went to bed.

The next morning Tom called Sara. No one answered again. Tom then decided to go to her house after lunch. He decided to wear his uniform to supply credibility to what he had to ask. After lunch he went to the address he had for Sara. It took him about forty minutes to get there. When he got there he got the same answer. He was about to leave when the neighbor who was outside sprinkling her flowers went up and spoke to Tom.

"Can I help you," she said. "The young lady who lives here has not been home for quite a while."

"I'm detective Tom Corely. I came to see Sara Brent," said Tom showing her his credentials. "Do you know what happened to her?"

"I don't even know if she is alive," said the neighbor. "Several police cars came here about a week ago and an ambulance came and carried Sara away. The police came later to talk with me. They wanted to know about her. I didn't know her. We never met. She was a very private person. The only thing I could tell the police that was strange is that one day at three in the morning when I went to the bathroom I looked out and saw a small black car in her driveway. At six in the morning I noticed it was gone. Being curious I checked often. It seems that she got a visitor after midnight every day, and then left before six the next morning."

"Thank you very much for that information" said Tom. "Have a good day." With that Tom left and went directly to the police station. At the Cleveland police station he walked up to the officer that was at the entrance desk.

"Hi," said the officer. "How can I help you?"

"I am Detective Thomas Corely from the Fairlawn police department. I would like to speak with someone about your police action about a week ago." Just then an elder gentleman walked out of the main office.

"I think you had better speak to Chief Benison," said the officer. The man heard the men talking and entered the conversation

"What can I do for you?" said the chief.

"I am Detective Thomas Corely, from the Fairlawn Ohio Police Department. I would like to speak to someone about a woman named Sara. Brent."

"Come with me," said the Chief. He then led him into an office at the end of the hall and introduced the officer that was sitting at the desk. "This is Detective John Anderson. He is assigned to the Brent case. I think you two should work together." The chief then left.

"I am detective Tom Corely. I am from Fairlawn Ohio. I am investigating the shooting of a woman named Tina Siden. I was told that Sara was a very close friend of Tina. However I have not been able to find her. Her neighbor told me that your police took her away last week."

"Come in," said John. "Have a seat. That is why we have not been able to contact Tina Siden. I have been calling her several times this week but no one answered the phone. Doesn't she have a family? I was about to travel to Fairlawn to find her."

"I would like us to work together as partners," said Tom. "Would you mind that?"

"I would love that," said John. "I could use all the help I could get. I also would like a companion to keep me company and have someone to discuss the case with. I am kind of lost at his time."

"Well, then let me start with what I know," said John. "I was assigned the case of the shooting of the Siden family. We found that the house was in a mess. Someone had checked every drawer and corner of the house looking for something. The husband and son were found dead. The wife Tania was also shot but is still alive. The bullet just skimmed her heart. After I was assigned the job I went to see her in the hospital. It was late in the evening and as I walked into her room I saw a masked person injecting something into her feeding hose. I stopped him but I did not chase him because I felt it was more important to save the patient's life. I pulled the hose out of her arm and called the nurse. We had the fluid check and it turned out to be poison. We then placed a police officer outside of her room twenty four house a day. I checked all of their relatives and friends and found that they all lived out of town and they all had good alibies. That's when I found that Tania had a very close friend here in Cleveland named Sara. So here I am trying to find her."

"Do you think there is a connection?" asked John.

"I think the possibility is good," said Tom. "So tell me all you know about Sara."

"We were called by her boss," started John. "She was to be in a very important meeting and since she didn't show up and didn't answer the phone he called us. We went there and found her lying on her kitchen floor. We called an ambulance but unfortunately it was too late. We found that her house had been ransacked. I think they were looking for something. However we did find her address book. That's where we found Tania's name. We tried to call the phone number given in the address book several times for about two days. That is when I decided to drive up to Fairlawn. I have checked all the people she worked with but I got nowhere."

"Is there anything else?" asked Tom, "that may be involved even if it is a very unlikely possibility."

"The only other thing that I'm involved with is the case that will be reviewed in court tomorrow. It is about who will inheritance the possessions of the famous singer, Nicki Lane. I'm sure you head of him."

"Of course," said Tom. "Who has not heard of him? He is the singer who is known as the sexiest available bachelor. What has he to do with all of this?"

"In my search in Sara's background," said John, "I found that she spent a few years as the manager for Nicki Lane. She was the one who set up all his performance dates all over the country. She traveled with him in most of the large cities in the USA. She quit about three years ago and settled here in Cleveland as a financial director for a clothing manufacturer."

"I'm beginning to see a possible connection with all of this," said Tom. "First let us check if there is a connection between the shooting of Tania and Sara. I presume that you have the bullet that killed Sara. I have the bullet's that hit Tania and her family. I will bring them tomorrow. I would like to go with you to the court review. Can you have your lab check to see if they were all fired by the same weapon?"

"Yes I can have our lab check them," said John. "Bring them tomorrow morning. The court review is for one o'clock tomorrow afternoon. It could be handy to have that information with us tomorrow."

"Sounds like a good plan," said Tom. "See you then." Tom left with a lot of thought running around in his head. He finally realized that he needed a lot more information.

That evening went just like all the evening for the last month. The girls came home had dinner and after a short discussion and a movie they all went to bed.

The next morning Tom got up early had breakfast and headed for the East Cleveland police station. He walked back to John's office. It was about ten thirty when he got there. John was there going through some papers.

"Good morning John," said Tom. "How are you this morning?"

"I'm fine Tom." said John. "Did you bring the bullets with you? I think we should get them to the lab as soon as possible." Tom handed a plastic bag with the bullets to John. "Just sit here and I'll be right back." He then left and was back after a few minutes.

"When did they say they will have the results?" asked Tom.

"Fortunately they were not that busy," said John. "They started right away. They should have the answer in less than an hour."

"What do you want to do in the meantime?" asked Tom.

"You know," said John. "I didn't have much of a breakfast. Let me take you to a favorite restaurant of mine. We should have lunch before we go to the court house."

"That is a great Idea," said Tom. "I thought you could have something else to take care of before we left for the court house."

"No," said John. "This is all I have been assigned for now." They left and John was right. The food there was fantastic. When they got back from lunch the results of the bullet test showed that they were all shot from the same gun. With that done they were ready to go to the court house.

It the meant time, back at the Hospital, Vicki was told that Margie was ready to be released. She quickly went to her room.

"Hi Margie," said Vicki. "I hear that the doctor is releasing you. Are you happy to go home?"

"Not really," said Margie. "I will be all alone. Not only that I can hardly walk so how can I take care of myself. I can't drive to buy food or other necessities."

"I was thinking of that," said Vicki. "I just wanted to hear what you thought about that. I think you will need a live in nurse. Do you think you could afford that?"

"I'm not too sure I want that either," said Margie. "I don't know if I would like a stranger living with me." Just then Ellie walked into the room. She had hear their conversation.

Hi Margie," said Ellie. "I was thinking about that. I was talking with your doctor and he felt the same. It is too soon to let you go out on your own. We wished that we could keep you in the hospital but we just could not pull it off. However I just interviewed a young nurse who needs a job. We don't have a position for her at this time. Perhaps when the hospital completes the extension they are working on we will have a position for her. She is very intelligent and very sweet. Why don't I call her and see if she is interested. I will have her come in here and you both can get together on the possibility. I'm not even sure if she would even consider the job."

"Go ahead and call her," said Margie, "What can we lose?" Ellie then went into her office to get the phone number. She called the young nurse. A few minutes later she returned to Margie hospital room.

"I gave her this room number, so she will be here in about fifteen minutes," said Ellie. It was only ten minutes when the young nurse showed up.

"Hi Ellie," she said as she walked in. "Please introduce me to your friends."

"Virginia," said Ellie, "this is Margarita Mellio and this is Nurse Victoria Graton. She is a good friend of Margarita."

"Please call me Margie. I am so pleased to meet you."

"Please call me Ginny," said Virginia. "That is what everyone calls me."

"Look," said Vicki, "I think we should leave you two alone to get to know each other." Ellie agreed and then Vicki and Ellie left.

"I agree that we should get to know each other before we discuss anything further." said Margie. "That would be a good place to start."

"Before we go any farther there is one thing that I would like to make clear," said Ginny. "Ellie said something about a live in nurse. If that is what you want I'm sorry but I can't do that. I moved back up here to be near my family. My parents live in Montrose and I have a brother that lives in Stow. I have a baby sister that lives with my parent. I moved up here so I could be with them."

"That would be better with me," said Margie. "I didn't like the idea of a live in nurse. Tell me, what do you see yourself doing if you got this job?"

"I would get up in the morning, drive to your house around eight. I would prepare breakfast for you and then I would do some house cleaning and do some shopping especially if we need food. At noon I would make you lunch and then do some chores that need to be done such as washing the dishes, washing your cloths and what else could come up. At about five I will start getting your supper ready. When you finish eating I will clean the kitchen and then go home."

"Would you be eating some meals with me?" asked Margie.

"It would be as you wish. I could pack my own lunch. Although, I think it would be nice to have a meal with you. I would like the company. However I don't want to be a burden on you."

"Tell me about your life," asked Margie.

"There is not much to tell," said Ginny. "I graduated from a Columbus University nursing school with honors. I got a job in a Columbus hospital, but I was too lonely. I quit the job and came back to Ohio to be with my family."

"I am the sole survivor of my family," said Margie. "I have no family and all my close friends have all passed away. So I know what it is like to be alone."

"I would like to keep you company," said Ginny.

"I think I would like that also," said Margie. "Let's talk details. How much will it cost me and how many days are we talking about?"

"I could work five or six days. It depends on how you feel after a few weeks. You may not need my help every day. At first I would suggest I come for six days."

"And what would you expect for salary?" asked Margie.

"At the hospital in Columbus I was getting $7.oo an hour. Is that two much for you?" asked Ginny.

"How about I pay you $100.oo a day," said Margie. "Some days you may have to work more than ten hours and some days lest then nine. You will still get $100.oo a day except the days you are off. All the meals you will have with me are all included at no cost to you. This set up will always be negotiable."

"Sounds like a great deal," said Ginny. "I like the idea that we should try it and then renegotiate after a few weeks if necessary." Just then Vicki walked in pushing a wheel chair.

"I think that it is time for you to go home," said Vicki.

"Margie and I have made an agreement," said Ginny. "So as her employee I will take over from here. I will driver her home."

"Fine," said Vicki. "I'm so glad that is taken care of." Ginny went ahead of them and got her car and drove it to the hospital entrance where Vicki had brought Margie. Vicki helped Margie get into Ginny's car and watched them as they drove away.

Tom and John arrived at the court house about ten minutes to one in the afternoon. Everyone was already there except the judge. He walked in exactly at one o'clock.

"Will Mr. George Lane please stand and plea his case," said the judge.

"I am George Lane," started George. "My father Walter Lane is Nicky Lane's brother. My mother is Liana Lane, Nicki Lane's

Sister-in-law. Mr. Lane was my uncle. As far as we know we are the only living relative of my uncle. In view of the fact that no evidence of a will is found I request that all of my uncle Nicki's possessions be transferred to my mother."

"Do I hear any objections to this request?" said the judge.

"Yes," said a man as he stood up. "I am Ronald Welch. I am Nicky's attorney. I took care of all Nicki's finances. I helped him write his will. He left everything to another woman. Unfortunately I don't remember her name."

"Could her name be Sara Brent?" asked Tom interrupting him.

"Yes, thank you," said Ronald. "Her name was Sara Lane."

"There is no record of such a will, and no relative whose name is Sara Lane." said George.

"That is because someone broke into my office and stole all my documents," said Ronald. "Someone also broke into Nicki's room and stole his document."

"Did you find anything unusual in your investigating of Nicki room?" asked detective John Anderson.

"I and a police officer searched the room for evidence of a robbery," said Ronald. "There was something very strange that we found out in that search. The maid who cleaned all the rooms told us that Nicki's bed looked like it seldom got slept in. The landlady also verified that something was strange. She told us that Nicki's car always left around one after midnight in the evening and showed up about nine or ten in the morning. It was strange that he always came home but didn't sleep in his bed. I'm curious. Why did you ask me that question?"

"I asked that question because I found something just as strange," said John. "The neighbor that lives next door to Sara told me that she got up one morning to go to the bathroom and happen to look out the window. She saw a car there that had not been there when she went to bed. In the morning when she got up it was gone. Curiosity got her to look out of her widow every night and every morning. It was always the same. Someone was coming in after midnight and leaving before seven in the morning."

"That is strange," said Ronald. "Could it be that Nicki was sneaking out every night and spending the evening with Sara?"

"This is a very funny story," said George being irritated by the discussion. "It would make a very great novel. But what has it to do with this case? There is no evidence with any of this."

"Your honor," said Tom ignoring George's comments. "Four people were shot, one in East Cleveland area and four in the Akron area. The lab has shown that the bullets all were shot from the same weapon. Four houses were broken into and only the important documents were stolen especially the victim's wills. The two women, Sara and Tania were best friends and were from the same city in Arizona. Your honor, there are too many unanswered questions. We request that you give Detective John Anderson and me a little more time to investigate this case."

"I think that is acceptable," said the judge. "I will give you one week. Let's meet at one in the afternoon next Wednesday. However I also request that you contact me immediately if you find some important evidence." With that said he dismissed the meeting and walked out of the court room. Tom and John quickly left before anyone could question them. On the way to John's office John questioned Tom.

"Do you have a plan of where to go from here?" asked John. "I have no idea of what to do from here."

"I have one very important witness to talk to," said Tom. "I think she has some information she had not told me. I didn't bring it up in court because I didn't want George to know that one of the victims is still alive. I'm going to interrogate her. I believe that George is our villain He is the same size as the fellow I caught in the hospital room trying to poison Tania. Also he had the same color hair" After they got to John's office Tom got into his car and drove home. Tom had no idea what Tania would tell him. He had no idea of where this whole case would lead him.

CHAPTER THREE

Unexpected Events

When Tom got home he decided that he would cook a nice meal for the girls before they got home. As he started to get some food out of the refrigerator the girls came home.

"Hi dad," said Ellie first. "If you are cooking a special dinner please make it for two. I have a date for tonight."

"Hi Tom," said Vicki. "I see that our young lady is starting to grow up."

"Who are you dating?" asked Tom.

"You met him," said Ellie, "he was the emergence room doctor that neutralized the poison that was injected into Tania's feeding tube. His name is Dr. Christopher Brian. He is on second shift and we can't date very often. He happened to have a day off so he asked me out to dinner."

"I remember him," said Vicki. "One day while he was still on second shift, when I was working late I stopped at the hospital cafeteria for dinner. He was also there for what was to him his lunch. When I saw him I recognized him and asked if I could join him. He said yes. I was surprised after he got his food that he hesitated to pray. I asked him if he was a Christian. He said that he was a Born-Again-Christian. I highly recommend him."

"Sounds like good fellow," said Tom. "Please be home before midnight." At ten miutes before six, Christopher showed up. Surprisingly Ellie was ready. Tom stayed out of view. Tom did not hear when Ellie got home. The next morning Tom got up at nine. Ellie and Vicki had their breakfast and had already gone to work. Tom had his breakfast and headed to the hospital. At the hospital he went directly to Tania's room.

"Hi Tania, how are you today?"

"Hi Tom, I'm much better. What brings you here this early?"

"I need you to tell me the truth," said Tom. "I know that you know more than you are telling me. I'm sure you know that Sara and Nicki are married. I need you as a witness to their relationship. We can't let all of Nicky Lane's possessions and money be inherited by his sister-in-law. Especially since I think Nicki's nephew was the one who shot four people. We checked the bullets and the lab proved that they all came from the same weapon.

"I think you are right," said Tania, "but why do you say four people. There were only the three of us, any way, you should ask Sara. That is her problem."

"Oh sweet Tania," said Tom. "I'm sorry. I guess you do not know. The fourth person shot and killed was Sara your best friend." Tom was surprise how Tania started to cry out loud. She took the death of her friend harder that Tom had expected. It took about fifteen miutes before Tom could settle Tania down to a tearful conversation.

"What happened," said Tania through tears.

"I think that his nephew George found out somehow that his uncle had a wife. So he broke into his apartment and found his will. He then destroyed it and broke into his uncle's attorney's office and destroyed all of the will in the attorney's offices. Then knowing that Sara was his wife he had to eliminate her and her will and any copy of his uncle's will. At Sara's house he broke in and searched for her will. He must have found enough evidence of your friendship with her that made him decide to get you out of way also."

"Well," said Tania sobering up a little. "We can't let him get away with that. How can I help?"

"Well first of all you have to be willing to testify," said Tom. "Is there anything that you can think of that could help us convince the court that Sara was his wife?" I can only testify that she told me in confidence because Nicki's popularity was that he was an available bachelor. If people knew that he was married most of his followers would vanish as his popularity would vanish. There is one thing however that I can do for you. I don't know if it would help."

"I will look into anything that could possibly help," said Tom.

"Well,' continued Tania. "Sara did give me a box to keep for her. I have no idea what is in it."

"Where do you keep this box?" asked Tom.

"I keep it in my secret safe," said Tania.

"I'm sorry," said Tom. "I think George went through your house with a fine tooth comb. I am planning to go through you home and help put it together before you go home. There is not a single drawer that is not empty with all its contents on the floor. All the pictures are on the floor probably they were searching for a safe that could be behind a picture. I don't see where you will have this secret safe"

"Well perhaps your right," said Tania. "What do you have to lose if you try?"

"All right," said Tom. "Where is this secret safe?"

"When you enter the bathroom that is off the family room," Started Tania, "you will find a cabinet on the left that has towels, blankets and other things stored there. The cabinet wall sticks out about six inches out from the sinks that are next after the cabinet. There are two sinks there. At the other end of the sinks is a wall that sticks out about six inches beyond the sinks. On the other side of the wall is about a two feet space to the outside house wall. In that space is the toilet. On the back wall above the toilet is a picture. If you remove the picture you will find a small safe." She then gave Tom the combination to the safe. Go and see what you can find."

"I will go right now," said Tom. "I see how you may be right. No one would guess that you would have a safe there. But will you be alright if I leave you?"

"I'll be fine," said Tania, "My mind will be occupied by the thought of what is in that little box Sara gave me." With that said Tom left and went directly to Tania's house. He was still amazed at the terrible shape the house was in. he decided that he would get one of the girls to come and help him get Tania's house back in shape. He then went into the bathroom of the living room. Everything was as Tania had described. Above the toilet was the picture Tania had said would be there. It was not disturbed. Tom removed the picture and sure enough behind it was a safe. Tom used the safe combination and the safe opened. Tom took out the small box that was inside and closed the safe trying not to disturb the other items that were in there. He then hung the picture and with the box went into the kitchen to see what was in the box. He sat at the table and opened the box. There were two documents and a letter in the box. Tom took one of the documents and read it. It was the will of Sara. It stated that after her death that her assets should be split three ways. One third is to go her brother Ralph Brent, one third is to go her best friend Tania Siden and one third is to go to Liana Lane. Tom was surprised that Tania was going to get the same as Sara's family. Tom then opened the other document. When Tom saw what it was he was stunned for a minute then he yelled "Horary," out loud with joy. It was the marriage certificate between Sara and Nicki. After getting his control back he checked the letter that was already open. The letter was addressed to Sara's attorney. It said that if Nicky died before her and left everything to her that he should contest the will so that one third of his assets went to his sister-in-law. Also in the envelope was the attorney's card with the attorney's name and phone number. He decided to call the attorney and see what he knew about the case He dialed the number on the card.

"How may I help you?" said a young woman's voice.

"I would like to speak to attorney Phil Belner," said Tom.

"I'm so sorry," said the woman. Mr. Belner passed away several months ago."

"What then have you done with all the wills that he wrote up for his clients?"

"We have mailed our copies of each will to each client he wrote them for."

"Thank you," said Tom and hung up. Tom then realized why Sara gave the extra copy to Tania. George must have taken the copy Sara had at home. Tom realized that George could not have seen the letter. Happy with what he got he headed straight to see Tania in the hospital. On the way he called Detective John Anderson.

"Hi John," said Tom when John answered his cell phone. I got very important information. I got all that we need to close this case and put the culprit in jail. Please call the judge and make an appointment. Tomorrow is Sunday so lets try for Monday. Please ask that it will be just us and the prosecuting attorney if he wants"

"I will take care of it right now," said John. "Please come here as early as you can so that we can discuss our action." With that he hung up. Five miutes later he arrived at the hospital.

"Hi Tania," said Tom as he walked into the room. "Guess what I found in your safe."

"I hope it will be something that will solve this crime," said Tania.

"It will do more than solve the crime and put the criminal in jail but you will gain something from the results."

"Alright now," said Tania, "cut the bull and tell me what you are talking about,"

"I found two documents and one letter," said Tom. "The most important is the marriage certificate. The other is a letter to Sara's attorney. It asked that if Nicky died before her and leaves all his assets to her, she wanted him to give one third to Nicky's Sister-in-law. Wasn't that so generous of her?"

"She was an angel," said Tania. "What was the other document?" Before Tom could answer he got a phone call. It was John.

"We have an appointment with the judge in his office for ten Monday morning," said John see me about eight."

"Great," said Tom. "Please try to find out what the total amount of assets we are fighting for."

"I have most it now," said John. "I will see that I will have it all Monday." With that they hung up.

"Where was I?" said Tom, "Oh yes it was about the other document. The other document was her last will and testament. It left one third of her assets to her brother Ralph Brent in Arizona. It left One third to Nicky's sister-in-law Liana Lane, and the last third she leaves to you, Tania Siden."

"You have to be kidding," said Tania in a state of shock. "How much are we talking about?"

"I don't know right now," said Tom. "That is what I just asked the Cleveland Detective, John Anderson. He is the one that I just talked to over my cell phone. I asked him to find out before our ten o'clock meeting with the Cleveland judge Monday morning." Tom stayed for a little while and then left to prepare dinner for his girls.

The next morning Tom got the girls up early to go to church. He wanted Vicki to become a member of his church. After the service he introduced her to the pastor. The pastor asked her to go with him to his office. He asked the rest of us to wait in the waiting room. Several minutes later she came out.

"Guess what," said Vicki joyfully, "I am a born again Christian. I feel like I'm at home here in this church." They then went home to prepare lunch. They were surprised to see Alex there.

"Hi Dad, and hi girls," said Alex. "I see you have a guest."

"Hi Alex," said both Tom and Ellie at the same time. Then turning to Vicki Tom said, "Vicki this is my son Alex. Alex this is our guest Vicki Graton."

"Nice to meet you, Alex," said Vicki. "I have been looking forward to meeting you and all of your father's family."

"You are right," said Tom. "When things settle down for both of us, I will take you to meet my parents. You two get to know each other and I will go up and make our lunch. I have two large pieces of prime steak. It will be more than enough for the four of us." Ellie went up with her father to help him. Vicki and Alex got to know each other while the steaks were being grilled. Vicki told Alex about her problem. However, Alex knew basic details of Vicki's problem. He had learned about it from his sister. Alex told Vicki that he was a general doctor working for the Medina Medical Group.

"That sounds great," said Vicki. "How are you doing?"

"I would like to open up an office of my own," said Alex. "They have too many strange rules that hold me back from some of the things I would like to do."

"Food is ready," yelled Tom. They all went up to the kitchen. After eating they sat around and shot the bull. The evening went by too soon. They soon all departed. Alex went home and Tom and the girls went to bed.

The next morning Tom got up early. He felt too excited to eat breakfast. Down stairs he found the girls were eating breakfast getting ready to go to work.

"Good morning Dad," said Ellie.

"Good morning Tom," said Vicki at the same time.

"Do you want some breakfast?" said Ellie.

"No," said Tom. "I have to go to Cleveland about the singer Nicky Lane's inheritance. I don't have time to eat. You girls have a nice day." With that said Tom left. He got to the office of Detective John Anderson at exactly eight o'clock.

"Boy you are exact in your timing," said John.

"It was just a coincidence," said Tom. "Now I think we should get right to how we are going to present this information."

"We have until ten," said John. "Tell me what you came up with."

"I think these documents point to the only guilty party that could do all this," said Tom. He then showed John the three items he had.

"Wow," said John. "I see why you are worried about how we should present his information to the judge. I also see why you only wanted us to be there."

"What order should we present this information?" asked Tom.

"Well my first thought is that we should settle that Nicky was married to Sara," said John. That will give all of Nicky's assets to Sara. Then we could show him Sara's will, to fix where all the possession of both Nicki and Sara should go. The letter is important to George. The shock may make him confess of his crimes." After a few discussions they left for the judge's office making sure they got there on time. They arrived a few miutes early. They sat in the car for a while so that they got to his office at ten o'clock on the dime. The judge was there with a woman who Tom and John assumed was a secretary.

"Good morning your honor," said John. "I think we have all that is needed to close this case."

"Good morning gentlemen," said the judge. "What information do you have?"

"This first item," started John, "it the marriage certificate that proves that Nicki Lane was married to Sara Brent, as Nicky's attorney insisted." John then handed the certificate to the judge.

"That pretty well settles that," said the judge. "Is there anything else you want to add?"

"Yes," said John. "I want to show you Sara's last will and testament. I want to make sure that each party gets their share." The judge handed the documents to the woman.

"Please make a copy of both of these," said the Judge. Then turning to John and Tom he asked. "Is there anything else?"

"Yes," said Tom. "As you can see that the only person who could benefit from all the shooting is George Lane. All the bullets of the four shooting match and if we find George's gun we could test to see if the bullets came from his gun. You honor I would like a court order to search his house and especially his car."

"That sounds reasonable," said the judge. "After you search his house and car, if you still think he is the guilty party, have him arrested. I will then set up a court hearing. I see you have another document. Is that relevant to this case?"

"It is a letter from Sara," said Tom. "In it she asks her lawyer that if she is the only one listed in Nicky's will, that she wants him to contest it so that His sister-in-law Liana Lane will receive one third of Nicky's assets. I think this will shake up George so that the shock of realizing that he didn't have to kill any one for his mother to get the funds she needed, could make him say something that could convict him. He may even confess to the shootings."

"All right," said the judge. "I will have the court order to search the house he lives in and his car in about an hour. Why don't you guys go to lunch and I will have it when you come back." Tom and John then went for lunch at a nearby restaurant. While there John called his office and asked that two officers meet him at the Lane house. He then gave them the address. After lunch they obtained the court order and proceeded to the Lane house. There they met the other two officers. They walked up to the door and knock. Fortunately both Liana and her son were home. Liana answered the door.

"Hello officer," said Liana. "How can I help you?"

"We have a court order to search you premises," said John. He then instructed his officers what to look for.

"Is your son home?" asked Tom.

"Yes" said Liana. She then yelled into the house. "George, come here please." George came to the door.

"I'm sorry," said George. "I have to leave. I have an appointment for a job and I am already little late."

"Your job can wait," said John. "We have to search everywhere and everything. So give me the keys to your car."

"Why do you want my car? I need it to go for my job."

"John grabbed him by the arm and took the keys from his hand. He had been ready to run. John then went and checked Liana's car and then George's car. There in the trunk he found a rifle that was the same caliber as the bullets they had retrieved from the victims. John then called one of his officers. "Sal" he instructed him, "please place George under arrest. Charge him with murder." Officer Sal then hand cuffed George and placed him in the police car. The other officer got in the back seat and left with them. After a short search through the house they left. Liana was sitting on her sofa in tears. Tom and John then went to John's office. There John quickly sent the rifle to see if it was the weapon that shot the bullet they retrieved from Sara, Tina and her family. About an hour later they got the results. It was the gun that had shot the bullets. John immediately called the judge.

"Your honor," said John. "We have all that we will need to continue the trial. We have the weapon that was used in the crime and we have arrested the suspect. We are ready for the hearing as soon as you can find an opening."

"Just a minute," said the judge. He was off the phone for about two minutes. "This is very unusual but I have an opening tomorrow at one o'clock. Let's get all the people together at that time"

"Thank you your honor," said John, "see you at one o'clock tomorrow." With that he hung up.

"That is a surprise," said John. "In the past I never had a hearing any sooner than a month."

"Listen John," said Tom. "I'm going to leave now. I don't think we have anything to discuss. I will see you at one o'clock tomorrow. I am going to drive directly to the court house. If things go as I expect there will no reason for me to go to your office."

"That's fine," said John. "See you tomorrow." Tom then left for home. When he got home the girls had not yet come home from work. He decided that he had not made a special dinner for them in a long time. He decided this was the time. He found that he had several packages of Baby back pork ribs. He remembered that the girls loved them the last time he cooked them. Each package had a large section with to rib bones in the piece of meat. He took out three packages. He had them all cooked when the girls got home. They all ate with joy.

"I'm surprised that you cooked for us," said Ellie. "You have been so busy. We hardly get to spend time with you except when you come to the hospital."

"I'll try to do better from here on," said Tom. "How about you, Ellie, don't you date that doctor, what is his name, Dr. Christopher Brian?"

"Not recently," said Ellie. "Since he is on second shift we don't get a chance to date, often. We date when he has a day off, however I see him often during the day." That evening went as most evening go, however it seemed like a week to Tom. Finally it was morning. He woke up at about six and could not sleep any longer so he just laid there till the girls left. Then he got up and had late breakfast. The rest of the morning he went over all the information they had.

Finally he ate a small early lunch and headed for the court house. He got there about ten to one. The others kept drifting in. The judge walked in exactly at one.

"Will everyone please stand," said the court clerk. After the judge got seated the Clerk asked everyone to be seated. As soon as they were seated George was brought into the court room.

"I think the first thing we should clear up is Nicky Lane's inheritance. We have here a marriage certificate that proves that Nicki Lane and Sara were married. We had all the signatures check and the certificate is valid. Therefore all of Nicky Lane's assets will be delivered to Sara Lane's account. Does anyone have any objections," asked the judge. When no one spoke up the judge continued. "Next I have document here which is the last will and testament of Sara Lane. It states that all of her assets to be divided into three equal parts to the listed recipients. I order that the request of this will be carried out immediately. Are there any objections?" There were no objections. "Do you detective John Anderson, have any information as to the amount of the assets?"

"Yes I do," said John. "The total of both Nicki and Sara assets amount to seven million two hundred thousand. That means that each recipient receives two million four hundred thousand."

"Thank you," said the judge. "There is one more document which has no effect on the results of this hearing, but I think that everyone should be made aware of its contents. It is a letter to Sara's attorney. In it she asks him that if her husband dies before her and he leaves everything he has to her that she wants him to give one third of her inherited asset's to Sara Lane's brother Ralph Brent who lives in Arizona. One third of her assets should go to her best friend Tania Siden. And one third of her assets should go to Nicki's lane's sister-in-law, Liana Lane." George was shocked. He yelled out his feelings of stress."You mean that I didn't have to do anything and my mother would still have gotten over two million dollars. Dear lord, what have I done? I have destroyed my life for no reason at all." George's attorney grabbed George and pulled him aside.

"Listen to me George," said his attorney. "They have a ton of evidence against you, and due to your loss of control you have just about admitted you crimes. Therefore I advise you to confess. It might get you a better deal."

"Your honor," said George. "I would like to tell you how I am involved in this case. You see my mother is very ill. She needs surgery badly. When my uncle had his heart attack I got very worried. I had to know if he intended to leave anything to my mother. You see my dad and Uncle Nicki had a very terrible fight. We hadn't see or hear from him in several years. So, worried about my mom, I unthinkingly broke into Uncle Nicki's room. I found his will. I was so devastated to learn that he left everything to a woman named Sara. I lost my ability to think strait. I destroyed his will and then broke into his attorney's office and destroyed his copy. I should have gone to Aunt Sara and asked for her help. I see now that she would have helped. I wasn't thinking strait. Since I had my hunting rife in my car, I stupidly shot her. I then ransacked her house and didn't find her will but I did see that she had a very close friend that she grew up with in Arizona. Since I already shot someone, it wouldn't be any worst if I shot someone else. In my state of stupidity I decided that I had to eliminate her also. Your honor, I cannot tell you how sorry I am at what I did. It hurt the most after finding out that I didn't have to hurt anyone. I deserve whatever sentence you give me."

"Well this turn of events," said the judge, "shows that a jury trial will not be necessary. Are there any objection or other comments?" Since no one responded the judge continued. "I think this session is over. I will determine the sentence after I review all the information I have." Then turning to George's attorney he added. "I will inform you after I have made my decision and we can discuss it." He then got up and left the room.

"Well John," said Tom. "I don't think I will be needed any longer."

"Actually neither of us will be needed any longer," said John. "Thank you for all of your help. I could not have done this alone."

I certainly needed your help also," said Tom. "We made a good team. If you ever get into a jam you can't solve give me a call. Perhaps we could help each other in difficult cases."

"Sound great to me," said John. "You have a great day." Tom then left and headed directly to the hospital. He had to inform Tania. About an hour later he arrived at the hospital.

"Hi Tania," said Tom. "How are you today?"

"I'm fine," said Tania. "So now tell me the good news."

"How do you know it is good news?" asked Tom.

"I can tell by the great smile you have on your face," said Tania.

"It could be that I am so very glad to see you," said Tom with a greater smile on his face.

"Come on now," said Tania. "I have never seen you with such a jolly disposition."

"Alright I'll tell you what took place," said Tom. "We caught the fellow who took all the shots at you and Sara. It was Nicky's nephew. He needed the money for his mother operation."

"What about the inheritance. Who gets what and how much?" asked Tania.

"All of Nicki's assets will go to Sara," said Tom. There was a total of about seven million two hundred thousand dollars to be divided equally among three recipients. "

"Wow," said Tania. "I didn't know they had that much. Who are three lucky people?"

"Well," started Tom. "Two million four hundred thousand will go to Sara's brother Ralph Brent. Two million four hundred thousand will go to his sister-in-law Liana Lane. Two million four hundred thousand will go to her best friend Tania Siden." Tom was surprised at the shocked look on Tania's face. She couldn't say a word for several minutes. She looked like she was going to pass out. When she did come too her voice showed the effects of her unbelief.

"You aren't kidding are you?" said Tania barely getting it out.

"Of course not," said Tom. "I wouldn't kid about something like that."

"Well then I have news for you," said Tania recovering from her shock. "I contacted my sister in Arizona. She told me that across the street from her there was a small ranch house that was for sale. She said she wanted me to come home. She wanted to provide the down payment for the house. She said I could pay her back later. I told her to do it. She called back later and told me that I was the owner of a nice ranch house. I contacted a real state lady and she is putting my house up for sale. As soon as things get settled here I'm going home. I will sell all the furniture I don't want and since I have enough money now, I will have the furniture I want to keep shipped down to my new house in Arizona. I never wanted to come here in the first place. I came here because my husband got a great job here."

"That is great," said Tom. "However I will miss you very much."

"I will miss you also," said Tania. "Thank you so much for all the help you have given me. You have saved my life and protected me from a killer. How can I thank you? Can I pay you something for your effort in this case? I have a lot of money now thanks to you."

"No, thank you," said Tom. "Besides it would be illegal. A police office cannot accept money from a client"

"Well I will never forget you," said Tania with tears in her eyes.

"Stop that now," said Tom. "You will have us both in tears. Besides I have to go home. I haven't spent enough time with my girls."

"Let me give you some advice," said Tania. "Don't let Vicki get away. I can tell from the way she talks about you and the look in your eyes that there is something beautiful there."

"She is just grateful," said Tom.

"Are you grateful too?" added Tania. "That is all I have to say. So now go. Have a wonderful life. Goodbye." Tom then left with tears in his eyes. He never felt this way for a client before.

Tom got home just in time to make a fish dinner for the girls. When they came home they were very hungry and quickly sat at the table.

"Dad," said Ellie, "Tell us what you have done this day,"

"I just came back from seeing Tania. I told her of the success we had in finding the shooter and closed the case. Until the next case comes up I'll be home. I am going to work on my latest novel."

"How many novels have you written?" asked Vicki.

"I am presently working on my sixth novel," said Tom. "How about you girls, what have you worked on this day?"

"We have bin doing what we always do," said Vicki. "There is nothing new."

"Don't you have any old woman who needs a friend like Tania and Margi did?" asked Tom.

"All the patients that we have right now have family members that keep them company," said Vicki. After dinner they all went back to their regular activities. The next several weeks went by without any unusual events. Vicki would pick up Margie on Sunday morning and take her to church. After the service they have Margie over for lunch. Vicki would then take her home. Sometimes Vicki would visit Margie during the week after Dinner. It was on Monday one day after the girls ate breakfast that Tom caught them before they left for work.

"Listen girls," said Tom. "Is there any way that you girls could take a day off this Saturday? I would like to take you girls to Grandma and Grandpa's house. I would like then to meet you Vicki."

"Dad," said Ellie with a smile on her face. "Where have you been these last few days? Don't you remember that Thursday is the fourth of July? Grandma and Grandpa always come here for the fourth of July."

"Dear Lord," said Tom. "Is it July already?"

"Do your grandparents come here for all of the holidays?" asked Vicki.

"No," said Ellie. "They come here for the fourth of July. They come to see the parade in the afternoon and after dinner we go to the park and see the fireworks. We alternate Thanksgiving. Sometimes she comes here and sometimes we go there. However Grandma insists that all Christmas holidays be celebrated at her house. On New Year's we all go our own way. When I get married I will hold one of the holidays. I'm not sure yet which one it will be."

"Sound like you are a very affectionate family," said Vicki.

"Ok then," said Tom. "Let's get ready for the fourth of July.

What do you girls feel we should have for lunch and what should we have for dinner?"

"I think we should have something simple for lunch," said Ellie, "because we will not have too much time. I think we should have one of your fabulous meals for dinner."

"We can have just a sandwich for lunch," said Tom. "What do you suggest we have for dinner?"

"Can I make a suggestion," said Vicki. "I love your Cavatelli dinner. It is a great Italian recipe. You can make it the night before and then just warm it up when we come back from the parade."

"That sounds like a great Idea," said Tom. "What do you think Ellie?"

"I think it would be nice but it will be too much work for you," said Ellie. "I would like something that we could help you with."

"That's alright," said Tom. "I don't have anything to do Wednesday." The days went by quickly and it was soon Wednesday. Tom purchased all that he need for the meal and started making the tomato sauce after lunch. It was an all day job. After he felt the sauce was done he put in the pork neck bones. An hour later he added the meat balls. It was late in the afternoon when he cooked the Cavatelli. He then put the meat in a large container and set it aside to cool off enough for him to place it in the refrigerator. He placed the sauce in another container to cool off. So that it could go into the refrigerator later. He left enough sauce out to use when the girls came home. He then cooked regular spaghetti and about four thirty he mixed it with the sauce and had dinner ready for the girls. When the girls got home they ate with great pleasure.

"Dad," said Ellie. "You have to do this more often. This pasta is terrific. You can just make the sauce and freeze it so that we can have it several times with pasta."

The next day Alex came early in the morning and had breakfast with Tom and the girls Tom's parents showed up at about eleven o'clock. Tom hugged them both. Ellie and Alex also hugged them.

"Mom and Dad," said Tom. "I would like you to meet Victoria

Graton. She is the guest that I told you about. Vicki this my mom Elaine Corely"

"Of course," said Vicki. "You named your daughter after her grandmother."

"Hi Victoria," said Tom's mom. "We are so glad to meet you. Tom has not stopped talking about you. I'm so sorry for all the problems you have gone through. I'm sure Tom and Ellie will take good care of you until you get back on your feet."

"So you have heard about the life I had to go through," said Vicki. "By the way please call me Vicki. And you must of course be Tom's father Alexander Corely," said Vicki, as she turned to Tom's father. "Tom's son is named after you. It is so nice to meet you."

"Nice to meet you too," said Tom's father.

"Now let's not delay," said Tom. "Let's eat lunch. The parade states at one. We want to get a good place to watch it from." They ate lunch and after lunch Tom place four folding chairs in the trunk of his car. Tom's mom and dad brought their own folding chairs. Tom's father followed Tom down Bancroft road to Trunko road. They turned left on Trunko and drove to Morewood Road. Tom then drove east on Morewood until he got to Blue Hill road. Tom drove down Blue Hill road. Just before he got to Market Street Tom turned into the rear drive way that led to the parking lot behind the office building. Tom took the back street to keep from having to go through heavy traffic on Market Street. Not only that but they usually block the traffic on Market Street about a half hour before the parade. Then they would have had to park at the mall. Tom and his father both parked in the parking lot behind the large building. They got their folding chairs and walked down the side driveway that led to Market Street. There they unfolded their chair and sat off the street curb.

"We got here just in time," said Tom's father. "We got a spot under the tree. The sun is too hot to have it over you for the hours of the parade."

"Yes," said Tom. "We got lucky this time. However we all brought a hat just in case we couldn't find a shady place."

"I don't think a hat does that much good," said Alex jointing into the conversation. The girls were all sitting together on the other side of the tree. They obtained the good location because they were very early. The parade would not start for over a half hour. The girls all had cheerful conversation trying to get to know each other. The men did the same thing. It was almost forty minutes later when they heard the sound of the band at the far end of the street. Soon they saw the police car that was leading the parade. Slowly the parade came into sight. After the police car came one of the Fairlawn Fire Trucks. It siren was almost making you deaf it was so loud. It moved too slowly. Finally it passed and behind it was the Fairlawn Copley High School band. Two students walked in front carrying a flag with the school's name on it. Behind them came another Fairlawn Fire truck. It went by to slowly thought Tom. Behind it was a car with the Fairlawn mayor driving. His wife was in the passenger side. He waved continual at the audience. Behind it was the Akron High School Band. Behind them came Two motor cycles that drove in circles around the street and once in a while they would lift up the front so that they were only driving on the rear wheel. Suddenly they heard a strange sound coming from the south. It was an airplane. It was flying so low that you could see the pilot. It flew just above the parade and then at the other end of the parade it turned around a came back over the parade now going south. Suddenly when it was over Summit Mall they saw something dropping out of the plane. A few seconds later a parachute opened and a fellow was parachuting down to the Mall's parking lot.

"I never saw that before," said Tom's father.

"I don't think it was performed before," said Tom, "at least not while I have lived here." Following the motor cycles was a group of young girls with white sticks that looked like batons in their hands. They flipped the batons spinning in their hands and throwing them in the air. They did this synchronized with each other. Their display was fantastic. Following the girls was an Akron Fire truck which then was followed with three convertibles autos which carried City and state representatives. The rest of the parade included School Bands from other schools and a few vehicles from other communities. The Parade lasted two hour. They finally got home at about three forty five.

They left their folding chairs in their cars and went inside. They needed an air-conditioned area.

"That was a very interesting parade," said Tom's father. "It is different every time I come here."

"That is planned," said Tom kidding his father. "If we didn't change it you wouldn't come here again."

"I wondered what that airplane and Parachute deal was all about?" asked Alex Tom's son.

"I think it was meant to salute our country," said Tom. After some small talk Tom went up and started to heat the sauce and the Cavatelli. At about six they all sat down at the table and ate the dinner.

"That was the best Cavatelli dinner," said Tom's father," that I have ever had." "What have you done that is different than your mother's Cavatelli dinners?"

"I have experimented and added a few ingredients that I learned from Rita's family. It is mostly in the meat balls. I have added bread crumbs and a few other ingredients to make them softer and tenderer." After eating they shot the bull for a while and about nine they drove to the park across from the police station. Alex went with them in Tom's car with all the girls. Tom and Tom's dad pulled into the police parking lot. Since Tom is well known by the Fairlawn police he was allowed to park there. They took their folding chairs and walked across the street to the park. They carried the chair to the front of the stage where the band was playing. The band played several songs that were faithful and devoted to the great American democracy. It was about ten when the band played its last song, God Bless America. As soon as the song was over the fireworks stated. It was a fantastic display. The shapes and colors were out of this world. While the fireworks was going on the band packed up and left the stage. They went behind the stage where they watched the fireworks. The fireworks lasted till almost eleven o'clock. After it was over everyone started to leave. Tom and family met at the police parking lot where their cars were parked. When the got there Tom's father turned to Tom and the rest of the family.

"I think we are going home from here," said Tom's father. "It is almost eleven o'clock. It will be midnight when we get home. So let's say good night here. We had a very wonderful time with all of you." They all hugged each other and after saying good bye they all went their way. When Tom got home Alex walked over to his own car.

"Dad and girls," said Alex. "I think I will go home from here. It is too late to come inside." With that said they all hugged and Alex left. Tom and the girls all when inside and being tired thy all went to bed.

The next several weeks went by with little change to their lives. Vicki would go and visit Margie at least once during the week. On Sundays, Vicki would always pick up Margie and bring her to church. After church once in a while she would come home to Tom's house for lunch. After lunch she would always want to go to her own house. Sometimes Margie would invite them all to her house for lunch. Seldom would they all go. Usually it was only Vicki. They did not want to burden Margie with the job of feeding four people. This went on for a few months. One day just before Tom and the girls were ready sit down to eat dinner, Vicki got a phone call. After answering it she became saddened.

"Oh no," she shouted out with a sadness to her voice. "I have to go. Margie just had a heart attack" immediately she jumped into her car and left for the hospital. When she got there she found out that she was too late. Margie had passed away. Vickie suddenly got tears in her eyes. Dr. Wilson, who happened to still be in the hospital that late, was there besides Margie's bed.

"I'm sorry Vicki," said Dr. Wilson. "I did everything I could think of to save her. But if you remember that after the surgery we found that her heart was very week. She lived longer than I thought she would."

"Where do we go from here?" asked Vicki thinking that it would be her job to take care of her burial.

"We already have orders to ship her to the funeral parlor," said the doctor. "Her attorney is in charge from here on." Vicki sat next to Margie's body until the funeral parlor came and pick her up.

"When will the funeral parlor have her ready to be displayed?" asked Vicki of the men who came and picked her up.

"She will be in the display area tomorrow from eight o'clock in the morning to noon," said one of the men who seemed to be the leader of the team. "After that she will be cremated."

"Who has decided all of that?" asked Vicki being surprised at all that was going on.

"Her attorney has the will and testament of the diseased," said the man. After they took Margie, Vicki went home. She was too sad to eat.

The next morning at eight o'clock, Tom, Vicki, and Ellie showed up at the funeral parlor. They were just opening the doors. They went in and one at a time they knelt by the casket and said a prayer for Margie. They all then sat down in the front row. A few miutes later Ginny walked in. She saw Vicki and after kneeling in front of the coffin and saying a prayer, she went and sat in the row in front of Vickie.

"Hi girls," she said as she sat down. I'm so sorry that we lost Margie. She was like a mother to me."

"I know how you feel," said Vickie.

"I'm sure you do more than anyone else," responded Ginny." As they sat there talking about their time with Margie Vicki noticed a woman who walked in and knelt in front of the casket. Vicki suddenly recognized her.

"Isn't that Mrs. Crawford," said Vicki. "What is she doing here?"

"I called her," said Ginny. "A few weeks ago Margie gave me an envelope with the phone number of four people. She said if anything happens to me first call for an ambulance and after that call the people whose names and phone numbers are in the envelope. I did just as she requested. I don't know some of them." Mrs. Crawford after getting up from her kneeling position turned and noticed Vicki. She then walked up to her.

"Hi girls," She said. "Can I join you?"

"Of course," said Vicki. "I'm surprised to see you here."

"Of course you wouldn't know," said Mrs. Crawford. "She didn't want to get credit for her kindness. To tell you the truth she was one of our biggest donors. She contributed a check every month."

"She is sweeter than I thought," said Vicki. After small talk for a while, Ellie notice a man she didn't recognize.

"By the way," said Ellie, "does anyone know who that is that is talking to the Pastor?" The pastor was in front of the casket getting ready to give the final prayer.

"It must be one of the persons I called," said Ginny. "I would guess that it is Margie's attorney." After a few words with the pastor the gentleman walked up to the group sitting together.

"I am Benjamin Richards, Margarita Millie's attorney. Please just call me Ben. Are one of you Victoria Graton?"

"I am," said Vicki.

"Is there a Martha Crawford," asked Ben

"I am her," said Martha. Ben then turned to Ginny.

"I guess you are Virginia Wender," he said to Ginny. "After the pastor gives the farewell sermon, I would like the three of you to come to the room across the hall. I have asked the pastor to meet us there also. I will read Margie's last will and testament. The rest of you are invited if you would like to come."

"I think I need to go home," said Tom.

"I also have to go work," said Ellie. At about eleven thirty the pastor said the farewell prayer. After the prayer everyone was dismissed from the funeral hall. Vicki, Martha and Ginny went to the office across the hall. Pastor Anders was already there. The attorney was not there yet. They all sat down and waited for him. They had no idea what was going to take place.

CHAPTER FOUR

The unexpected Results

They all sat there wondering why they were asked to be there for the reading of the will. No one felt like they were part of her family.

"I wonder why they asked us to be here," said Vicki. "We are not family members."

I don't think she has any family," said Ginny. "I think we are the only family she has. She never talked about any one."

"I wonder if we are mentioned in the will to just thank us for our friendship." It was about ten minutes later that the attorney walked in.

"I am Ben Richard," He said as he walked to the head of the table. "Please relax. This will not take too long. I am Margie's attorney. I was requested by Margie that if anything happens to her that I should read the will to the four of you and to perform all that she requested of me." He then opened an envelope and took out a document, and began to read it. "I Margarita Mellio hereby wish to leave all my processions and assets as follows. I leave one hundred thousand dollars to the West Hill Baptist church. It was there that I became a Born Again Christian. I also leave One Hundred thousand dollars to the Charity House in Montrose. I am very impressed with their accomplishment. Especial for how they saved Victoria Graton. I will leave one hundred thousand dollars to Virginia Wender. She was like a daughter to me." Before Ben could continue Ginny jelled out.

"I can't believe it," she said with tears. "It must be a mistake."

"It is not a mistake," said Ben. "I helped her write it." Ben continued to read the Will. "I leave the rest of my investments and bank account to my wonderful friend Victoria Graton who was more like a daughter to me. I also leave my car and house to Victoria.

"How much are we talking about," asked Vicki being surprised that she had left her anything.

"The total monetary value is approximate five hundred thousand dollars," said Ben. "I have no idea what the car and house are worth. Well that is it," concluded Ben. He then handed each an envelope. "These envelopes have all the required documents for you to receive you inheritance." He then handed Vicki the auto keys and the keys to the house. Vicki was in a complete state of shock. She couldn't even thank him.   "Does anyone have a question?" Everyone was silent being completely shocked that Margie had that much money. After a few minutes of silent, Ginny spoke up.

"How are you paid for the work you are doing?" she asked.

"I was paid when I helped her write the Will," said Ben. "She also left me a little sum for her burial and my service. Is there any more questions?"

"Where will the burial take place," asked Ginny.

I'm sorry I didn't tell you this before." said Ben. "According to her request she will be cremated. The body remains will then be scattered in a secret place that she wants no one but me to know. Is there any other questions?" Since no one answer he then concluded with final remarks.

"It has been a pleasure to meet you," said Ben. "In the envelopes you also have my card. If you ever need help I will be glade to help you. Have a great day." With that said he left. The pastor and Martha got up and left. Vicki and Ginny sat there in a state of shock. It took several minutes before either one spoke.

"I think we should leave," said Vicki "I should probably go to work." They both got up and left and stopped in front of Ginny's car.

"I don't think we will see each other from now on," said Ginny. "I have no reason to come back to the hospital."

"What are your plans from here on?" asked Vicki.

"I don't know said Ginny. "I never dreamt that I would get so much money. I have to think about it. One possibility is that now that I have all this money I could go back to school. I could get my master degree. As a matter of fact, with all this money I may just go on to get my doctors degree. I have a lot of thinking to do. I live with my parents. I'm sure they will have some advice for me."

"I have a lot of thinking to do also," said Vicki. "I didn't expect anything. Well I wish you the best in your future. If you decide to go back to school come back here after you get your degree. I'm sure Ellie will find a job for you. God bless you."

"God Bless you too," said Ginny. "Have a great life. Goodbye."

"Goodbye," said Vicki. They both got into their own car and each drove away. Vicki wondered if she would ever see Ginny again. She drove away in a state of shock not knowing what the future would bring. She decided to go home instead of going to work. She was to shaken up to go to work. When Vicki got home, she went directly to Tom's home office.

"Tom," she said with a shaky voice. "I need your help."

"What happened to you," said Tom seeing that she was emotionally upset. "You look like you saw a ghost. What in the world happened at the funeral during the readying of Margie's will?"

"It was the most unexpected results of the reading that anyone expected," said Vicki recovering slightly. "You will never believe what happened."

"Well don't leave me in the air," said Tom. "Tell me what happened."

"First I have to tell you that Margie had a total of eight hundred thousand dollars not counting her car and house," said Vicki still sounding very excited.

"That doesn't surprise me," said Tom. "I didn't know her very well. I just saw her a few times mostly when we ate lunch after church."

"Well here is the unexpected surprise," started Vicki. "One hundred thousand dollars were given to the church. One hundred thousand dollars were given to the Charity house in Montrose, and one hundred thousand dollars was given to Ginny who took care of her after she left the hospital."

"I'm sure that was not expected," said Tom. "But what happened to the five hundred thousand dollars that is left?"

"That is the strangest of all," said Vicki. "The five hundred thousand dollars, her car and her house were left to Victoria Graton."

"That is such wonderful news," said Tom. "I'm really not surprised. You treated her like she was your mother. I'm so happy for you."

"However that brings me a big problem." said Vicki. "How do I get all of this under my name? I could call the Stock Broker that Margie had, but I don't know anything about him."

"I can make a suggestion," said Tom. "I could recommend my stock broker. I trust him completely. He used to be a pastor until the church changed direction away from the bible and he then decided to be a broker following in his father's shoes. I highly recommend him. He will take you through all you need to do."

"That would be great," said Vicki feeling a little relieved. "Thank you so much Tom."

"His name is Vincent Summers," said Tom. "I'll call him right now and see when he will have an opening to see you."

"Hi Vince," said Tom when Vincent answered to phone. "I have a good friend who needs your help. She just inherited some money and a bunch of stocks. She would like to talk with you about you possibly being her stock broker."

"I have tomorrow available," said Vincent. "Have her come to my office at nine in the morning." Tom then turned and notified Vicky of the appointment.

"Since we have the rest of today available let me take you to get your car needs taken care of," said Tom. "First let's eat lunch. I was about to make myself a sandwich. I don't believe you have anything for lunch"

"I didn't even think of lunch "admitted Vicki. After they had lunch Tom turned to Vicki.

"So get all the documents and let's go and take care of you needs." He then got Vicki in his car and they drove to the Ohio bureau of Motor Vehicle. There she had the title of the auto transferred to her name. They had to go to two different places. The Ohio Bureau of Motor Vehicle did not provide auto license plates. They had to go to Ohio License Bureau. There Vicki got new license plates for her car. After that was done they headed for home. On the way Tom made a suggestion.

"Since we still have a lot of time, let's go to my bank and see if all the currency you inherited can be placed in your own account." They then went to the PNC bank. It only took about fifteen minutes to open a new account and to transfer all that Margie left Vicki. She ended up with thirty thousand dollars in a new check book account, and two hundred seventy five thousand in a money market account. Apparently three hundred twenty five thousand dollars were invested in stocks and bonds. After they were finished with the bank they went home and after dinner they rested the rest of the day.

The next morning Vicki was at the stock broker's office exactly at nine.

"Hello Vicki," started Vincent. "How are you today?"

"Hi Mr. Summers," said Vicki. "I'm fine but a little nervous."

"There is nothing to be nervous about," said Vincent. "And please call me Vince. I would like us to be friends."

"Thank you," said Vicki, "that makes me feel more at ease."

"Please hand me all the documents that you got at the inheritance meeting," said Vince. Vicki opened her brief case and handed him all the documents she had.

"These are all the documents involved with the stocks," said Vicki as she handed him the documents. "The other documents I received were for bank accounts. That has been taken care of." Vince reviewed them and then went onto his computer. After several miutes on the computer he filled out two forms which he gave a copy to Vicki and kept the original copy into his folder.

All the stock you have will be under the Lincoln Financial Group," said Vince. "I will be your manger. All changes will be made through me with your approval. They will mail you an account of your investments every quarter" If you want information sooner and more often, I will get you a method through your computer. I will often look over all your investment and suggest changes when I feel it will be better for you. I will mail you more information when everything goes through." Vicki gave him the address of her new home. She intended to move there as soon as she could.

"I don't have a computer yet," said Vicki. "I will give you my E-mail as soon as I get a computer set up." They then said their goodbyes and Vicki left. She went to Tom's house. When she got there she found that Tom was home working on his novel.

"Hi Tom'" she said as she entered. "I got everything taken care of at last. I now have to go to work. I would like you to know that after I get off from work I'm going to my new house. I have so much to do there."

"Before you go tell me what took place with Vincent," asked Tom.

"He transferred all my holding to his company and will now be my stock broker," said Vicki. "Before I go, I should go upstairs and pack my suit case."

"Listen Vicki," said Tom. "You can have any of my wife's clothes that you like. I am going to give it all to a charity soon anyway. You can also have the large suit case that is in her room. However I would rather have you stay here. You can sell the house. I will miss you terribly."

"I would like to stay in my own house for a while as part of my getting back on my feet. I will give your suggestion serious consideration."

"As you wish," said Tom with a very disappointed voice. Vickie went upstairs and packed her belongings. There was not very much to pack. There were only the few items she had and what she had purchased while living in Tom's house. She did take as few of Tom's wife's dresses that she liked very much. She then left with a hug from Tom.

After work Vicki went directly to her new home. She first started to go through the kitchen refrigerator. It had a few items that looked so old that Vicki decided to throw them away. In the freezer that was located on the upper part of the refrigerator she found a few items. There was a small package with chicken breasts. There also were a couple of packages of wieners and a few packages of frozen vegetables. She then went to the large freezer which was located down stairs in the basement. The freezer was empty and was unplugged. Vicki then went back up stairs and started to look through all the cupboards in the kitchen. She was surprised when she found a box of Mothers Oats, a box of Farina and a box of Oat Meal in one of the cabinets. She also found three different sized frying pans and a Waffle cooking device in one of the other cabinets. That was more than enough for future breakfast. Vicki then decided that she needed to go to the grocery store to buy food for the rest of the week. When she got back she filled the refrigerator with all the food she bought, and had an early dinner. She had not had anything for lunch. After she ate she checked all the other rooms. First she went to one of the smaller bedrooms. She decided to go to the main bedroom last. She knew that there would be much stuff there that she had to get rid of. In the first small bedroom she found a nice bedroom set. All the furniture drawers were empty. The closet was also empty. She then went to the farthest small bedroom. It had no bedroom furniture. It seemed like Margie used it as a storage room. It had many empty cardboard boxes. Vicki was glad to see them. She knew that she was going to need some of them. She next went into the main bedroom. She took two of the larger boxes with her. She checked the closet first. In the closet she found several nice dresses. They were too small for Vicki. Margie was short and husky. Vicki was slim and tall. She put all the dress in one of the boxes. She then went through all the dresser drawers. It was the same thing. None of the clothing she found would fit her. She then filled the other box she had brought with her. She had to go back and get another box to empty the bedroom of Margie belongings. She then brought all the boxes to the small back room.

Next she opened her suit cases. She hung her dresses in the closet and then fill the dresser drawers with all her other cloths that she had. She then stored the suit cases in the back room with Margie's boxes of cloths. She was tired so she spent the rest of the evening watching TV. She had to play around with the controller to learn how to operate the TV. She was surprised that she was able to use the TV. Apparently, Margie's last payment had not run out yet. The next morning Vicki had breakfast and went to work. She kept what she had obtained from the other hospital employers. After work she went home had dinner and started her research in the little room off the family room. It was Margie's office. Vicki spent all evening going through all the information in each folder in the desk drawer. It was going to be a big job. The desk had four drawers. There also was a cabinet which had four drawers. It took Vicki the rest of the week to review all the information in the office. She threw a lot of the unimportant folders but placed the doubted ones in a cardboard box and placed it with the other boxes in the last room where she had stored Margie's cloths. She thought that she would check the doubted folders some time later when she had time. Sunday she went to church. She walked in and sat next to Tom.

"Hi Tom," she said as she sat down. "It's so good to see you."

"Hi Vicki," responded Tom. "I was hoping we would see you today. We missed you very much."

"I know," said Vicki. "I missed you two. Unfortunately, nothing happened at the hospital that brought Ellie and I together. I have been very busy supporting several surgeries."

"Why don't you come for lunch," suggested Tom. "Ellie and I would like to spend a little time with you."

"I have so much to do to make my house livable," said Vicki.

"You can just have lunch with us and you can leave after you eat," said Tom. "Come on, it will only be a little while. We would like a little time with you."

"Alright," said Vicki, "By the way where is Ellie? I thought she would be here with you."

"The girl that watched the children in the nursery is sick," said

Tom. "Ellie is temporally taking her place." After the service was over Vicki followed Tom home. Ellie hugged Vicki when they got home.

"Vicky, it is so nice to see you," said Ellie. "You have been so busy at work that I don't get a chance to see you."

"I know," said Vicki. "I think this next week is going to be slower. Let's try and see each other."

"Lunch is ready," yelled Tom from the kitchen where he had gone to cook lunch. He had prepared stuffed peppers and set the oven timer so that the lunch was ready when they got home. They all enjoyed the special lunch. When they had finished Vicki excused herself.

"I'm sorry but I have so much to do. I have to go now. I will try to see you again soon." With that said Vicky left. She spent that afternoon and evening going through all the folders that she had put aside to study. It was Wednesday evening after Vicki had finished eating and had gone back to review the documents in the last folder that she heard a knock at the door. She wondered who would be visiting so late. When she opened the door she was surprised to see who it was.

"HI Vicki," said Tom.

"Hi Tom," said Vicki. "What are you doing here? I hope that everything is alright. Is Ellie alright?"

"Everything is fine except me," said Tom. "I missed you very much. I think we have to talk."

"Come on in," said Vicki. "Can I get you anything, a cup of coffee?"

"No thank you," said Tom as he sat down on the living room couch. "I think we have to talk about us."

"I'm sorry Tom," said Vicki with a sad look on her face. "I know what you mean. I have the same feelings that you have, but let me tell you what is on my mind at this time. Tom, I have been thinking only of myself these past months. I was only concern on getting back on my feet. I was depressed and thinking only on getting back my respect. A few months ago I was a street vagabond and today I have found my respectable self. I have to think of other important things. First of all, Tom, my husband died only about four months ago. When I think about another romance I feel like I am cheating on my husband Walter Like I didn't really love him. Tom, I loved him very much. I need to mourn over his death. I am thinking of going back to Chicago and have his body sent to Columbus where his parents and relative could mourn with me."

"Have you contacted his father and mother?" asked Tom.

"I tried to call them to notify them of their son's death, but no one answered. I then sent them a letter telling them all that I went through trying to save him."

"I understand," said Tom. "Let me know if there is anything I can do to help."

"Thank you Tom," said Vicki with tears in her eyes. "I will be gone for only a couple of days. I have already called the Chicago funeral parlor to make arrangement to move Walter. I also called an attorney in Columbus to set up the funeral. I asked that the casket unopened of course to be viewed in the morning and have the burial in the afternoon. I'm going to Chicago tomorrow. I will be gone over the weekend. I hope to be home on Monday."

"I will pray that you will be successful in what you want to do and to come back safely." said Tom as he got up to leave. "Let me know when you get back." Tom then left and sadly went home.

Vicki arrived in Chicago on Thursday at one in the afternoon. She went directly to the funeral parlor and made arrangement for the shipping of the casket. It took about two hours before the truck left Chicago. Vicki followed in her car. They arrived in Columbus at about five in the afternoon. The casket was delivered to the Columbus funeral Parlor. She asked them to notify the relatives that were on the list she had given them the day she make the arrangement by phone. Vicki then drove to the motel that is in Grandview heights, a western suburb of Columbus. It was the area that was close to the house of Vicki's in-laws. She ate dinner and after a while went to bed. The next morning she was at the funeral parlor at eight in the morning. As she walked in she saw a young lady that had arrived just before her. The young lady saw Vicki walk in.

"Hi Vicki," said the young lady. "It is so good to see you."

"I didn't know if you would come," said Vicki, "knowing how your Uncle Harry felt about his son. Do you think he will come?"

"Oh dear Vicki," said Adele, "Have you not heard. Uncle Harry passed away about five months ago. I'm sorry we should have notified you."

"Is your mother or father coming?" asked Vicki.

"No said Adele," my parents are both gone."

"How about your Aunt Helen will she come?"

"My brother Gabe is bringing her," said Adele, "she can hardly walk. I don't know if you are aware but she had a bad stroke about a year ago." Just then Adele's husband walked in.

"Hi Todd," said Vicki. "I am so glad to see you. How are you?"

"I'm fine," said Todd. "I'm so glad to see you. I hope we can be like a family now that Uncle Harry is gone." Just then Gabriel walked in pushing Helen who was in a wheel chair.

"Hi Gabe," said Vicki. "And who is this beautiful girl you are rolling in?"

"Hi Vicki," said Gabriel. "I'm surprised you remember me." Vicki didn't have time to answer when Helen yelled out.

"Vicki, my dearest daughter," said Helen. "I was so looking forward to seeing you. Come here and give me a big hug and a kiss. Vicki went to the wheel chair bent over and hugged Helen and kissed her on the cheek.

"I didn't think you even wanted to speak with me," said Vicki, "let alone called me your daughter."

"When you married my son you became one flesh according to the Bible," said Helen. "Therefore you became my daughter."

"Then," said Vicki, can I call you mother?"

"That would thrill me to death. You couldn't do anything that would please me more."

"Why then if you feel that way about me and Walter," said Vicki, "why didn't we see you when we lived here in Columbus?"

"That was my husband Harry's fault," said Helen. "He was very stubborn. He always had to have his way. He always kept his feeling to himself. He was a very arrogant man with very little affection for me or anyone. I once tried to make contact with you but he threatened me. I know that he would not hesitate to punish me. One time after an argument I threatened to divorce him. He told me that the only way I would get away from him is in a coffin. Anyway, I would not divorce him. I am a Born-again Christian. "

"I'm so sorry," said Vicki. "I had no idea of what you were going through. I thought you went along with all that your husband said." Then looking past Gabe Vicki saw Gabe's wife.

"Hi Vicki," said Sally Gabe's wife when she noticed that Vicki had turned her head towards her.

"Hi Sally" said Vicki. "It is so good to see you. How are your children? I believe they are Ryan and Gina."

"Yes," said Sally. "They are fine. I'm surprised that you remember them."

"All of you were always in Walter's heart," said Vicki. "He tried to learn all he could about you and Adele and your families."

"Tell us all about your life since you left Columbus," said Helen.

"Well let's all sit here on the bench in front of the coffin and I will tell you all that has happen since we left here," said Vicki. They all sat on the benches as Vicki asked. Helen sat next to her on her right, Adele sat next to her on her left, and Gabe and his wife Sally sat in the bench in front of her. Vicki then started to tell them her story. She related how Walter got cancer and that the Columbus doctors and hospitals could not help. She told them how she had to take Walter to Chicago to a cancer research center. She told them how she eventually had to sell her house and all she had to pay for the surgeries that were necessary to keep him alive. She related how she had run out of money after paying for the rent she had live in while they were in Chicago and that she only had enough gas to get her to Aunt Nicolina in Montrose Ohio.

"You stayed at Nicolina's house?" asked Helen with a surprised look on her face. "Please tell me all about her. You had to be the last one to see her alive"

"She was a very sweet woman. She accepted me like one of her kids. We were happy to be together. I tried to look for a job but I had to sell my car to pay for a Chicago debt that I had to pay. So I couldn't look for a job. Aunt Nicolina didn't have a car. So if she were still alive I probably would still be there."

"So what happened to her house and possessions?" asked Helen.

"One of her nephews was the only one that was listed in her will," responded Vicki. "It was written years before her husband died. She never changed it. Tell me mom, how come you and her were not close?"

"It was my husband's fault," said Helen. "He had an argument with his brother. He was angry that he, like Walter, refused to work in the store. He worshipped the store because it was started by his grandfather and he wanted to keep it going."

"Anyway, after she died her nephew sold the house and I was left without money, without a car, and no place live," continued Vicki. "I was left as a street walker begging for food. Sometimes I slept on the entrance way of a store that was closed for the night. One day, while I was going down a street knocking on doors to get some help I came across a house where no one answered. They had a nice swing in the front porch that had pillows on the seats. I found that it made a nice bed for me. I slept there several days until the owners came home from where ever they had been. They called the police who then took me to the charity house in Montrose. That is where a volunteer fellow named Thomas Corelli, rescued me, gave me food, and a place to sleep. Several days later he helped me find a job that got me to where I am now."

"Wow," said Helen. "That is a story that would make a great novel"

"I'm not finished yet," said Vicki. "I got the job at University Hospital in Fairlawn Ohio. I was the surgeon's assistant. One day I assisted in the surgery of a little old lady who had a heart attack. I helped her recuperate. We became great friends. She was in her eighties and had no family. After she was released and went home I continued to see her. I took her to church on Sundays and I got a nurse to watch over her. We invited her to Tom's house for dinner several times. To make the story short she passed away a few weeks ago. In her will she left me her car, her house and a large sum of money. So you see I went from riches to poverty and back to riches." Everyone was so astonished by her story that no one could say anything. After about an hour Adele spoke.

"Do you know," Vicki. "I think God loves you very much. I bet you never stopped believing and trusting in Him."

"You are very intelligent Adele," said Vicki. "I am a born-again-Christian. I never doubted that he would take care of me in the long run. Perhaps he was testing me. I never stopped praying either." They all sat there considering all that was said. At about ten miutes to twelve the pastor came in. He gave the final sermon. After the sermon the Funeral Parlor director and four helpers came in to move the casket. The director asked the people in the room to follow him. The four men carried the casket out the door into the grave yard which was just west of the funeral parlor. They carried the casket into the building which was on the other side of the grave yard across from the funeral parlor. They entered the building and stopped in front of the above ground crypt that looked like a large hole in the wall with a door in front of it. The door had Walter's name, date of birth and the date of his last day on the earth. After the pastor gave a last goodbye prayer the casket was put into the crypt and the door was closed. The Funeral Parlor director then invited them all to the luncheon that was given in the lower level of the parlor.

"We can't go to the luncheon said Gabe. Sally and I have to go to work. I am already late. I will be even later since I have to take Aunt Helen home."

"I can take your aunt home," said Vicki. "I am not going to leave for Ohio until Monday. I would like to spend a little time with her."

"I have to leave also," said Todd. "I am so behind in my work."

"I can stay with you and Aunt Helen" said Adele. "I would like to spend some time with you both. However, Can I come with you in your car?" I came with my husband and I will need a ride to Aunt's house and then to my home later tonight."

"That will be no problem," said Vicki. "We would love your company" They then went to the Funeral Parlor for lunch. After lunch they all got into Vicki's car and started for Helen's house.

"That was a fantastic lunch," said Adele. "I couldn't help from taking a little of everything on the self-serve counter. That pasta and pork ribs were so good. I couldn't stop eating them with all the other food to choose from on the counter."

"I know said Vicki." I ate more then I should have. I don't think I will have anything for supper. I will just have a large breakfast tomorrow." Helen just smiled as the girls talked. That was the first regular meal she had since she got her stroke. However she was careful in not eating too much. Her stomach was not used to anything but sandwiches and soup. They just sat around talking about their lives. Adele talked about her son Ronald. She was very proud of him. Vick talked about Tom and how much she cared about him. It was about five when Adele got up.

"Vicki," she asked "Would you mind taking me home now. I will have to cook dinner for Todd. He probably didn't have much for lunch so he will be very hungry."

"Yes I would be glad to take you home. I think I will go to my room in the hotel."

"Please check out of the hotel and come and stay here with me," said Helen. "I have two unused bed rooms. I would love it if you will take one of them. I want to spend more time with you."

"I am only going to be here one night," said Vicki.

"That is fine," said Helen. "That will give me reasons to have you stay a little longer. Vicki, I think of you as a lost daughter. I love you with all of my heart."

"Oh Mama Helen," said Vicki with tears in her eyes. That is so sweet. I love you too. I will see if I could stay a couple of days longer." Vicki then took Adele home and then went to the hotel packed her suit case and checked out. When she got back to Helen's house she saw her with crutches trying to get lunch meat out of the refrigerator.

"Mama, what are you doing?" asked Vicki seeing how much trouble Helen was having getting something to eat. "Is a sandwich all you want for dinner?"

"That has been the only dinner I have had since I got the stroke," said Helen. "I usually only have a slice of toast in the morning a carrot or a fruit for lunch and a sandwich for dinner."

"That is not acceptable while I'm here," said Vicki going to the refrigerator. Opening the refrigerator she noticed that it only had a couple of carrots, three apples, and a head of lettuce. She then opened the freezer door. She was shocked. The freezer was empty. "How do you exist without a decent meal?"

"Every once in a while," said Helen, "Adele or Sally invited me over their house for a great dinner. They always invite me over for any holiday. Their husbands of course pick me up. They are doing the best they could."

"That is not good enough," said Vicki. She then grabbed the keys to her car and left. About an hour later she returned with several bags of groceries she had purchased at the Giant Eagle store that was near her house. She place most of them in the freezer compartment and the rest in the refrigerator.

"What are you doing?" asked Helen. "I will not be able to cook any of that food after you leave."

"You are going to eat regular meals while I'm here," said Vicki. Before I leave we will have to figure out a way to keep you eating regularly meals. I will have to talk with your niece and nephews."

"Are you going to stay until you solve my problem?" asked Helen with a smile on her face.

"Of course," said Vicki. "I can't leave you with the way things are. I love you too much."

"Well you had better start cooking," said Helen, "because I didn't have the sandwich for dinner."

"Have you thought of moving in with one of your nephews?" asked Vicki.

"They both have offered," said Helen, "but I declined. I would still be alone because they all work. Then I would be worried about their children. No thank you."

"Have you considered going into a nursing home?" asked Vicki.

"Yes I have," said Helen. "They want thousands a month. I can't afford that even if I sell my house." Vicki then went on her phone and after a few phone calls she called the nearest Nursing home. She was shock at the rate they charged. They said that the cost included all her meals and the cost of a private nurse.

"Have you considered hiring a private nurse to come every day and take care of you?" Vicki then described the situation that Margie was in and the plan she had with nurse Ginny.

"No way," said Helen. "I will not have a stranger come in and take over my house. I don't trust having someone I don't know having full access to everything in my house, no way."

"Well I will find a way to take care of you,' said Vicki in deep thought.

"You already found a way," said Helen. "You just won't admit it yet."

The next few days went by to slowly. Vicki could not come up with an answer to her problem. However she could not leave her mother-in-law alone without help. That Sunday she took Helen to church. It was that effort that made Vicki realize how helpless Helen really was. After they got home from church Vicki made a nice meal for their lunch. She liked to eat her big meal on Sunday at noon and a sandwich for dinner. It was because she never ate breakfast before going to church. This day was no different.

"That was a great lunch," said Helen. "Is it the last meal before you leave?"

"Very funny," said Vicki thinking that Helen was kidding. Helen was not really kidding. She was worried that Vicki made the big meal because she planned on leaving.

"You know that I can't leave you," said Vicki. "This morning I almost had to carry you in and out of church. I'm still working on finding a way to take care of you. Until then you have to put up with me."

"How long," asked Helen with a smile on her face, "are you planning on staying?"

"I will have to stay as long as I'm needed," said Vicki, suddenly deciding that she had to stay until she could find some kind of help for her. "You know Mom," said Vicki trying to be daughterly like. "I think we should go and see your doctor. He may have some medication or some help. You can't even standup by yourself."

"There in the desk drawer is my phone book," said Helen. "My doctor has his office right in the hospital." Vicki got the phone book and called the doctor. She got an appointment for eight in the morning. At eight the next morning they were there at exactly eight. The doctor's nurse called them into the doctor's office at eight forty five.

"Hi Helen." said the doctor as he walked into the room.

"Hi doctor Rayland," said Helen. "This is Victoria, my daughter-in-law."

"Hi, doctor," said Vicki. "I would like you to examine my mother-in-law for her sudden loss of energy. I took her to church Sunday and she couldn't even get out of her wheel chair. Just a week ago she was able to get up and walk to the refrigerator and get food. She can't do that anymore. Can you give her some medication that will give her some energy back?"

"Well let me examine her first," said the doctor. "Will you wait in the waiting room please?" Vicki left and waited in the small room just outside the doctor's office. It was about fifteen minutes later that the doctor came out. A nurse was wheeling Helen to the hospital elevator.

"What is the problem?" asked Helen.

"I am sending her to the lab to make a few tests. It shouldn't be too long." It was about an hour later that the doctor showed up coming out of the elevator.

"What have you found out?" asked Vicki.

"She is not in very good health," said the doctor. "I came up to talk to you before she comes down from the lab. Her heart is about fifty percent of what it should be. Her blood pressure is to low so her feet do not get the blood flow it needs. I am giving her a prescription that could help a little"

"So what do you think are her chances?" asked Vicki starting to worry.

"I think that she could go any time," said the doctor. "I would say that the most time she has with good care is about two to three years." When Helen came down from the lab Vicki took her strait home. She immediately made lunch.

"You know what," said Vicki when they had finished eating. "I think I will stay for a few more days. I just can't leave you alone without help." It was then that Vicki decided that she would stay as long as she needed help. However she hoped that she could find someone to take care of her that she would accept. It was then that she realized that finding someone was near impossible. Vicki realized that Helen would reject anyone that was suggested to her.

"You know," said Vicki, "I think I will stay with you until you get well enough to take care of yourself."

"That's great," said Helen realizing that she had won what she was praying for. She loved Vicki and wanted her to stay under any circumstances. The joy she felt was very obvious by the look on her face. "Are you going to move in with me?" she asked.

"I suppose, however, I have to go back to Ohio and get all my belongings and settle all other things that need to be done." Vicki was thinking of whether she should keep her home or sell it. She had time to think about it because she realized she couldn't leave Helen for the few days that she would need. Then a thought came into her mind. Why couldn't one of her niece stay with her for the few days that she would need. Vicki then went into the desk and located Helen's private phone book. He immediately looked up the phone number for Adele. He figured that she was the most likely one that could do it. She only had one son and he was much older than her sister in law Sally's children. Vicki wrote the phone number on a piece of paper she found in the drawer. She waited until evening and then called Adele's phone number. Fortunately it was Adele that answered the phone.

"Hi Adele," said Vicki when Adele answered. This is Victoria. How are you?"

"I am fine," said Adele. "Is Aunt Helen ok," she asked worried that Vicki called with bad news.

"We are all fine," said Vicki understanding Adele's concerns. "The reason I am calling is to inform you that I decided to move in with your Aunt Helen. I am going to stay and take care of her."

"That is so wonderful," said Adele with joy in her voice. "We would love to have you back as a permanent member of the family."

"I have one problem," said Vicki. "I need to go back to Ohio to get all my belongings and settle all my other affairs."

"How can I help?" asked Adele.

"I need someone to take care of your Aunt during the few days that I am away," answered Vicki. "I can't leave her even for a day let alone for a few days. Can you take a few days off perhaps some vacation time and take care of her while I'm gone?"

"How soon," said Adele, "will you need that help?"

"Well," said Vicki, "I could wait a few days."

"Can you wait about a month or more?" asked Adele.

"More than a month?" asked Vicki. "What is the problem?"

"Well I have to cook for my family," said Adele. "However, Ron will leave for college at the end of august. Also after Ron leaves Todd has to go out of town for a couple of weeks. That would be a great time for me."

"Let's plan on that time," said Vicki. "I don't have to be in a hurry." With that agreement Vicki hung up. She then informed Helen of the agreement. Helen was thrilled at the prospects. The days went by to slowly. Finally it was September. Adele came at eight o'clock on the first Monday of the month. She brought a suitcase full of her cloths. She was ready to move in and take care of her Aunt Helen. Vicki left the next day feeling sad that she had to leave.

CHAPTER FIVE

Back To Unending Love

Vicki got home to Ohio at about one in the afternoon. She went directly to Tom's house. She had called him Monday and told him that she was planning on selling her house. She asked him to find a good real estate person to help her red tag the furniture she will not want. She also wanted a truck to take the furniture she wanted to keep, to a storage area. She also asked if he could find her a hotel room for her to stay in, if she would need one, for the short time while she was in Ohio. He had agreed. When she got there Tom met her at the door. He had waited near the door waiting for her to arrive. When he opened the door neither one spoke a word. Tom just grabbed Vicki and gave her a big hug. After a while they parted and Tom grabbed her hand.

"Come on in," said Tom. "Come sit and relax. I'm sure you are tired from that long drive. I'm also sure that you have not had lunch. I will get you something to eat. Vicki, it is so good to see you. I have missed you so much."

"I've miss you too," said Vicki. "Now did you get me a room nearby?"

"Yes," said Tom, "it is just up the stairs on your right."

"OH come-on Tom," said Vicki. "I can't take advantage of your kindness."

"Oh stop it," said Tom with a smile on his face. "You knew that I would never let you go to a hotel"

"You are too smart for me," said Vicki smiling back. Tom then pulled out three kinds of lunch meat and the One Hundred Percent wheat bread he knew Vicki liked. Vicki made herself a sandwich. She used one slice of each type of lunch meat and a slice of cheese. She ate it with a nice warm cup of coffee.

"I think we should wait until tomorrow," said Tom, "to start your clearing and evaluating what you want to keep and what you want to save, besides packing all the cloths you want to keep. I thing Hana, the real estate lady I asked to come will help you in making all your decisions. She will meet us at your house at eight tomorrow morning."

"Sounds great to me," said Vicki. The rest of the afternoon they spent bringing each other up to date as to what they had done the last few months. At six Tom brought out eight Lamb chops, grilled them, and they had a great dinner.

"Where is Ellie," said Vicki. "Isn't she coming home tonight?"

"She is out with her boyfriend. He is now on day shift so they go out to dinner most of the evenings" After dinner they watched a movie on the TV. After the movie they listened to the news until ten thirty and then they went to bed. The next morning Vicki got up at seven. She got dressed and went down stairs. Ellie had come home after Vicki went to bed last night and had already gone to work when Vicki got up. To her surprise Tom had already make Mother's oats.

"Hi," said Vicki, "you are up early."

"I had to," said Tom. "Remember that Hana will be there at eight." They ate breakfast and were at Vicki's house at eight. They just opened the door to enter when Hana arrived.

"Hi Hana," said Tom. "I would like you to meet Vicki."

"Hi Vicki," said Hana as they shook hands. This is a very nice house you have here. Too bad you have to sell it."

"I am going to live in Columbus for the next two or three years. It doesn't make sense to keep it and pay all the costs of keeping it."

"I understand," said Hana, "but it's a shame that you can't stay here now that Ellie is engaged. Tom will be all alone."

"Ellie is engaged," said Vicki being shocked at the news. "When did that happen?"

"It happened a couple of days ago," said Tom. "I haven't had the time to tell you."

"Well let's get to work," said Hana as she took out her tape measure and started to measure each room. When she got done, she called Vicki who was starting to pack all the cloths she wanted to keep.

"Why are you measuring all the room?" asked Vicki.

"It is part of the system to get the true value of your house," said Hana. "I find that using all the information I have that you should get about three hundred twenty five thousand for the home after paying all the fees and costs."

"That sounds great," said Vicki. "By the way, I am going to leave a lot of clothes that belonged to the previous owner and some that I don't want. What do you suggest I do with them?"

"Just leave them," said Hana. "I will red tag them with the furniture you leave and what doesn't sell I will give to charity. Now let's look at the furniture."

"I have not completely decided on what I want to keep," said Vicki. Tom who had been waiting in the living room got up to help. "I think that you should keep the book case," said Tom. "It is tall enough for many books, but it is narrow enough to fit in any room."

"I agree," said Hana. "Not only that, it is a very well built unit and is hard to find one like this." They then circulated the house, reviewing all the furniture. Vicki was amazed how Hana was able to tell what the original price of each unit was and what she felt it would sell for.

"I definitely want to keep the lounge chair," said Vicki. "I love that chair. I would also like to keep the love seat that is in the living room."

"You have a good eye for valuable furniture," said Hana.

"What else would you suggest I should keep," asked Vicki.

"First I would suggest that you keep the folding chairs," said Hana. "They are of the highest quality. They are very expensive. I don't think you can sell them for a decent price. I would suggest that you keep several books. It looks like a few are first editions. They will be very valuable someday. If you like I could pick them up for you."

"I would appreciate that," said Vicki. "I would like to make a final quick tour of the house before I leave it all up to you." She then did a quick tour of all the rooms and stopped in the kitchen. She went through all the drawers and took what she thought she wanted to keep. "I don't see anything else that I would want to keep."

"Then you guys pack everything in the truck," said Hana. "I will make up all the red tickets and have a document for you to sign in just a few minutes." While she was writing the tickets and writing the document, Tom and Vicki loaded everything in the truck. When they were done Hana was also finished with all that she had to do. She asked Vicki to come inside and use the counter to sign the document that gave Hana the authority to sell the house and everything in it. Vicki read it over quickly and then signed it.

"Does that take care of everything?" asked Vicki.

"Yes," said Hana. "I will call you with the result when I am done." Tom and Vicki then said goodbye and left for Tom's house. When they got home it was two in the afternoon.

"It is a two hour drive," said Vicki. "I should leave right now."

"You have not packed yet, said Tom, "and you have not had lunch. What is your hurry? Let's have lunch together and tonight I will make your favorite dinner. Please stay another day"

"How could I say no to that," said Vicki. That night they had a very enjoyable evening. Ellie showed up after dinner. She had eaten dinner at a restaurant with her fiancé.

"Hi Ellie," said Vicki. "It is so nice of you to come home so early. I missed you so much. By the way, I would like to congratulations you on your engagement to Doctor Brian. God Bless you both. Have you set a wedding date yet?"

"The only date we could get to do all that is necessary is late in June," said Ellie.

"Let me know the date and I will try to make it," said Vicki. That evening they discussed all that they had been up to the pasted months. Soon it was late and they all when to bed. The next morning they had breakfast together and Ellie was the first to leave. Vicki hugged Ellie as she went out the door.

"I will keep in touch," said Ellie and drove away. Vicki stayed a few minutes to finish her coffee and spent time with Tom. Tom got get her to stay until lunch. It was about two in the afternoon when Vicki decided that she had to leave. Tom grabbed and gave her a great hug.

"I wish you would stay a while longer," said Tom. "Actually I wish you would come back permanently."

"I would like that too," said Vicki. "I just can't leave my mother-in-law alone. She can't take care of herself and will not except a stranger to take care of her and she will not move in with her niece or nephew. They can't take care of her because, first they have children, and then they all have jobs they need to survive. We will have to trust the Lord." Tom gave her another hug and Vicki left for Columbus.

Vicki arrived in Columbus at four thirty in the afternoon. Adele met her at the door. She had seen the car pull into the drive way.

"Hi Vicki," said Adele "It is so good to have you back home. We missed you, especially Aunt Helen. She kept asking me when you were going to come back."

"It's good to be back," said Vicki, "How is Your Aunt doing?"

"Sometimes she can't walk at all," said Adele. "Sometimes she hangs on to me with her hands around my neck."

"Where is she?" asked Vicki.

"I put her to bed," said Adele. "She gets so tired in the afternoon. Around six I have been getting her up for dinner. After dinner she is all right."

"Yes," said Vicki. "I had been doing the same thing, although not this early. She always wants what she called an afternoon nap."

"Come on in," said Adele. "I have prepared an early dinner. I suspect you did not have one."

"I am starved," said Vicki. "I also suspect that you want to go home."

Not really," said Adele. "As a matter of fact I was hoping that I could stay a few days more, if it is OK with you. I would like to spend some time together with you and Aunt Helen."

"You don't need my approval," said Vicki. "She is your family. I should ask your permission to stay here."

"Great," said Adele. "My husband will not be home until Tuesday next week. I would like to spend the days until then with you and Aunt Helen."

"That would be great," said Vicki. "That will be like taking a short vacation for all three of us." They then got Helen up and the three of them ate a fantastic dinner that Adele had prepared. That evening they enjoyed being together very much. Vicki brought up some funny stories that she had heard and they all enjoyed laughter. The next days they sometimes played cards in the afternoon. Sometimes they just enjoyed each other's company. Most of the evenings, they watched movies. Helen liked Romantic movies the most. The days went by too quickly. Soon it was time for Adele to go home. She left the afternoon the day before her husband got home. She had to get some groceries to make him an exceptional dinner. They were all very sad to see her go. It took several days for Vicki and Helen to settle down to their own routine. It was about two weeks later when Vicki got a phone call from Hana her real estate agent.

"Hi Vicki," said Hana. "I want to tell you that an offer has been made for your house and most of the furniture. The offer is somewhat less than the value that we talked about."

"How much less?" asked Vicki.

"Well the offer for the house and the furniture minus all the fees will leave you three hundred thousand dollars." After a slight delay Vicki answered.

"Go ahead Hana," said Vicki. "That is good enough. How soon do I have to be up there?"

I will have everything done by tomorrow. The buyer has the money in his check book and will give it to me when you sign over the deed to him. We will meet here in my office the day after tomorrow at eight the morning. That will give you time to get here" Vicki then hung up.

"Who was that?" asked Helen. "It must be something important from the shocked look on your face."

"It was my real estate agent," said Vicki. "She has sold my house. I'm surprised that it sold so fast."

"Do you have to go back to Ohio," asked Helen with a worried look on her face.

"Yes," said Vicki. "It will be two days at the most. "I will try to make it back in one day."

"Don't do that," said Helen. "That is too much to do in one day. You will have to go there do all the business and come back the same day. I understand it is a two hour trip. Please don't try that."

"Okay," said Vicki. "I will come back the next day." Vicki then called Adele that evening.

"Hi Adele,' said Vicki. "How are you?" Vicki then explained all that she had to do."

"You go ahead and do what you have to do," said Adele. "I will take care of her for two days. I will bring her lunch and super. I will leave breakfast within her reach."

"You are so good," said Vicki. "Thank you so much."

"You go and have a safe trip," said Adele. "I don't know what we would do without you."

It was on Wednesday that Vicki got up early made breakfast for Helen and at about nine she was on the road to Ohio. She got to Tom's house at about eleven thirty. Tom answered the door.

"Hi Vicki," said Tom. "It is so good to see you."

"Would you let me stay here for one night," asked Vicki.

"You don't even have to ask," said Tom. "This is your home."

"Thank you," said Vicki. "I have a meeting with Hana tomorrow."

"I know all about it," said Tom. "I talked with Hana yesterday after she called you. Come on in. Make yourself at home. Since I knew you were coming I got some Tilapia. I know that you loved it.

I also have a small sandwich with Turkey Baloney. I don't think you stopped to eat anywhere."

"I knew better than that," said Vicki. "I figured you would expect me to eat lunch with you." They ate lunch and afterwards sat in the family room to talk.

"Tell me all that is going on in Columbus," asked Tom. "How is your mother-in-law doing?"

"She is getting worse every day. She has no strength in her legs. She can hardly walk even with her crutches. I think she will be stuck in her wheel chair for the rest of her life. Her mind however is still pretty good. She still has a good memory."

"I hope that she appreciates the time you are spending with her."

"How about you," asked Vicki? "What have you been up to?" Tom explained that he had nothing at this time to do as a police officer. He then explained that he spent most of his day working on his novel. Tom could see that Vicki was very tired from her drive. He then asked her to relax on the family couch and rest.

"I think we have said enough for now" said Tom. "You need a little rest time. Just sit here and relax. We will talk more during dinner."

"Thank You," said Vicki as she laid back on the couch. Tom left her there and went in to get her a cup of coffee. When he got back Vicki was fast asleep. Tom drank the coffee and went into his office and started to work on his book. It was about six o'clock when Vicki woke up. She walked into the kitchen where Tom was cooking the Tilapia.

"Glad you are up," said Tom. "I was just ready to come and get you. Super is ready."

"I can't believe that I slept for over two hours," said Vicki. "I'm sorry. I think that my mind was more tired than my body. I have so much going on at this time."

"Just relax, said Tom, "I will do all that I can to make you feel at home." After dinner and after Ellie got home, they shot the bull for a while. Vicki told a few of the jokes she had heard. After a few laughs they all went to bed feeling relaxed.

The next morning Vicki got up about six thirty. The first thing she did was pack up her suit case and brought it down stairs where she found Tom making breakfast.

"Are you all packed to go back to Columbus?" asked Tom seeing her suitcase.

"I am going to put it into my trunk. Hopefully the meeting will not take long and I could leave from there after all is complete."

"So this is goodbye again," said Tom.

"I will try and come back soon," said Vicki. "I miss you guys as much as you miss me." Tom then hugged her and she left not wanting to be late for the meeting with Hana.

Vicki got to Hana's office at five to eight. Hana's secretary told her to go right into the office. She went in and stopped at the doorway being surprised at the man she saw sitting at the table in front of Hana's desk.

"Dr. Brian," said Vicki with a shocked look on her face. "What are you doing here?"

"I have business with Hana Miller, said Chris. "Please call me Chris. You are not one of my patients."

"Ok Chris," said Vicki, "what is your business here?"

"Dr. Brian is purchasing your house and some of your furniture," broke in Hana.

"Why didn't you tell me?" asked Vicki. "I could have negotiated a better deal with you."

"That's why we didn't tell you," said Chris. "Ellie said that you have such a sweet heart that you would not have make a deal that was fair to yourself. This way, it will be just business. Besides, with your good heart you sold it to me way below what it is worth."

"All right," said Hana. "Here are the documents that you both have to sign." Both Vicki and Chris read the documents. After a few questions they both signed them. "Now Vicki, you have to sign the deed to the house signing it to Christopher Brian and Elaine Corely." Vicki then signed the deed over to the new owners. "Now Dr. Brian has paid me the agreed sale price for the house and furniture he has purchased. I have deducted all the fees and costs and have here a check in your name for three hundred thousand dollars."

"Thank you so much," said Vicki. "I will call you if I need any other help." Then turning to Chris she expressed her joy in the sale. "I'm glad that you bought the house. It will be a nice home for you and Ellie. She is like a daughter to me. Give her my love. I have to go now. I have to go to the bank and after that I have to be in Columbus by early afternoon. Goodbye" with that Vicki left and went directly to the bank. After depositing the money in her account she headed for Columbus. She stopped on the way to have lunch. Vicki arrived at Helen's house at about six. As she pulled into the drive she saw Adele starting to get into her car. When she saw Vicki's car she started to walk toward it. When Vicki stopped the car she opened the door to greet Adele.

"Hi Vicki, I was hoping you would be home this afternoon. In fact I was very sure I relied on it."

"Hi Adele, it is so good to see you. I didn't expect to see you. I thought you would be gone by now. What did you do that needed me to come home now?"

I cooked enough extras food for the two of you. I have only been here long enough to bring in the food. You are just in time. The food is still nice and hot."

"That is so kind of you," said Vicki with a loving smile. "What did you bring us?"

"I brought you Chicken casserole," said Adele. "I'm sorry but I can't stay and talk with you. My husband is waiting for me so we could eat our share of the Chicken Casserole"

"Thank you so much," said Vicki. "See you later." With that Adele left and Vicki went inside. Helen was there in the door way to meet her. She had heard the commotion outside.

"Vicki, sweet heart," she said as she extender her hands out to embrace her. It was very difficult from her wheel chair. "I have missed you so much."

"Come on now mom," said Vicki, "I was only gone for two days."

"Never mind that," said Helen. "Let's go and eat. I am very

hungry." After they ate, they sat down and discussed all that Vicki had done during the two days. Helen seemed very happy at the outcome. She had Vicki now living with her forever.

It took two days for things to get back to normal. Every day Vicki noticed that Helen was getting a little worse. Now she could hardly walk even with crutches. The days went by quickly. It soon was October. About the middle of the month, Vicki went out and bought two packages of small candy bars. She wanted to be ready for Halloween. The night of Halloween, Vickie moved the stature that was on the right side of the front door. The front door had four glass panels lined up on each side of the door opening. Helen wanted to sit in her wheel chair on the right side of the doorway. From there she could see all the children in their costumes. When the door opened to the right it blocked her so that no one outside could see her. She felt comfortable that way. Even when the door was open she could still look out the window to see the children who came for the treat.

"The trick or treat time is from six to eight," said Vicki. "That is two hours just sitting there waiting on the trick or Treaters. Aren't you going to get bored?"

"Not at all," said Helen. "I will have you around all the time. You are the one that will give out the treats." Vicki turned on the porch light to let the children know that treats were available. It was at exactly six when the children began to come to the door. Vicki and Helen both were amazed at the fantastic costumes that they saw. Since it was a nice day there came more children than they had expected. It was about seven thirty when they ran out of candy. Vicki then turn off the porch light and the children stopped coming. The trick or treat day was over. Helen enjoyed the evening very much. Vicki was surprised how happy Helen looked that evening.

The days of October went pretty fast. Soon it was November. On November fifteen Vicki took Helen to the doctor. The doctor gave Helen a complete examination. Just as he had done the last time Vicki brought Helen to the doctor, he pulled Vicki aside before Helen was brought down from the lab.

"I have fully examined her," said the doctor. "She is still very ill; however, her heart is a little better than the last time I examined her. I think you have given her more joy and perhaps a little exercise."

"I try to get her to walk a little every morning," said Vicki. "She has to hang on to my shoulder, but I don't want her to be stuck in her wheel chair for the rest of her life."

"I think that it is working. I see that her heart is a little more regular. Still it is not good, it is only slightly better. Keep her walking. I think that the walking caused her blood to flow better." Helen was then brought into the doctor's office.

"How am I doing doc?" asked Helen. "Am I going to live?"

"You are doing fine," said the doctor. "I would like you to continue trying to walk. Stop anything you are doing if you feel a pain in your chest. If that happens sit down and rest until the pain goes away. If the pain doesn't go away in a few minutes call me." Vicki then took Helen to the car and they drove home.

The next weeks went by without any trouble. Soon it was Thanksgiving Day. Gab and Sally invited Vicki and Helen to spend Thanksgiving at their house for the celebration. They of course accepted. Before they left Vicki called Tom. She wished him a very great Thanksgiving. They told each other how much they missed each other. Tom also told Vicki that Ellie and Chris were engaged. Tom didn't know that Vicki already knew. After the call Vicki and Helen left for Gab and Sally's house. They arrived at twelve o'clock. The dinner was set for one o'clock. At the house they met Gab and Sally of course, and their son Ryan and daughter Gina. They all treated them like they were close family and they were all so thrilled to see them. About fifteen minutes later Adele, Todd, and their son Ronald arrived. They were all so happy to be together. There were nine of them altogether. They were all very excited to be together. Apparently it only happened during a holiday.

"Are your parents coming here to celebrate the holiday with us?" asked Vicki.

"At present my parents are in Germany visiting relatives there," said Todd. "They go there every year."

"How about your parents," Vicky asked of Sally.

"My parents are at my uncle's house in Florida. They go there every year for about two months. They don't like the weather here in Ohio."

"Will they be back for Christmas?" asked Vicki.

"I hope so," responded Sally. Sally had made a twelve pound turkey. At exactly twelve thirty she brought it out on to the table. Before Gab cut up the turkey, he said a very loving prayer thanking God for all that He had done for him and his family. Gab then cut the turkey. Helen loved turkey wings. So she was given a wing. Most of the children loved slices of the turkey chest. Gab made large slices of the chest. Vicki liked a leg so she was given a leg. It was a great dinner. After dinner Sally brought out a large Pumpkin Pie. They were all very full from the turkey dinner, but the pie looked so good they all had a piece. The rest of the afternoon went by with jolly conversations. Vicki noticed that Sally's daughter Gina was the only one that didn't have a wrist watch.

"Why don't you wear a wrist watch?" Vicki asked Gina.

"I don't have one," said Gina sadly.

"Maybe Santa will bring you one," responded Vicki. Sally looked at Vicki with her hands out like asking why. Vicki smiled at her and pointed to herself. Sally then smiled and shook her head saying OK. That evening they enjoyed each other's company and were all so happy that they got together. At supper time they all had sandwiches of what was left of the turkey. After they finished they each had a piece of pie until it was all gone. They were enjoying the day so much that no one wanted to go home. However, around eleven, Vicki noticed that Helen was getting very tired. Vicki decided that she had better take Helen home. Helen fell asleep in the car on the way home. Vicki had a very difficult time getting her inside and into bed. Vicki didn't realize how tired she was. So as soon as she got Helen undressed and in bed Vicki went to bed. She fell asleep before her head hit the pillow.

The following days went by faster than they realized. It soon was December. At about the middle of December Vicki decided that they had to talk about the coming holiday.

"Mon," started Vicki one day after breakfast, "we have to prepare for the coming Christmas holiday. What are we going to give your two families for Christmas gifts?"

"I am going to do the same this year as I did last year," said Helen. "I will give Gab and Sally a Christmas card with a check for five hundred dollars in it. I will do the same for Todd and Adele. I will give a card to each of their children with one hundred dollars in them. So all I need from you is to get me ten Christmas cards."

"Wow," said Vicki. "You have it all planned. I need your help to pick out all that I have to give to the seven. The only one I have planned is to give Gina a nice wrist watch. What should I give the other six?"

"I think that Both Todd and Gab could use a nice shirt and a matching tie. They kind of hinted that they would need good clothes for the special holiday that is coming. The boys could use new backpacks. The ones they now have are about six years old."

"That is great," said Vicki. "All I need now is what to buy the two mothers."

"Well we have about two week to think about it," said Helen. "You can consider some kind of jewelry. In the meantime why don't we, or should I say you, fill in what we have already decided?" The next morning, after breakfast Vicki went out shopping. First she went to a card shop and purchased twenty Christmas card. She had to buy a few that were identical. They only had six different kinds. She then went to the clothing store. She had no trouble finding the shirts and ties for the men.

Vicky had notice that Gabe always wore Brown clothes. So Vicki bought him a nice light green shirt with a matching tie. She had also noticed that Todd always wore blue cloths so Vicki bought him a light blue shirt with a matching tie. Vicki then went to the jewelry store that was only a block away. She went there to buy Gina a nice wrist watch. She had no trouble finding a beautiful one. However looking around she saw beautiful jewelry. Since she was there she decided to buy the gifts for Adele and Sally. She found a beautiful bracelet for Sally. Looking around she found a nice necklace with matching ear rings for Adele. By this time it was close to lunch time so Vicki decided to leave the rest of the shopping for later and went home. Helen met her at the door

"How did you make out?" asked Helen.

"I got all that I need for the girls and the men," said Vicki. "All I need now is the gifts for the boys." She then showed Helen what she had purchased. After lunch Vicki went out to a general store at the mall. There, after much searching, she found the back packs. She bought the best they had. She was on her way out of the store when she was attracted by the kitchen appliance counter. She spotted dishes that were exactly like the ones Helen had. An idea then entered her mind. She didn't like eating on Helen's dishes because they were the larger set. They never ate enough to need the large dishes. Vicki then looked around and found some that were exactly the same design but in the smaller size. She then decided that the smaller size would make a great Christmas gift from her to Helen. There were eight dishes in each package. Vicki bought a whole package. Before she left she bought a necklace with matching ear rings for Ellie and a shirt and match tie for Tom. She paid the sales lady extra to wrap the gifts and then took them to the post office. She mailed both packages to Tom's address. Helen, while Vicki was shopping, wrote all the Christmas cards and inserted in them the checks as she had planned. Vicki and Helen spent the next day wrapping all the gifts and attaching Christmas cards to them. Vicki had kept the dishes she purchased for Helen in the car. After she put Helen to bed she got the package of dishes from the car, wrapped it, and attached the Christmas card to it. She then hid it under her bed and went to sleep. All that they had to do for Christmas was now complete.

In Ohio, Alex was in the Medina General Medical center to check on one of his patients. As he walked down the aisle on the third floor he heard someone crying in one of the hospital room. He looked inside and saw a woman in bed crying. She was all alone in the room. Alex then when back to the nurse's counter.

"Hi," said Alex to the nurse at the counter. "I walked by the room that is about the third one down the aisle and found a woman crying. "You should go and see what the problem is."

"Hi Doctor Corely," said the nurse recognizing him. "That is Liana Pilsner. She hear the doctor telling me that she had only hours to live. She has no one that we can call. She has this strange desire that she doesn't want to die alone. I am too busy to spend time with her. I am the only nurse on this floor at this time."

"That is OK," said Alex. I will go and spend time with her." Alex went directly to her room. He then grabbed her hand a squeezed it tight.

"Who are you?" asked Liana, hardly getting the words out.

"I am your new friend," said Alex. "I will hold your hand and I will not let you go."

"The doctor said that I was going to die," said Liana. "I didn't want to die all alone."

"Don't worry," said Alex. "I will not let you die. As long as I hold your hand you will not go anywhere."

"I hear the doctor tell the nurse that I had just hours to live," said Liana.

"He was probably talking about someone else," said Alex trying to encourage her. "I will not let you die. I am very attracted to you. I want to see if maybe you are my true partner in life." Alex was not lying. Her voice thrilled him. He also looked at her when he first came into the room. He thought that she was the most beautiful girl he had ever seen.

"How do you know all this?" asked Liana.

"I guess I should introduce myself," said Alex. "I am Doctor Alexander Corely. I am going to take care of you."

"Please come up close to me," said Liana trying hard to open her eyes. Alex got up and leaned over her so that his face was directly over hers. "Did I die and am in heaven?" asked Liana. "You look like an Angel."

"I want to be your earthly angel," said Alex siting down again. A few minutes later the doctor that did the surgery walked in.

"I am Dr. Bentley. "Are you a relative?"

"I'm Dr. Corely," responded Alex. "I am a good friend."

"Is she still alive?" asked Dr. Bentley not realizing that she was awake and could hear everything."

"Her blood pressure is acceptable, said Alex, "but her heart is not beating. Can you tell me what happened to her?"

"She was shot in the chest," started Dr. Bentley. "We brought her directly into surgery. We had no idea that the bullet cut a large slice on her heart. Had we known this we probably would not have operated. However since we had her there and had her chest opened I closed the wound in her heard and hoped for a miracle."

"She was awake for a little while," said Alex. "She feels a little better now. I think she is not as depressed as she was when I first walked in. I think she is ready to fight for her life."

"Has she spoken at all?" asked Dr. Bentley.

"Yes she has said a few words," said Alex. "She could only whisper."

"I came in here to disconnect her from the heart machine. It is designed to reduce the load on her heart not replace it."

"I feel she has a good chance of recovery. Please let it stay for a little while longer."

"Alright," said Dr. Bentley. "We really don't need it at this time. Since she is awake, I will give you three days at the most."

"Thank you Doctor," said Alex. The doctor didn't answer but just turned around and left.

"Liana honey," said Alex trying to make her feel like she was with her family, "did you hear any of that?"

"Enough to make me fight for my life," said Liana. "If for no other reason that I want to get to know you better."

"That's the girl," said Alex. "I'm going to stay here with you as long as they will let me. I will only leave you for lunch and dinner. I will sleep in this nice comfortable chair until it is safe to leave you during the night." Liana slowly fell asleep. It was about ten o'clock when the nurse came in.

"How is she doing?" asked the nurse.

"She just fell asleep," said Alex, but she feels better. She said that she is going to fight for her life."

"That is great," said the nurse. "The doctor told me to give her a sleeping drug. It will make her body relax and sleep through the night.

"Can I stay here all night to watch over her?" asked Alex. "I would like to keep track of her. I can make sure she keeps on breathing."

"Well you are a doctor," said the nurse. "You can stay as long as you want." Alex held her hand until he fell asleep. He woke up about eight. He immediately went down to the hospital cafeteria and had a big breakfast of eggs and toast. He had not had supper the day before. After eating, he immediately went up and grabbed Liana's hand. It was about ten miutes later that a police officer walked into the room.

"Hi," said the officer. "I am Officer Peter Dartner. I am here to see that who shot our victim will not get another chance. Who are you?"

"I am Doctor Alex Corely," said Alex. "I am a good friend. Does your department have anyone investigating the shooting?"

"I know we should," said Peter. "But the two who are in that department are busy investigating the murder of the three at Gino's bar in down town Medina. We don't have anyone else that will know what to do."

"Perhaps I can help," said Alex. "My father is a Detective. He is licensed to operate anywhere in Ohio."

"You aren't the son of Detective Thomas Corely are you?" asked peter. "He is the center of our investigating training. Do you really think you can get him to help us?"

"A simple phone call will tell us," said Alex as he picked up the phone. While he was calling his father peter called his captain to make sure it would be politically OK. "Hi Dad," said Alex when his father answered the phone.

"Hi Alex," said Tom. "Do you have a problem?"

"A young lady got shot in the chest," said Alex. "I am taking care of her. What I wonder is if you have time to investigate her shooting?"

"Don't the Medina police have someone to do it?" asked Tom.

"They are tied up in that shooting that went on in the down town bar," answered Alex. "They don't have anyone else."

"All right," said Tom. "I will look into it if the Medina Captain approves." Just then Peter walked up to Alex.

"If you are talking to your father," said Peter, "tell him that his help is approved by the Medina Captain."

"I heard that," said Tom. "I will come right over as soon as I finish my breakfast." With that said they hung up. Peter then walked out to be the guard in the doorway.

"Liana," said Alex. "Are you awake?"

"Yes," said Liana. "I am listening to all you are saying."

"Do you think that you can be interrogated by my father?" asked Alex.

"Yes,' said Liana, "I think I can handle that. I will do my best." About a half hour later Tom walked into the room.

"Hi Alex," said Tom. Then turning to Liana he addressed her.

"Hi Liana," started Tom. "My name is Tom. It is my job to find out who it was that shot you. I need some information from you."

"Thank you," said Liana. "I am ready. What do you want to know?"

"First of all do you have any Idea who wants to kill you?"

I can't think of any one. I just started working here less than a year ago. I moved here from Scranton Pennsylvania. I don't have any family or friends here in Ohio."

"Well first tell me about your family," asked Tom.

"My mother and father died in an auto accident when I was about six years old. I was raised by my grandmother, who pasted away about three years ago. I have no brothers or sisters."

"Did you have any friends in Scranton that perhaps you had a problem with?"

"No," said Liana. "I had one girl friend, but she has moved to California. I have had no contact with her. I went to college in New York and I have no contact with any of my class mates."

"I guess that leaves only someone where you live and where you work," said Tom. "Is there anyone at work that is unhappy with the job you got that they had expected for then selves?"

"The only one I could think of is Betty Cishop," said Liana. "I think that she was worried that I was stealing her boyfriend. That is silly because Troy is more than ten years older than me.

"What is her job there?" asked Tom.

"She is the head of the sales department," said Liana. "All the sales girls report to her."

"I think I have enough to go on for now," said Tom. "Get well, and God Bless you. I'll let you know what I find out." Tom then left. Alex then sat down next to Liana and grabbed her hand.

"Alex honey,' said Liana. "You have been here two days; don't you have a job to go to?"

"This morning before I came here," said Alex, "I called my office and told them that I was taking a two week vacation. So as long as you need me I'll be here. I will only leave for a few minutes while I have lunch and when I have dinner. After it looks like you are over the critical part I will leave at night after you are put to sleep and I will be back before you wake in the morning." Just then the nurse then walked in with a syringe.

"What is that for?" asked Liana. She had never given her a shot of any kind before.

"It is some fluid food," said the nurse. "You have had nothing to eat for over two days. We don't want you to die from starvation. After giving Liana the shot in the arm she left.

"I think that I am going down to the cafeteria for lunch," said Alex. "I will be right back." It was less than an hour when Alex came back. When he got back he grabbed Liana's hand.

"I missed you terribly," said Liana. "It is very strange, I don't even know you, but somehow I love you."

"I know," said Alex," I feel the same way. There is some kind of radiation coming from us and it must be the same frequency. You know I learned something in school that was like that. They had a dead body in a glass coffin like box. They had come up with a piece of equipment that detected this radiation. The strange thing was that the radiation was seen coming out of his body even from the arm that was missing."

"I know," said liana. "I remember something like that when I was in college, except in was a plant instead of a body. It also radiated from a stem that was missing."

"We are getting to technical," said Alex. "Let's just say that it's just what is known as Love at first sight."

"You do love me then?" asked liana.

"From the first time I saw you," said Alex. "I had never felt the thrill I got from holding your hand. I never wanted to let it go."

The first place Tom went was to the apartment Liana was renting. The first person he talked to was the land lady.

"High," said Tom when she answered the door. "My name is Detective Thomas Corely. I would like some information about a tenant of yours named Liana Pilsner."

"What is the problem?" asked the landlady.

"Liana was shot and is in the hospital recovering," started Tom. "I'm wondering if you know of anyone in the apartment complex that she had any problems with."

"First of all I hardly know her myself," said the landlady. Secondly she works late every day except Sunday and so no one sees her and last of all the two apartments next to hers are empty."

"Thank you very much," said Tom and left. Tom figured that it was unlikely that someone in the apartment building was the shooter. He next went to the Macys where she had her job. When he got there he introduced himself to the first sales lady he saw and asked to see the manager. The young lady led him to the manager's office.

"Hi," said Tom when he entered the office. "I am Detective Thomas Corely. I need to ask you questions about Liana Pilsner."

"I hope she is alright," said Troy. "I need her help very badly."

"Do you know," asked Tom, "anyone who would want to hurt her?"

"No," said Troy, "she is a very sweet and talented young lady. Why would anyone want to hurt her?"

"Do you and her have any romantic feelings for each other," asked Tom.

"No," said Troy, "first of all she is too young for me, secondly I have a girlfriend. The time we spent together was strictly business. She has reorganized the financial Department so that we have increased our income by almost fifty percent. We have worked together to get all her idea's installed."

"Was there anyone in the building?" asked Tom that was jealous of her position here in this company?"

"Not that I know of," said Troy.

"How about your girlfriend," asked Tom, was she at all jealous of the time you spent with Liana?"

"She did say that she wasn't happy with all the time that I was spending with Liana," said Troy. "I explained to her what we were accomplishing. And I assured her that there was nothing going on between Liana and me. I told her that the most important thing in any relationship is trust. If she can't trust me then she better look for someone else."

"I would like to talk to your girlfriend," said Tom. "Is she around here somewhere?"

"She took the day off," said Troy.

"Thank you very much," said Tom. "You have a great day." Tom left and was sure now who the shooter was. He went directly to the Medina court house, to get a court order to search through Betty's possessions. After the judge made a few phone calls to verify that Tom was approved by the Media police department, he gave Tom the order. Tom went directly to the apartment building where Betty lived. He found the car in the apartment parking lot. He got the required tool from his car and opened the car door. He didn't have to look far because he found a pistol in the glove compartment. It was of the same caliber of the one that had shoot Liana. He took it directly to the Medina police station.

"Hi" said Tom to the police in the front office. "I am Detective Thomas Corely. I would like to speak with Captain Ruso." He was lead to the office of the captain.

"Hi Captain Ruso," said Tom as he entered the office. "I'm Tom Corely."

"Hi Tom, said the captain. "I was waiting to hear from you. What have you found?"

"I found what I believe is the weapon that was used to shoot Liana Pilsner," said Tom. "I believe you have the bullet that had been removed from Liana. I got the pistol out of the car of Betty Cishop. She works at the same company that Liana works at." Tom then gave him all the information he had on Betty.

"Let me have the pistol," said the captain. Tom gave him the pistol. The captain took the bullet out of his desk drawer. "Wait here a few minutes." He then took the pistol directly to the lab. A few miutes later the captain came back.

"Do you need me here any longer?" asked Tom.

"They began the test immediately. So if you are not in hurry just wait a few minute. Tell me about your life as a detective. I understand that you are retired. You are a hero here in Median." They talked for a while. Tom told the captain about some of interesting investigations he had been assigned to. About fifteen minutes later the captain got a phone call. When he hung up he turned to Tom.

"Well Tom, said the captain. "You were right. Betty was the shooter. The bullet that was taken from Liana came from the pistol owned by Betty. Thank you so much for your help. I don't believe we will need your help any longer. If you are needed when she goes on trial we will call you. It probably will not be necessary. The information you have given me will be enough to put her in jail. Thank you again for your help. Have a great day." Tom then left and drove home. He had a great feeling of success and a feeling of satisfaction in his heart.

CHAPTER SIX

Love Is In The Air

It was on the first day of October when Tom had finished his investigation of the shooting of Liana. Tom got up early that day, ate breakfast and went to the Median Hospital. He went to inform Liana and Alex that the shooter was found and was arrested. He entered the hospital room, said hello to Alex and Liana who was wide awake, and was about to explain what he had accomplished when the doctor came in.

"Hello Alex," said the doctor. "I see that Liana is awake. This is the third day when I was supposed to remove all the equipment from Liana's body. But I see that Liana is awake and alive. How are you Liana?"

"I feel better Doctor," said Liana removing the air tube from her mouth. Do I really need this?" Before she could answer Tom broke in.

"Doctor, if you will look at the heart monitor you can see that her heard shows a beat every once and a while."

"Dear Lord," said the doctor in amazement. "Her heart is trying to start beating. That is wonderful. I will lower the blood pump equipment so that the heart could do a little of its job."

"I think she is breeding a little better. Does she really need that mouth piece?" asked Alex. "I have removed it when we spend time talking" The doctor then removed it and checked her breathing.

"Does it take any effort to breath?" asked the doctor.

"No," said Liana. "I don't even know that I am breathing. It actually takes an effort to hold my breath."

"Alright," said the doctor. "You may leave it off during the day if it doesn't require an effort to keep breathing. However at night I want you to keep it on all night after the nurse gives you your evening sleeping shot. I will also tell the nurse to start feeding you. You have not eaten for three days. We don't want you to dye from starvation. I will be back tomorrow morning and we will see what else we can do. I'm glad to see the improvement you are showing." With that said the doctor left.

"You came in here like you had something important to tell me," said Liana to Tom. "Have you any idea who tried to kill me?"

"Yes said Tom. "I found a pistol in Betty's car. I had it checked to see if it was the weapon that shot the bullet that they took from you. It matched so she was arrested and is in jail waiting for a trial. So you are no longer in jeopardy."

"Thank you so much Detective Corely," said Liana.

"Please call me Tom. If that bothers you because of our age difference, and that I am Alex's father just call me sir. I hope soon you will be calling me Dad."

"I can hardly wait," said Liana. Tom then said goodbye and drove home. The rest of the day went by joyfully for Alex and Liana.

The next morning Alex got to the hospital before Liana woke. He walked up to the bed and sat down and grabbed her hand. Liana must have felt Alex hand and woke up. She reached up and removed her mouth piece.

"Hi Alex," she said when she turned and looked at him.

"Hi Liana," said Alex. "How do you feel today?"

"I feel fine," said Liana. "Now that you are here I feel perfectly safe and greatly loved." Before Alex could answer the doctor walked in.

"Hi you two," said the doctor. "Wow, I see that Liana's heart beats have tripled. That is good news. If tomorrow we have the same improvement I will take her down to the lab. I want to check all her organs. The last time I checked they were all partly shutting down. See you tomorrow." The doctor then left. The rest of the day Alex and Liana enjoyed their time together. The next day when Alex got to the hospital Liana was not in her room. Alex hoped that the reason was that she was in the lab going through all the required tests. He sat there and waited. It was about an hour later that Liana was brought back to her room. She was very glad to see Alex there.

"Hi Alex," she said "Have you been waiting long"

"I have been here about an hour," said Alex. "Have you heard anything yet?"

"No," said Liana, "but the girls that run the test said that things look good." It was almost noon when the doctor walked in.

"Hi you two," said the doctor with a great smile on his face. "I have very good news. The tests show that all her vital organs are back to normal. She is going to recover like new. She will be very week for a few weeks because of the illness and that she hasn't had any food for the last three days. I will instruct the nurse to start her feeding process. We will have to start feeding her soup and gradually get to solid food. I will check up on her daily. I think she should be able to go home in about two more weeks. You guys have a great day."

The doctor was right. Alex took a leave of absence for the next month and spent the next two weeks by Liana side. The nurse took Liana for a walk after the first week. She however needed a cane to stay stable. The days went by too slowly. The nurse slowly increased the type of food she was giving Liana. Finally after about three weeks in the hospital, in the middle of November the doctor decided to release Liana. The nurse brought back Liana's insurance and credit card they had obtained from her purse when she was omitted in the hospital. Alex and Liana were over joyed. Liana was wheeled to the entrance way in a wheelchair. Alex got the car and drove to the front of the hospital entrance where Liana was waiting. Alex helped her in the car and they drove off too Liana's apartment. It was a two bedroom apartment in a large apartment building. Alex helped Liana get inside the building and into her second floor rooms. She had a hard time getting there.

"How do you feel?" asked Alex.

"I feel very tired," said Liana. "Let me sit here for a while. I will be OK."

"You know Liana," said Alex. "I think this is a big mistake. You will not be able to take care of yourself." He then went to her refrigerator. He opened the door and found that it was pretty empty. "You don't even have any food here."

"You can buy me some before you go back to work," said Liana.

"That is not acceptable," said Alex. He then grabbed the phone and called his father. "Hi Dad, How are you?"

"Hi Alex," said Tom. "Do you have a problem?"

"Yes Dad. Do you have a minute to discuss a problem I have?"

"I have all day," said Tom. "How can I help you?"

"Liana was released from the hospital today and I brought her home to her apartment. It's an apartment on the second floor. She has no food and can hardly walk. I thought of hiring a nurse for her, but she can't afford one and I have to go back to work. Can you recommend some place like a nursing home that will be cheaper than a private nurse?"

"Yes," said Tom. "I have the perfect place and cost nothing."

"Are you suggesting a charity house?" asked Alex.

"No, "said Tom. I am suggesting my house. I have five bedrooms where two are empty at the present and soon another one will be empty. So bring her here. I can take care of her while you are working.

"Oh Dad," said Alex. "Will you really do that?"

"Do you really love her?" asked Tom.

"With all of my heart," answered Alex.

"Then bring her here," said Tom. "I will take care of my future daughter-in-law."

"I will help her pack up her cloths and we will come there." After hanging up he turned to Liana.

"Liana," started Alex. "I love you with all of my heart. Do you really love me?"

"I love you more than you love me. I will not be able to live without you. I'm crazy in love with you. There are not enough words to express my love for you."

"Then will you do as I tell you?" asked Alex

"Without question," said Liana with a smile on her face.

"Liana," said Alex with a smile on his face. "I will always try to make you happy."

"You are already doing that," said Liana. "Now what is this all about?"

"I want you to come with me and live in my father's house," said Alex. "At least until you are well enough to go back to work."

"Will your father go along with this?" asked Liana.

"It was he that suggested it," said Alex. "Now help me pack what you want to take with you." It took most of the afternoon to check all her belongings. They both knew that Liana would probably not go back to live there. It was about five in the evening when they got to Tom's house.

"Come on in," said Tom as he opened the door. "Glad to see you guys." They walked in, but Alex had to hold Liana up so that she would not fall.

"Glad to be here," said Liana. "I hope that I will not be a burden on you Mr. Corey."

"Not at all," said Tom. "I will appreciate the company. Anyway please don't call me Mr. Corely. I hope that someday soon you will call me Dad. Just call me sir or something like that."

"Which bedroom are we going to put her in?" asked Alex.

"The only bedrooms that are available," said Tom, "are yours and Vicki's old room. But they are both at the far end of the hall. I would like her to be closer so that I could watch over her. Let's wait until Ellie gets home and see if she would be willing to move to one of the back rooms and give her room to Liana."

"Hello everyone," said Ellie as she walked into the room. "Give my room to whom."

"Hello Ellie," said Tom. "First I want you to meet Liana."

"Hi Liana," said Ellie. "I have heard about your problem. Welcome to our home."

"What we were talking about was which bedroom we should give Liana," said Tom. "I would like her to be in the bedroom across from me, your room. Do you mind moving to one of the rear room?"

"Don't be silly," said Ellie. "We can both occupy the same bedroom. We have two single beds in there. That way I can be there if she has a problem during the night. We are about the same age. We can be like sisters. I am only going to be here a few months anyway."

"That would be fine," said Tom, "if you don't mind that setup Liana."

"That would be wonderful," said Liana. "I could use the company. I wonder however why do you have two beds in Ellie's room?"

"It originally was Alex's room. The doctor told my mother that the child she was about to give birth to was going to be a boy. So it was decided that the two boys should sleep together. So instead of a boy mom had me. Alex then preferred the far bed room, so I became the one who sleeps here.

"All is settled then," said Tom. "Let's go up and eat dinner. I have enough for the four of us."

The days went by slowly. Liana got better every day. She was now walking alone with a cane. Ellie and Liana became great friends. They obtained a sisterly affection for each other. When Ellie learned that Liana was a Financial Manager she got a great idea.

"Liana," she said one evening. "I wonder if you would like to take over my job when I am promoted."

"You know for sure that you are going to be promoted?" asked Liana.

"Yes," responded Ellie. "My boss Julia Donavon is retiring at the beginning of the year. She has promised me the job because she and the board of directors are very impressed of the changes I've make since I started to work there. What do you think?"

"I think it is great," said Liana. "Are you sure I can do the job?"

"Tomorrow I am going to bring my suitcase home with the things I will need and I will train you here in our bedroom. We can use this desk I have here in the bedroom and I will see what we can do. When you are feeling well probably around thanksgiving I will bring you with me and I will train you right at hospital office where the computer is with all the financial Information." For the next week they spent going over all that Liana had to know. Ellie was impressed with Liana's intelligence. After each lesson, they spent the evenings in the bed room shooting the bull before they went to sleep. Everything seemed great. Tom was happy, Ellie was happy and Liana was thrilled at the attention she was getting. The only one that was unhappy was Alex. He could only see Liana on Wednesday, Saturday and Sunday after church. During the week days it was too far to go back and forth to see her. He missed her very much. He let them all know it when he came home on those days. Liana missed him too, but there was too much new things going on that took her attention. It was on Monday the week before Thanksgiving that Ellie felt that Liana was ready to go with her to the hospital. At breakfast she brought it up.

"I think that Liana is ready to go with me to the hospital," said Ellie "I will inform my boss Julia and if it is OK I will take her with me tomorrow."

"I think you should wait a few days," said Tom. "I would like to take her to my doctor to make sure she is ready to go to work."

"Why don't you call him now," said Ellie. "Perhaps he could see her tomorrow and I could take her on Wednesday," said Ellie. Tom took her advice and called his doctor.

"University Medical group," said the nurse. "How can I help you?"

"I would like to make an appointment with Dr. Clemen Please," said Tom.

"I'm sorry said the nurse. Dr. Clemen or the other doctors will not have an appointment available until Tuesday of next week. If it is an emergence please go to the emergence Department."

"Thank you," said Tom and hung up. Then turning to Ellie he said "They will not have an opening until Next Tuesday. That is ridiculous."

"Let me take her with me," said Ellie. "I have some influence there. Let me see what I can do." After breakfast Ellie got Liana dressed up nice and they went to the hospital. Ellie took Liana to her office.

"Wait here," said Ellie to Liana. "I will go and see what I can do. I will not be long" Ellie then went into Julia's office. She informed Julia what was going on. She had told Julia earlier about Liana and that she wanted to teach her to take over her job after Julia retired and Ellie moved up to her job. Julia had given her permission. From Julia's office Ellie went to the medical Group office.

"Good morning Stella," said Ellie to the office secretary in the waiting room. "I would like to talk to Doctor Vera." The secretary got on the phone and talked to Doctor Vera.

"You can go right into his office," said Stella. Ellie went down the hall way to the doctor's offices. When she got to Doctor Vera's office she knocked on the door.

"Come in Ellie," said the doctor. "How are you? What can I do for you?"

Hi doc," said Ellie. "You are aware that Julia is retiring the first of the year and that I am taking her place."

"Yes," said Doctor Vera, "I am aware of the plan."

"Well I am training a young lady to replace me," started Ellie. "I need her to have a complete checkup before she can start. When my father called to make an appointment he was told that there will not be an opening until around next Tuesday. Can you somehow fit her in sooner?"

"How soon can you get her here?" asked the doctor.

"She is sitting in my office right now," said Ellie.

"Bring her to my nurse," said the doctor. "I will have her do all the tests that we can do here. I will write up a test request which you can take down to the lab."

"I will go get her right now," said Ellie. "If I can ask," said Ellie why is it a problem to get an appointment here?"

"We have lost two doctors who have moved back to their home town to open their own practice. We are short of doctors."

"I think that maybe I can help you," said Ellie. "I will get back to you." Ellie then left and brought Liana back to the Doctor Vera's office and went back to her office. She had a lot of work she had put off. The nurse at Doctor Vera's office was ready and performed all the required tests. About two hours later Doctor Vera's nurse called Ellie and asked her to come to the doctor's office.

"What's up?" said Ellie as she walked in the waiting room. The doctors nurse was there waiting for her.

"I have performed all the tests the doctor requested, however the results of the urinary test have not yet returned. The doctor will review them when all the tests are complete. Here is the lab request form. Take it and the patient down to the lab. They have been requested to perform all the tests listed as soon as possible." Ellie took the document and getting Liana they went down to the lab. They were ready to receive her and after a few questions they took her inside. Ellie decided to wait. It was about thirty minutes later that Liana came out.

"How was it?" Ellie asked Liana.

"I never had so many test performed on me in all of my life," said Liana. "Besides the audio tests and the X-ray test they pushed me on my back through three other machines." Ellie laughed at Liana statements.

"Let's go back to my office," said Ellie. "I am so far behind in my work. Come you can watch me perform what I will have you doing after I catch up a little." They did just that. Liana just sat next to Ellie and watched what she was doing. She never bothered Ellie with a question. That afternoon before they were getting ready to leave Ellie got a call from Stella, doctor Vera's nurse. She asked Ellie to come to Doctor Vera's office before she went home. They wasted no time going to the doctor's office.

"Hi doctor," said Ellie when they entered his office. "What are the results of the tests?"

"Hi girls," said the doctor. "She is perfectly healthy. The results of the test could not have been better." He then reached into his desk drawer and pulled out a business card. He handed it to Liana. "I hope you will accept me as your primary Care physician."

"It will be my good fortune and the smartest thing I could do to have you as my physician," said Liana. "I will keep this in my purse."

"May I have a card also," said Ellie. "Dr. Clemens is my father's doctor. I don't have one yet."

"Of course," said the doctor as he got another card and gave it to Ellie. Ellie looked at it and saw that it read 'Doctor Donald Vera AMD'. She then placed it in her purse. "Have a good evening doctor," said Ellie.

"Thank you very much for your excellent job of taking care of me," said Liana as they left his office. They went back to Ellie's office to gather up all the belongings they wanted to take home and left. When they got home Tom had a nice dinner ready for them.

The next two days went by slowly. Ellie had Liana at her office every day. She finally let Liana take over all the financial activities. She did great. Soon it was Thanksgiving Day. Tom bought a twelve pound turkey. As he was dressing it to get it ready to cook he got a phone call. It was Vicki. Tom felt so good talking with her. They spent fifteen miutes talking. After they finish talking Tom felt so much better. He finally placed the turkey in the oven. At about eleven o'clock Tom's mother and father showed up.

"Hi mom, dad," said Tom as he hugged his mother and shook hands with his father. "You both look so wonderful. How do you guys keep so young?"

"We love you to son," said his father indicating that they looked good because of his love. As they came in and removed their coats Ellie came down from her bedroom.

"Hi Grandma and Grandpa," said Ellie and greeted them as Tom had done. Just as they were talking, Alex walked in. He greeted them just as Ellie had done.

"The turkey will be done in about an hour," said Tom. "Ellie, is Chris coming to eat with us?"

"No dad," said Ellie. "He is going to Cleveland to be with his parents." About an hour later they sat down at the table. Tom said grace and they all had a great diner. Tom's mom and dad wanted to know all that they have accomplished since the last time they saw them. Alex gave the full story of how he met Liana. After they all ate, Tom brought out a large pumpkin pie. They all enjoyed it very much. The time went by too fast. At about six thirty they each had a turkey sandwiches and continued their small talk. At about eleven Tom's parent decide to go home. They thanked Tom and after hugging him and the girl they left. Alex was the next one to leave. After Alex left every one decided to go to bed. Thanksgiving holiday was over.

On Saturday afternoon, two days after the Thanksgiving holiday, Alex came to his father's house for dinner. He stayed overnight so that he could go to church with them. He wanted more time with Liana. After church, Chris, Ellie's fiancé, showed up. He had gone to his own church. He had been a member of that church for years. He was not ready to leave it yet. They all had lunch together. Alex and Liana went to the TV room to watch a movie. They wanted to spent time alone together. Tom and Ellie and Chris watch a movie in the Family Room. At around six they all had a sandwich and spent the rest of the day enjoying their time together. At about ten o'clock Chris decided to leave. He had to get up early the next day. They all said goodbye and he left. Alex decided to go home also.

Alex was about to leave when Ellie grabbed him by his arm.

"Alex," she asked, "could I have a few minutes of your time? I have something I would like to discuss with you."

"Sure sis," said Alex, "what do you have in mind?"

"I know that you and Liana miss each other badly," started Ellie. "I have a suggestion to make."

"I would like to hear it," said Alex.

"I would like to hear it to," said Liana.

"Me to," added Tom.

"I know that you would like to start a practice of your own," said Ellie ignoring Liana and her dad. "Maybe you can someday, but I think you should consider what I am suggesting."

"I can't wait," said Alex getting impatient.

"At the University Hospital, there is an east wing where an

organization called University Medical Group is located," continued Ellie. "They have doctor's offices where people can get personal care. It is similar to the one you work at Medina. This organization, however, I believe gives you more freedom to practice. It so happened that two of the doctors left for another state to start a practice of their own. Therefore they are short of doctors as Dad can tell you. Dad had a big problem getting an appointment with his Primary Care physicians. So they really can use another doctor. I can take you there and introduce you to Doctor Donald Vera, the head of the center."

"It sounds like a fantastic opportunity," said Alex. "When do you want to go?"

"How about tomorrow morning," said Ellie. Alex started to take off his jacket.

"I think I will spend tonight here so that I can go with you tomorrow."

"That is a great," said Tom. "I will pray that you get the job so that I could have my family here together for a while."

"Tell me Alex," asked Ellie. "Why are you so unhappy with the place you now work?"

"They are to controlling," responded Alex. "To give you an example, I have an elderly lady that has been my patient for several years. When she came in they asked her what her problem was. She said that she had Urinary infection problem. They then assigned her to another doctor telling her that Dr. Seder was better in curing Urinary problems. So I sat in my office waiting for my next patient that is if they would have let my patient come to me."

"That is terrible," said Ellie. "I will never let that happen at our hospital." About an hour later they all went to bed.

The next morning Alex and Ellie got up about six. When they got downstairs they were surprised that their father was up making breakfast for them. Liana was also there.

"What are you guys doing up?" asked Alex.

"I didn't sleep all night," said Liana.

"I knew that you guys would not have time to make breakfast so I thought I would help," said Tom.

"Thank you dad," said Alex. They all ate quickly and Alex and Ellie left for the hospital. Alex drove his own car thinking that he would leave after the meeting. They arrived at the hospital at about fifteen before eight. Doctor Vera was already there.

"Hi Doctor Vera," said Ellie. "I want you to meet my brother Doctor Alex Corely. He is currently with the Medina Medical Group. He would like to change and come to work here."

"I can understand that," said Doctor Vera. "I have heard how badly they operate there. Ellie, why don't you go to your job? Your brother and I will sit here and discuss the possibilities." After Ellie left the doctor turned to Alex. "First of all I would like to call you Alex and I would like you to call me Donald. Then I will like to hear about all your education and all the experience you have had since you graduated." Alex spent the next hour telling Doctor Vera all that has happened since he graduated.

"I guess that is all that I can think of that you would be interested in," said Alex.

"I am very pleased to hear that you graduated from the same university that I did. I also think that you will be perfect for this job."

"Sounds great," said Alex. "When can I start?"

"How about right now," said Doctor Vera.

"I would love that," said Alex. "However I have to resign from my present job and move into my father's house. When will I have time to do that?"

"Why don't you start now?" said Donald. "I will get all your paper work for you to sign. Then I will show you to your office and introduce you to all the other members of this group. Then you can leave this afternoon to take care of all that personal business."

"Sound doable," said Alex. Doctor Vera then took him around as he had suggested. First he took him to Alex's new office. It was about noon when they were done with all that was to be accomplished. Alex was now a member of the University Medical Group.

"Well I guess it is time for you to leave," said Doctor Vera.

"Tomorrow you will have a day full of new patients ready for you." Alex left and went directly to the Median Medical Group. He resigned and settled all the financial requirements. He then went to his apartment. He explained to his landlord what was happening. He settled all the rent that he owed and started to pack all his belonging. He filled all his suit cases three cardboard boxes and what he had left he placed in the back seat of the car. Late that afternoon he arrived at his father's house. It took him an hour to move back into his old bedroom. He was finally finished by the time the girls got home. The girls were thrilled that Alex got the job at the hospital and that he was moving in with them. They all joyfully had a wonderful dinner. Tom was the happiest of all. He had all of his family together again

In Columbus, Vicki was spending most of her time preparing for Christmas. She wanted to decorate Helen's house. She removed the lamp from the small table that was in the front window and replaced it with a small three foot Christmas tree. She decorated the rest of the house with flowers and all the Christmas decorations she could find. That evening after dinner Vicki got a call from Adele.

"Hi Vick," said Adele. "How are you and Aunt Helen?"

"Hi Adele," said Vicki recognizing her voice. "How are all in your family?"

"We are all fine," said Adele. "The reason I called is that I want to make sure that you knew that Christmas will be celebrated at my place and it will be on Christmas Eve, not Christmas day. On Christmas day, Todd and I will be going to Todd's parents and my brother and Sally will be going to Sally's parents to celebrate the holiday."

"That sounds like a well thought out plan," said Vicki. "Your' Aunt Helen and I will be at your house at five PM on Christmas Eve."

"Great," said Adele. "I just wanted to be sure you knew. See you then." Adele then hung up.

The days went by to rapidly. On the morning of Christmas Eve Vicki called Tom.

"Hi Tom," said Vicki when Tom answered the phone. "Merry Christmas Tom, how are you?"

"Merry Christmas Vicki, how are you? We are fine. We are very busy preparing for Christmas."

"We are celebrating Christmas tonight," said Vicki. "On Christmas day Helen's niece and nephew are going to their in-laws for the holiday celebration."

"We are doing the same," said Tom. "Ellie and Chris are going to celebrate Christmas with his family on Christmas day. By the way, we got the gifts you sent us. It was so sweet of you to do that. We loved what you picked to send us."

"I also got the gift you sent me," said Vicki. "It was beautiful." After a few minutes talking about the past days, they wished each other a happy holiday and hung up. Later that day Vicki got dressed up and helped Helen dress up. They then left for Adele's house. They were received with affection from Adele, Todd and their son Ronald. Gabe, Sally and their children Ryan and Gina were already there. They saluted each other with a hug except the men and the boys said hello with a hand shake.

"So glad to see you both," said Adele to Vicki and Helen. "I'm so glad you could make it. I was worried about you Aunt Helen. Are you feeling alright?"

"I'm fine and very hungry," said Helen. "That should tell you how well I am."

"Very funny Aunt Helen," said Adele. "I'm happy you still have your humor." A few minutes later they were called to the dinner table. Adele had cooked a twenty pound ham. It was very tender and very tasty. They all enjoyed the dinner including the Pumpkin Pie they had for desert. After dinner they all sat around the Christmas tree. Ronnie was chosen as Santa's helper. He distributed the gifts to each, one at a time. He waited until each recipient opened his or her gift before he presented the next gift. That took the rest of the evening. They were all very pleased and happy with the gift they received. Soon it was late and Helen was getting sleepy. Vicki didn't receive a gift from Helen and Helen did not receive the gift from Vicki. They wanted their gift exchange to be private the next day.

In Ohio on Christmas Eve, Tom, Alex and Liana, Ellie and Chris all went to Tom's parent's house. They had a marvelous dinner. After dinner they sat around the Christmas tree and exchanged gifts. On Christmas day, Ellie and Chris went to Chris's family for dinner and the exchange of gifts. Tom Alex and Liana spent the day together. They enjoyed being together for the two days.

On Christmas day in Columbus, Vicki got up before Helen and pulled the Helen's gift from under her bed and placed it under the tree. When she got to the tree she was shocked to see a gift siting under the tree address to her. Vicki couldn't figure how the gift ever got there. Soon Helen woke up. Vicki helped her to the kitchen. Vicki had prepared breakfast. It was Mother's Oats that Helen loved. After eating they went into the living room and sat next to the Christmas tree. Vicki reached for Helen's gift.

"Please Vicki," said Helen. "I would like you to open your gift first."

"When did you get this gift for me?" asked Vicki.

"While you were out shopping, I had Adele do it for me," said Helen. "Please open it." Vicki opened the gift Helen got for her. It was a large picture of Vicki and Helen in a beautiful fifteen by fifteen inch wooden frame. It was a picture that was taken on Thanksgiving Day and enlarged to fit the frame.

"Wow," said Vicki honestly impressed. "This is beautiful."

"I wanted you to have it so that you will never forget me," said Helen with a loving look on her face.

"I could never forget you," said Vicki with a loving smile. Vicki then handed Helen the gift she had bought for her. Vicki helped Helen open the gift. When Helen saw the dishes Vicki had bought for her she was socked.

"Dear Vicki," said Helen with tears showing up in her eyes. "I have never had a more wonderful gift in all of my life. It is perfect. They match the larger dishes I have perfectly. We really needed a smaller version of my dishes. The larger dishes are too large for the little that we eat."

"I'm glad that you like it," said Vicki. "Now I'm going into the kitchen to prepare you a special lunch."

"It's too early to have lunch," said Helen. "We just had breakfast."

"This is a special lunch," said Vicki. This meal will take about three hours to cook. I would have normally made a dinner like this for the evening meal. However, it is Christmas day. We are going to celebrate it at lunch time."

"Sound fine to me," said Helen. "I can't wait to see what you will cook." Vicki cooked a tomato sauce with some Pork Neck bones and meat balls. When the sauce was finished, she cooked some Cavatelli in the sauce. They enjoyed the food with great pleasure. At the end of the meal, they found that they had some pork Neck bones left over. They ate them late in the evening with some leftover meat balls. It was a great holiday.

The next few days went by quickly. Soon it was New Year's Eve. Helen's niece and nephew's had private plans of their own. Vicki and Helen spent the day by themselves. At night they watch TV until the New Year's ball came down at Times Square. Vick had some champagne ready to drink when the New Year was announced. They wish each other a Happy New Year, drank the champagne, hugged each other and soon went to bed.

In Fairlawn Ohio it was the same. Tom was alone on New Year's Eve. He stayed up to see the Times Square ball come down and afterwards went to bed. The next day they all got together for a delicious ham lunch and a sweet Blueberry pie for desert. That afternoon Tom got a call from Vicki. They wished each other a Happy New Year and after a short discussion about what they had been doing since they last spoke they hung up. Late that afternoon Tom and his family all had sandwiches with left over ham. Tom and his family all enjoyed being together as a family for the holiday. Too soon it was eleven o'clock. They all decided to go to bed. The holiday season was over.

CHAPTER SEVEN

Unexpected Turn Of Events

In Columbus the days of January went by with no unusual events. Each day was exactly like the day before. Every morning Vicki would make breakfast and after it was done she would go to Helen's bedroom and get her dressed. They would then go into the kitchen and eat breakfast together. Vicki then would do the required chores and at least twice a week she would go out shopping. In the evening after dinner they would both watch TV. Helen seemed happy with the arrangement. Vicki was glad she was able to help Helen.

At Ohio everything was the same for January. In February it was the same for a while. However things changed on February tenth. On the morning of that day Tom got a call from Ellie.

"Hi Ellie," said Tom. "Is everything OK?"

"No dad," responded Ellie. "We have a problem. Early this morning, Chris's apartment building caught on fire. Chris was on the second floor when he became aware of the fire. He tried to leave the building but the stairs gave way and he fell. Fortunately a young man saw him and carried him out of the building. An ambulance that was called by the firemen brought Chris here to the hospital. I don't know how badly he is hurt. Dr. Wilson checked him up and sent him to the hospital lab for tests. I think he would like some company."

"Did you call his parents?" asked Tom.

"I tried," said Ellie, "but no one answered. Anyway I think they go to their condo in Florida for the winter."

"I'm leaving right now," said Tom. "I'll see you in a few minutes." He then hung up and headed for his car. He arrived at the hospital about ten minutes later. He went directly to the hospital room he was told that was Doctor Brian's room. Tom sat there for about an hour. Finally a nurse brought Chris in from the lab. Doctor Wilson was with them.

"Hello there Doctor Corley, how are you?"

"Hello doctor Wilson, said Tom. "I see that you are back. I thought you had moved to a hospital in a southern state."

"I did but I was not happy there, said Doctor Wilson. "So I came back here."

"Good to see you," said Tom. "How is our patient?"

"He has a broken arm, a badly bruised shoulder and a slight bruise on your head," said Doctor Wilson. "He also suffered from smoke inhalation."

"Is he going to be OK?" asked Tom.

"Yes, said Doctor Wilson. "May I ask you why you are here? Is there some question about the fire?"

"There will be an investigation on how the fire started," said Tom, "but that is not why I'm here. Doctor Brian is engaged to my daughter. I am here to keep him company."

"Fine," said Doctor Wilson. "Have a good day." The doctor then left the room. It was over an hour later that Chris woke up.

Chris looked at Tom as he turned his head to see who was sitting next to him. He had expected it to be Ellie.

"Hi," said Chris when he realized who it was. "Where am I? What am I doing here?" He was confused as to what happened. The last thing he remembered was getting up in the morning getting ready to go to work.

"Your building was on fire and you got hurt trying to escape the building," said Tom. Chris began searching his memory. Finally he remembered trying to leave the burning building.

"Yes I remember now," said Chris. "I remember that the building was on fire and I tried to leave. The last thing I remember is I was going down the steps and the steps collapsed. That is all I remember until now. How badly am I hurt?" Tom was about to answer when Ellie walked in.

"Hi sweetheart," she said to Chris. "I will answer that question. But first let me say hello to my dad. Hello dad. Thanks for come." Then turning to Chris she added. "I asked dad to come and keep you company. I am so busy I can only come once in a while. Remember I run this place. Now let me tell you about your injuries. You have a broken arm, a badly bruised shoulder, a slight concussion. But the doctor said that you will be alright in a couple of days.

"Thank you Honey" said Chris. "I understand. I will be alright. Just drop in once in a while" Then Chris turning to Tom.

"I hope this is not a burden on you. I'm sure you have a lot of things you would rather do."

"Not at all," said Tom. "I think it will give us time to get to know each other. After all you are going to me my son-in-law. Besides, I am retired and have nothing else to do except write novels"

"I will like that, "said Chris, "I don't have anything else to do ether."

"Well at least you have your sense of humor," said Tom. They spent the next hour discussing their past. Tom told him about his past life. Chris asked Tom to tell him some of the interesting cases he solved. Tom told him about the cases that he felt would be the most interesting to him. Chris told Tom of his high school events and his college years. After they had both finished Chris turned to Tom.

"How are we going to spend the rest of the long hours in the days to come?"

"Well I brought one of my books that I think you will like," said Tom. "It is called 'A Time Before Time' I will read from it from you if it's OK with you."

"I would love that," Chris. "I hate the idea that it will trap you. I would not like it if you leave without finishing the novel."

"I promise that I will not do that," said Tom. "It may take a couple of days." Tom then opened the book and stated to read the first chapter. Tom read the first chapter and when finished Chris asked question about the event of the story. He was very interested in the story like it was real. This went on until noon. Tom then decided to go down to the cafeteria to have lunch. In the meantime Nurse Colene went in to feed Chris. After lunch Tom went back up to Chris's room and read the next chapter. It was about five in the afternoon when Tom had finished reading chapter four and was about to turn to chapter five. He was surprised that Chris did not ask any questions. He had asked question after each other chapter. Tom got up and looked a Chris. He had fallen asleep. Tom then put the book down and waited for the nurse to come to feed Chris. She came about five thirty. She woke up Chris to feed him.

"I'm sorry Mr. C," said Chris when he was awakened. "I didn't mean to fall asleep. I guess I am more tired than I thought."

"That is alright," said Tom. "You need some time to heal. I'm going to leave now. I have to cook for the rest of my family. See you tomorrow morning."

"Goodbye dad," said Chris. Tom smiled at him as he left. Tom got home about six. Every one was home waiting for him.

"Sorry guys," said Tom. "I should have left earlier but Chris fell asleep and I didn't want to wake him and I didn't want to leave without saying goodbye. Anyway, I have some pizza I made just in case this happened. All I have to do is warm it up." That evening they all enjoyed the pizza. They knew that Tom made fantastic Sicilian pizza. They spent the rest of the day as usual. The next morning Tom arrived at the hospital at eight. The nurse was just finishing feeding Chris.

"Hi Chris," said Tom. "How are you today?"

"I'm a little better today," said Chris. "I however can't wait to hear what happens next in your book." Tom opened the book and started to read. He started to read from where Chris remembered before he fell asleep. They stopped for lunch and after Tom got back from lunch he started to read from where he had left of. At about two in the afternoon Ellie showed up.

"I'm sorry I couldn't come sooner, said Ellie. I had a lot of work to do. However I have good news. I got a call from our wedding Planner. A wedding was cancelled and March 20 is now available. I told the planner to go ahead and move our wedding to March 20. I hope that is alright with you."

"It is still not soon enough," said Chris. "But if that is the only time available lets go with it."

"Also I want you to know that yesterday while you were asleep I got all your clothes from the closet and washed them. I put them back this morning."

"Thank you sweet heart," said Chris. Tom continued reading until about four. Then he excused himself.

"I have to go home now and cook for the family, I will see you tomorrow morning" He then said goodbye and left.

The next morning Tom showed up as promised. Chris had just finished breakfast.

"Good morning Chris," said Tom as he walked in and sat down next to Chris.

"Good morning," said Chris. "I hope everything is fine with you."

"I am fine," said Tom. "I think I can finish my first book today. So in case I finish early I brought my second book called 'Terror in Green Valley'

"I can't wait to hear the end of your first book," said Chris. It was early in the afternoon when Tom finisher his first book. Chris could not stop talking about how much he loved the story. Tom was about to open the next book when Ellie walked in.

"Hi fellas," said Ellie. "I have good news. The doctor examined Chris early this morning and said that everything was fine. He said that he will release him tomorrow morning. He wants to see him in two weeks from now to take off his casts. Isn't that great?"

"That is wonderful," said Tom. "What do you think Chris? You don't seem excited from the news."

"It sounds great," said Chris, "but where am I going to live. The building where I lived is demolished. I can't get a room in a hotel.

I don't think that I could take care of myself. Do I go to a Nursing Home? That would be worse than staying here."

"Don't be silly," said Tom. "You are coming home with me."

"Oh I don't want to impose on you," said Chris. "I'm sure you have a lot better things to do rather than taking care of me, besides where would you put me?"

"I have a spare bedroom," said Tom. "It is the room that Vicki lived in. I can set you up so you can read my book by yourself. After you get up and have breakfast I can set you up in the TV room. There you can read the book and when you want some rest from reading you can watch TV."

"Are you sure you want to do this?" asked Chris.

"Positive," said Tom.

"Not only all that," said Ellie. "When I get home from work, I can take care of you. I can feed you and take care of you until bed time."

"I can hardly wait," said Chris.

"By the way Chris," said Tom. "I forgot to tell you. I contacted the Police and the Fire Department. The firemen went into you rooms and filled up two large boxes from all that they could save of you stuff before the building collapsed. I placed them in the bed room I was sure you were going be in for a while."

"You were sure that I was going to move in with you?" said Chris with a smile.

"Well I have got to leave," said Ellie. "I have a lot of work to do." Before she could leave Tom grabbed her by her arm.

"Let's go in the hallway. I need to talk with you about something."

"You got some secret you don't want me to know," said Chris, with a joking voice.

"Its business," said Tom. "I don't want you to be loaded down with my problems." With that they walked out into the hallway out of Chris's hearing.

"What is the problem Dad?" asked Ellie.

"I was wondering about Chris's stay in the hospital," said Tom. "How are we going to take care of the cost?"

"Chris was not dumb," said Ellie. "When he left his apartment he made sure he had his check book and his wallet with him. I have taken care of everything. His insurance is paying for most of it."

"That is great," said Tom. Tom then went back to reading from his number two novel. He had only read about three pages when the nurse came in with a set of crutches.

"Since you are going home tomorrow," said Nurse Colene, "I think we better train you to walk with crutches," She then helped Chris get up. She informed him to keep his weight on the crutch and not on his bad leg. She then took him around the hospital third floor hall way. They came back after about fifteen miutes.

"How did you make out?" asked Tom of Chris.

"It is hard," said Chris. "I instinctively want to put weight on my bad leg. I also still have a little pain in my left shoulder." Tom then went back to reading from his second novel. He read until about four.

"I think I will have to leave now," said Tom. "I will see you early tomorrow morning. I will have your bedroom ready for you." With that Tom left to cook, for the family, what the girls said was a fantastic dinner.

The next morning Tom was in the hospital at eight.

"I'm sorry but you will have to wait a little while," said Nurse Colene. "Ellie is helping Chris dress. She asked that I don't let anyone in until Chris was fully dressed. They will be ready in a few minutes." A few miutes later Ellie came out pushing Chris in a wheel chair. The crutches were on his lap.

"Hi dad,' said Ellie. "I was hoping that you would come in time. "Chris is ready to come home. If you will pull your car in front of the entrance way I will bring him down to you."

"I'm on my way," said Tom. "Hi Chris," he said as he left.

"Hi Dad," said Chris at the same time. Tom got his car out of the parking lot and pulled in front of the entrance way. Ellie was already there waiting for him. Ellie helped Tom get Chris in the front seat of the car. She then placed the crutches in the back seat.

"See you tonight," said Ellie as they left. A few minutes later Tom pulled into his garage. He then walked around and opened the door to help Chris get out of the car. There were three steps from the garage into the family room. Tom had a hard time getting Chris up into the family room. Finally with Chris's arm around Tom's neck Tom lifted Chis up one step at a time. Fortunately Chris was not too heavy. Now there were eight steps from the family room to the kitchen. Fortunately there was a railing on the right side. Chris, used his crutch for his left side, and grabbing the railing with his good right arm was able, pull himself up one step at a time. When they got to the top they both decided to rest for a while.

"I think we had better rest," said Tom. "There are eight more steps to get to the bedrooms."

"I think you are right," said Chris. "That sofa in your living room looks good. "Maybe I could sleep there for my stay."

"Nonsense," said Tom. "We have a wonderful bedroom upstairs and you will not need to come down until you are able. We have a TV room upstairs that has a very confortable couch. We also have a folding little table that had feet that slip under the couch to give you a place to eat and do any other thing you want to do. You can read one of my books or you can watch TV. If you want to read, you can set the book on the table and turn the pages with you good right hand."

"Sounds great," said Chris. "Does that mean that I don't have to go up and down any stairs?"

"Not until you are able," repeated Tom. "Ellie can take care of you after four thirty when she comes home. She can feed you and eat with you if she wants and afterwards she can stay with you watch TV with you."

"Sounds great," said Chris. "I'm ready. Please take me up stairs." With much effort Tom got Chris up to the TV room. He sat Chris on the couch and set the table next to him.

"Just rest here," said Tom, "and at lunch time I will bring you your lunch," At noon Tom brought Chris A cup of coffee and a Turkey Baloney sandwich. After he ate, Chis asked Tom to bring him to the bed room. He was tired and wanted to take an afternoon nap. Tom did as Chris asked. Chis had no trouble walking with the crutches. At four thirty when Ellie go home she went upstairs to see Chris. She was surprised that Chris had used his crutches and moved to the TV room. He was watching a movie.

"Hi sweet heart," said Ellie when she found him in the TV room. "It is so good to have you home."

"It is so good to be here," said Chris. "Your dad has taken good care of me. The bed room he gave me is perfect. I had my afternoon nap there."

"From here until you go to bed, I will be your nurse," said Ellie. "When dad finishes cooking I will bring the food up here and we will eat together."

"I'm almost glad that my apartment got destroyed," said Chris jokingly. This went on until it was time for Chris to go to the hospital to hopefully remove his casts. It was February 26 when Chris had all his casts removed. After that Chris was able to walk with only a small limp. He was happy to be able to go up and down the stair and eat with the whole family. One day, when they were all at the kitchen table eating, Alex went down on one knee besides Liana.

"Liana, honey," he started. "I love you with all my heart. Will you marry me?" Liana didn't answer right away. Instead she threw herself into his arms. "I guess that means yes?" asked Alex.

"Yes with all my heart," said Liana with small tears in her eyes. "When do you want it to take place?"

"Being hopeful that you answer was yes, I contacted the Wedding planner that is taking care of Ellie and Chris. I asked if the date in June that Ellie has before she got move up to March was available. The wedding planner said that it was available; however there was an earlier date available. It was May 10. I told her to hold it for us. I hope that is OK with you."

"That is perfect," said Liana. From that day on they were all very happy. The next thing they were looking forward to was the wedding on March 20 of Ellie and Chris. Tom was happy to have his whole family together even though it was for only a few months.

Down in Columbus, Vicki and Helen were enjoying their time

together. Vicki days were all the same. She would get up in the morning make breakfast and then get Helen up to eat. This went on day after day. On Sunday March 7 Vicki had a hard time getting Helen to church and back. She decided that it would be the last time she would take Helen to church on Sundays. Vicki would have to go by herself.

On Monday morning Vicki went back to her old routine. She got up early made breakfast and then went up to wake up Helen and bring her down to eat. She had made Mother's oats which Helen loved. As she walked to the bed room she yelled.

"Mother, it's time to eat. Wake up and get up." When she walked into the bed room she saw that Helen was still lying on her side. "Get up mom," said Vicki as she grabbed her shoulder and turn her towards her. Then she saw the cold look on her face. She quickly checked for a heartbeat. There was none. She touched her face and found that it was very cold. She quickly got on the phone and called for an ambulance. The ambulance got there in five minutes. The doctor that came with the ambulance checked Helen and then turned to Vicki.

"There is nothing we can do," said the doctor. "She must have passed away sometime during the night. We will take her to the Funeral Parlor. I believe they have all the information that is needed." Vicki followed the ambulance in her car to the Funeral Parlor. When she got there she went up to the Funeral Parlor Director.

"Good morning," said Vicki. "I am Victoria Graton. I am the one who called the ambulance for Helen Grafton. What do I have to do to get Helen prepared for the funeral?"

"Yes of course," said the director. "We have everything under control. You do not have to do anything. Mrs. Graton had everything taken care of years ago. We have notified her attorney. We have also notified her niece and nephew."

"When will she be displayed in the Parlor?"

"She has been delivered to the undertaker. He will need tomorrow to prepare her for the funeral. She will be on display on Wednesday morning until noon. She will then be placed in the crypt above her husband. After the final prayer, we will have lunch down stairs. After lunch we will come up to the office across from the display area where we will have the reading of the will."

"Thank you so much for the information," said Vicki. "I will see you Wednesday." With that said Vicki left the parlor and went home. She realized that she had all day tomorrow to pack her stuff and get ready to return to Ohio. However she decided to check the kitchen very carefully for anything she wanted to take. She decided to take the special dishes she had purchased and the larger ones Helen already had. She also loved the toaster. She also picked out several kitchen items she liked. She packed them all in a cardboard box she found in the basement. It was then time for lunch. She cooked herself three Lamb chops she found in the refrigerator. After lunch she packed all her belongings in her own suitcase. At about five in the evening she called Adele and Gabe. They both answered with tears. After a few minutes expressing their sorrows Vicki went and searched the freezer and refrigerator. She didn't want to leave any food she liked if it could not be taken home in her car. She found two beautiful filet Minion steaks. She had one that evening and saved the other for the next day. The next day she spent most of the day searching through every closet and drawers in the house. She found one of Helens suitcases and filled it with all of Helens clothes that she liked and could wear. She finally went to bed.

The next morning she arrived at the Funeral Parlor at eight in the morning. Vicki walked by the coffin and knelt down on the little stool that was there. She said a little prayer for her. She then walked back and sat at one of the chairs. Soon Adele, Todd and their son Ron arrived. After walking past the coffin Adele threw herself into Vickie's arms they both stood there with heavy tears

"I am going to miss her like I never thought I could miss anyone," said Vicki after they both recovered.

"You are only going to miss one person," said Adele. "I am going to miss two persons. That is because I suspect that, after the funeral you will be leaving to return to Ohio."

"I will be missing all of you." said Vicki. "That is much more than two." Adele hugged Vicki again. Just then Gabe and Sally walked in. They all hugged each other. Gabe and Sally then went to the coffin and knelt down like Vicki had done. They then went and sat with the rest of the family.

"I'm so sorry," said Sally to Vicki. "I know how close you two were."

"Thank you Sally," said Vicki. "I know how much you guys loved her too. By the way, where are your two children, Ryan and Gina?"

"They are in college," said Sally. "It is too far for them to come here. They would not make it in time."

The time went by too fast. Soon it was noon. The pastor came in and said a prayer for Helen. They asked everyone to walk past the coffin for a final look and proceed to the burial site. Then two parlor men closed the casket. At the burial building they set Helen's coffin in the opening above where her husband was placed. They then closed the door of the crypt. After a final prayer they were asked to go to the Funeral Parlor basement for lunch. When they arrived there they saw self-serve tables full of delicious food on the right side of the room. They all got into line and got the food they wanted. They then sat at one of the small table in the room. Vicki, Ellie, Todd, and their son Ronald sat at one of the tables. As they ate they discussed the sadness they were going to feel for a long time. After everyone was nearly finish eating one of the parlor men spoke up.

"When you are finished eating," said the parlor man," you are asked to go upstairs to the office room across from the display room. The reading of the Will is scheduled to be done there." When Ellie and her family got up to go upstairs Vicki grabbed Ellie and hugged her.

"I am not going up to the office," said Vicki. "I am going home and start packing."

"Are you not coming to hear the reading of the will?" asked Ellie.

"No," said Vicki. "I am not in her will."

"I can't believe that she would not leave you anything," said Ellie.

"She is right," said the man standing next to them. "I am Steve Marten. I am Helen Grafton's attorney. Except for small charity gifts she left everything to her niece and nephew." Ellie and all her family, as well as Gabe and Sally, all hugged Vicki and sadly said goodbye. It was a very sad moment for all as Vicki left the funeral Parlor. Vicki got home to Helen's house and started to place all the things she had packed in boxes and suitcases in the truck of her car. She left only the clothes she was going to wear tomorrow and her pajamas she was going to wear that night. She spent the next few hours doing a final search through every inch of the house. She found that she had packed everything she wanted. She then went into the refrigerator and got the Filet Minion steak and had a great dinner. After she finished eating she called Adele.

"Hi Adele," said Vicki. "I want to talk with you about your aunt's possessions before I leave."

"Hi Vicki, said Adele. "I am going to miss your calls."

"I wanted to ask you if it was alright for me to take some of Helens belongings," said Vicki. "Mostly I want the dishes I bought for her and some of the other kitchen items that I would like to have in memory of her."

"Listen Vicki," said Adele. "You can rent a truck and take everything in the house. With all that you have done you deserve it."

"Thank you so much Adele," said Vicki. "I may just take a little of Helen's clothes that I like. I suggest that you come and get all that you want and then call a Real Estate Agent and have her put a red flag on all the furniture you want to sell. The flags will have the price you want to sell it for. Then have her put the house on sale. She will tell you what the value of the house is. So listen, I am going leave for Ohio early in the morning. I will leave the house keys in the mail box. I will greatly miss you most of all. So have a great life and God Bless you and your family."

"I will miss you too," said Adele. "May God bless you to and guide you to great happiness. Goodbye Vicki"

"Goodbye, Adele" said Vicki and hung up.

The next morning Vicki got up around six. She couldn't sleep.

She felt if she got away from Columbus she would not feel so bad. She had a quick breakfast and left the house about seven-thirty. After a long trip that seemed like it would never end Vicki arrived at Tom's house around nine thirty. She pulled in to the end of the drive way behind the house. The garage door was located in the rear of the attached garage. As she got out of her car she noticed that Tom was just pulling out of his garage. Tom pushed the button in his car that shut the garage and then noticing that Vickie's car had pulled in. He got out of his car and walked over to where Vicki was.

"Hi Vicki," said Tom. "Listen, please lock your car and get in my car. I am in a hurry. Captain Richard called me for a special assignment. We can talk on the way there." Vicki did as Tom requested and soon they were on the road.

"Hello Tom," said Vicki as soon as the car was on the way. "How are you? What is this assignment that you have and where are we going? Also I thought that you were retired?"

"I am on a special assignment," said Tom. "I get one every once in a while. Anyway, a woman was shot in the neck, shoulder and in the ribs," continued Tom. "The information I got from the police who went to the scene of the crimes suggests that it was an attempted murder. The only information we got was that a neighbor said that she saw a black car around for several days surveying the Rineli house."

"So where are we going?" asked Vicki, "and how can I help?"

"We are going to the University Hospital," said Tom. "She is in surgery to remove the bullets from her body."

"And how can I help?" asked Vicki.

"With all my experience," said Tom, "I have seen many crimes that are similar to this one. I have a suspicion as to what happened. In this case if I am correct I may need a woman to ask questions."

"I will help in any way I can," said Vicki. "By the way, can I have a room at your house until I could find a place to live?"

"I'm sorry," said Tom. "I gave your room to Dr. Christopher Brian, Ellie's future husband. If you need some place to sleep for a day or so you could sleep on the couch in the TV room upstairs."

"That is alright," said Vicki. "I will find a place, perhaps in a motel for a day or so."

They soon arrived at the hospital. Tom got directions as to where the victim was and he and Vicki when into the room. Sitting at the chair next to the bed was the husband.

"Hi," said Tom. "I am Detective Thomas Corely. I am here to investigate the shooting of your wife. This with me is Victoria Graton. She is my assistant in this case."

"I am Andrew Rineli, Colene's husband. I hope you can solve this problem soon."

"Can you tell me Andy," asked Tom, "if there is anyone that you suspect that would want to hurt one of you?"

"NO Detective Corely," said Andy. "We have only lived in Ohio about one year. We moved here from Arizona. My company sent me here to fill an engineering spot here in good year Aerospace Corporation. What do you think this could be about?"

"First," said Tom. "Please call me Tom. There are four possibilities. The first is that it could be a random shooting. I don't think this is the one because of your neighbor and you seeing a black car around your house. The second possibility is that someone wants to kill both of you. I think that this is very unlikely. The third is that someone is after your wife and the fourth is that someone is after you. The last two are the most likely. However we will investigate all four possibilities."

"What can I do to help?" asked Andy.

"Tell me what you can tell me about the shooting. I understand that your house is on a street corner. I understand that you have an attached garage. Why was your car outside?"

"Last night when I got home I found that the switch I have above my rear view mirror did not work. I could not open the garage door. I went inside the house and tried from the switch in the garage. That didn't work either. I have called the repair people and they are to come tomorrow to fix it.

"You never got the car started," said Tom. "Is that correct?"

"I heard the shots before I could get it started."

"That bring up an important question," said Tom. "The shooter was across the street with his car parallel with your so how did three shoots miss you and hit your wife?" Andy thought for a few minutes, then as if it suddenly dawned on him he yelled out.

"Oh my God," Andy said with a load voice. "I forgot all about it. Just as I was about to put the key in the ignition, I dropped it on the car floor. I bent over to get them when I heard the gun fire. I was so shook up with the sound of the bullets breaking the car door window that I forgot all about it."

"That puts the possibility that the gun man was after you in a first place."

"Tom," said Vicki, "can I see you in the hall for a miutes."

"Of course," said Tom. Vicki and Tom then walked out in the hall way.

"I don't think you need me for a while," said Vicki." I have written down all that has been said. I would like a little time to go and visit Ellie and Liana. I will be back as soon as the doctor says that Andy's wife is brought back to her hospital room. I will be there when you get to talk with her."

"That is fine," said Tom. "I will call you on your cell phone if she arrives sooner than we expected." Tom then walked back into the hospital room.

"Is there a problem?" asked Andy.

"No," said Tom. "Vicki felt that since we were finished here that she would handle one of the other tasks. I will stay with you until your wife is brought here and is able to talk. I would like to ask her a couple of questions before I continue on with this case."

"While we sit here and wait," said Andy, "why don't you tell me about some of the interesting cases that you have worked on."

"First," said Tom. "I have a few things I have to do. First since I believe that you were the intended victim, I am going to call for a police back up to watch this hospital room." Tom then went to hall way to make his calls. First he called his captain. He explained all the he knew. Next he called the personnel manager in Goodyear Aerospace and explained what he wanted. He got an appointment after lunch. Feeling secure he then went back to the hospital room. Tom then told Andy about the cases that were the strangest he had worked on.

Vicki, after leaving Tom and Andy, went directly to Ellie's office.

"Hi Ellie," said Vickie as she entered her office.

"Vicki," said Ellie, "is that you?" she then got up and hugged Vicki.

"It is me in the flesh," said Vicki

"When did you get here," asked Ellie, "and how long are you going to stay in town?"

"I just got here," said Vicki. "I am moving back to Ohio."

"Are you looking for a job?" asked Ellie. "Did you know that Dr. Wilson is back working here? He would love to have you back."

"I would love to come back here to work," said Vicki. "Do you have an opening that I could fit into?"

"Yes," said Ellie. "We have an opening for a nurse to help Dr. Wilson. He would love to have you. He has complained ever since he got back. However, it would be more to your advantage if you work for the hospital instead of working directly for him. You will get some benefits that you will not get working for him directly. I then can assign you to be Dr. Wilson's assistant nurse. Are you interested?"

"Will there not be a cost difference," asked Vicki.

Not at all," said Ellie. "The doctor already pays for a nurse. If he hired you he will stop paying us for a nurse."

"Will you show me the papers I have to sign," said Vicki. "I am very interest. I would love the job." Ellie then did all that was required to hire Vicki. After it was over Ellie put her hand out to Vicki.

"Welcome as a member of the University Hospital medical staff."

"Thank," said Vicki. "However I cannot start for a couple of days. I just came in from Columbus and don't even have a place to live. "

"Let's go to Liana's office," said Ellie. "I think she would like to meet you. Then we can go to see Dr. Wilson."

"Sounds good to me," said Vicki. When they entered Liana's office Liana looked up to see who was entering her office.

"Vicki," said Ellie. "I want you to meet Liana. She is Alex's finance'. Liana, this is Victoria Graton. We all know her as Vicki."

"Hi Vicki," said Liana. "It is so good to meet you. I have heard so much about you. I feel like I already know you."

"I am so glad to meet you to," said Vicki. "It is so nice that you all work for the same company. I see that you are very busy. I will see you often from now on especially since I will be working here also. But now I also have to go and help Tom with the investigation of the shooting of a woman. I will see you later." From there they walked into Dr. Wilson's office.

"Hello Dr. Wilson," said Vicki as they entered his office. Dr. Wilson was looking down signing a document and didn't notice who had entered his office. Suddenly he looked up and recognized Vicki.

"Vicki," he said out loud. "Is it really you? I have missed you as a friend and as the best assistant I have ever had. I hope you are coming back to work here. I need you very badly."

"I am hired by Ellie as a member of the University Medical Center. If you want Ellie could assign me to you as your nurse."

"When can you start?" asked Dr. Wilson.

"It will probably be a couple of days. I just go here from Columbus. I don't even have a place to live."

"Perhaps I can help you in that area," said Dr. Wilson. "I have an apartment off of Rosemount Boulevard. It is the most beautiful apartment that you could ever find in this area, and it is very reasonable in the monthly cost. If you don't know where that is, it is the road that is the extension of Elgin drive across from Cleveland Massillon road. I don't know if they have an opening at this time, but they will in a couple of days. My wife and I have bought a house in Fairlawn and we are moving this weekend." He then got a piece of paper and wrote down the address. Hope this will help you." Vicki and Ellie then said goodbye and left his office. In the hallway Ellie turned to Vicki.

"Look Vicki," said Ellie. "I am way behind in the work I have to do. Go to the victim's room and say hello for me to my dad." After that she left and Vicki headed back to the hospital room.

It was a few miutes after Vicki left to see Ellie that Colene, Andy's wife was brought into the hospital room. She was still asleep. Andy grabbed her hand and with tears talked to her.

Sweet heart," said Andy. "I almost lost you. I would have died with you." Just as she was beginning to moan in waking up a police officer walked into the room.

"Hello Tom," said the office. "I am here to protect the Rineli family. I will be siting just outside the room. So if you want to leave I will be here. "

"Hi Brian," said Tom. "I will be here for a little while yet." Tom waited a few minutes until Colene was fully awake and Andy was finished telling her how much he loved her when Tom interrupted them.

"Hello Colene," said Tom. "I am Detective Tom Corely. "I'm sorry but I have to talk with you Colene."

"I'm sorry detective," said Andy. "I should have introduced you. Honey this police office needs to talk to you. It is his job to find out who shoot you."

"How Can I help?" asked Colene.

"First tell me about all of your family and any personal friends you have," said Tom. Colene then told Tom about all of her family. She told him that they all lived in Phoenix Arizona.

"I don't have any friends or relatives in this area," concluded Colene.

"Tell me where you work and do you have any problems with any of your co-workers?" asked Tom.

"I work at the Woman's Dress Shop at the mall." said Colene, "I have no problems with my coworkers. They are all like family to me. They are all so nice and affectionate friends."

"Can you tell me the name of your boss?" asked Tom.

"Yes, her name is Martha Wellington. She is the best boss I ever had."

"Well that is all that I need for now," said Tom. Just then Vicki walked in the room. "Colene, I want you to meet," started Tom when Vicki broke in.

"I will introduce myself," said Vicki with a gentle loving voice. "My name is Victoria Grafton. I am a nurse practitioner. I assist Dr. Wilson in his operations. When I am not assisting in an operation, I will be taking care of patients like you."

"Nice to meet you too," said Colene. "I though you where Detective Corely's assistant."

"I am today and tomorrow, but I just got rehired a little while ago. I was Dr. Wilson's assistant for several years. I left for an emergence and am now back. I start my job with the hospital two days from now," said Vicki. "Until then I will be helping detective Corely fine the one who shot you."

"Listen Vicki," said Tom. "We have an appointment in the investigation of the shooter at one this afternoon. Let's go to lunch and I will tell you all about it."

"Should I go to lunch with you?" asked Andy.

"No," said Tom. "I think you will be safer here. I have asked the nurse that brings Colene her food to bring food for you too. In a little while she will come and ask you what you want for lunch. We will see you later." Tom and Vicki then left for the hospital cafeteria. At the cafeteria Tom informed Vicki of the job he wanted her to do. Vicki agreed to do her best. After lunch Tom drove to the Aerospace Company. They entered the employment office and asked for the Employee consular Marlene Wendsen. They were pointed to her office. When they entered Marlene spoke first.

"You must be Detective Tomas Corely?" asked Marlene. "Please come in and sit down."

"This is my assistant Victoria Graton that I told you about," said Tom. "We all call her Vicki."

"As I mentioned on the phone," started Marlene, "We generally sent my assistant to speak to all the managers. She asks them how they like their job and if they have any suggestions that would make their job more productive. It is kind of early for this task but they will not realize it. I have already notified them of your coming. If you walk down the hall on your left you will find a door that will take you to the southern section of the area. There on your right you will find three of the section manager's offices. All the workers for that section will be located in front of them. At the end if you turn left you will find the Department manager's office. Next to it is the last of the Section Managers office. If you continue you will go into the lab. Instead turn left and you will go to the Division Managers office. We don't usually go there but if you have any question you can go and ask him. You can go any time you are ready. Here is a list of the Section Managers and their job. Do you have any questions?"

"No, I thing you have made it very clear," said Vicki. "Thank you so much,"

Thank you so much," said "Tom. "It was so nice of you to give us this opportunity." Then turning to Vicki Tom said, "Listen Vicki, I am going to check another possibility. I will be back to pick you up in about an hour. If you are done sooner call me." Tom then left. Vick followed Marlene's instruction and found herself in front of a Section Manager's office. She walked into the office

"Hi, I am Vicki Graton. "I believe you are Steve Medman."

"Yes," said Steve. "Come on in and have a seat."

"As I understand you are the manager of the Drafting Department," said Vicki. "I'm sure you have answered these questions a hundred times. So let's do it again in case things have changed. Do you have any problems you want to complain about, and do you have any suggestion how they could be corrected?"

"The only problem I have," said Steve, "is that I do not have enough drafting people. I am about three months behind in my required drawing."

"I will mark that down in my notes," said Vicki as she wrote in her note pad. "I have another question," said Vicki. "What do think of Andy your Department manager?"

"He is the best boss I ever had," said Steve. "He is more like a helper than a boss."

"I have one last question," said Vicki. "Can you think of anyone who does not like Andy?"

"The only one that I heard complain was George the Simulation Equipment Manager. He felt like he should have been promoted into the Department Managers job that Andy got."

"Well thank you very much," said Vicki who then walked out and into the next office.

"Hi Vicki," said Ralph as she walked in, "come on in and have a seat. "I am Ralph Costa, the Hardware Section Manager. I will save you some time by answering the most asked questions. I love my job and I don't have any suggestions to making my section better. So do you have any other questions?"

"I have two other questions," said Vicki with a smile on her face. "First I would like to know what you think of Andy your new boss."

"He is the best I ever had," said Ralph. Do you know what he told me? He said that I should not think of him as a boss. He said that we were both just workers for the same company. We just each had a different assignment. He said that if in his research he found anything that he thought would improve our hardware product that he would tell me what his idea was, but it would just be a suggestion. I am the hardware designer. Can you beat that?"

"Sounds great," said Vicki. "My second and last question is do you find anyone in this division that is a problem especially with Andy?"

"Yes," said Ralph. "George has gone crazy. He felt that he should have had the job of Department Manager. He feels that Andy somehow bought his way into the job. He feels because he has been here five years and Andy only one year that he should have be promoted. He forgets that Andy worked for the company in Arizona for six years and was sent here to improve the software designs."

"Thank you very much," said Vicki getting up to leave.

"I would recommend when you go to talk to George not to get him too excited about the job he didn't get. He could get ruff."

"Thank you," said Vicki. "I will remember that." Vicki then left and went into the next office around the corner.

"Hello Mr. Wendell," said Vicki as she entered his office and sat down.

"Hello, Vicki," said David. "Please call me Dave. I guess you want to know if I like my job and do I have any suggestion to improve the section. Well, first of all I just was promoted to this job. I worked for Andy for a year. He had everything so well set up that there is nothing to improve. I think I like my job. I hope I could fill Andy's shoes."

"I guess that you thought a lot of Andy," asked Vicki.

"Yes," said Dave. "I have worked for him since he moved here from Arizona. He was great to work for."

"What do you think of George," asked Vicki.

"I thought he was going to attack me he was so furious about losing the promotion. He never left me alone. He is always here telling me what to do like he was promoted."

"Thank you so much for that information," said Vicki. "I hope I will get through him quickly. I am worried about his reaction to my questions." Vick then walked down to George's office. She walked into his office. He just looked up at her.

"What do you want?" he finally said.

"My name is Victoria Graton," said Vicki as sweetly as she could. I am here to find out if you are happy at your job."

"Yes," said George, "you are Vicki. They told me you would be coming. I like my job and I am happy on it."

"Have you anything to add that will make the job easier?" said Vicki trying to stay away from the obvious promotion problem he had. It didn't work. George flew into a rage. My job should have been the job they gave to the incompetent Andy. He stole my job. He must have used some unethical pressure on the upper management." He kept raving on how he was betrayed and many other statements that Vicki couldn't understand. Finally Vicki walked to the door and just as she left she yelled back.

"Goodbye, have a great day." She then walked to the other end of the hall to the Division Manager's office.

"HI Mr. Beck," said Vicki still a little nervous from the time with George.

"Hi Vicki," Said Robert. "I thought you would come up here. I hear the commotion George made. Come sit dawn. Please call me Bob. What do you want to know?"

"First of all," started Vicki now beginning to feel angry. "Why haven't you fired that idiot?"

He is a very great engineer. He has developed an aircraft simulator that the product that is tested on it acts like it was on a real aircraft. He is a little arrogant. The success he has had in all the equipment he has designed has gone to his head. Please don't repeat this to anyone. Forget that I told you," said Bob. "I think with all the problems you had you deserve to know. We are training one of his assistant to take over his job."

"My mind just erased all that you told me. My coming here was for nothing. I think I had better go now. Thanks for seeing me. Have a great day." With that Vicki left and returned to the Employee's Consolers office. There she gave her notes to Marlene and called Tom.

"Hi Tom she said when he answered the phone. I am sure that George Medelsen is our man. I think you should get a court warranty to search his car. Anyway, I am ready to be picked up." After her phone call Vicki sat with Marlene and discussed all she had learned waiting for Tom.

After leaving Vicki to the job of talking to all the section Managers, Tom went directly to the mall to the Woman's Dress Shop. Tom walked in and walked to back of the store where the offices were. He asked one of the sales ladies where he could find Martha Wellington. The young lady directed Tom to the office in the rear of the store. Tom knocked on the door with was already open. The lady at the desk turned around.

"What can I do for you?" she asked.

"I am Detective Tomas Corely," said Tom. "I would like to ask you a few questions about one of you sales ladies."

"Please come in and have a seat on the other side of my desk and tell me why your here." Tom went around to the other side of her desk and sat down.

"I'm here to ask you if you know of anyone who would want to hurt Colene Rineli."

"Why do you ask? Is she alright, is she hurt?" said Martha with a concerned look on her face. "I was worried when she didn't show up to work this morning."

"She has been shot," said Tom answering her question. "But she will survive. Did she get along with all of your other sales people?"

She was like a sister to most of us," said Martha. "But let's check all possibilities." Martha then called each of the sales ladies and all the other store employees one at a time and asked each if they knew anyone who didn't get along Colene. One at a time they all declared that she was a close friend to everyone. They could not find anyone who had a problem with Colene. Tom then left and was on the way to pick up Vicki. On the way he got the call from Vicki. He then went directly to the court house to get the search warrant from the judge. After he obtained the warrant he drove to pick up Vicki. When he got there he went into Marlene's office.

Hi girls," said Tom. "Are you done, Vicki, with what you need to do?" I am ready to go home," said Vicki. "I have all that I need and so does Marlene I hope."

"I'm satisfied with what you have given me," said Marlene.

"Before we leave I would like ask you a question," said Tom. When I came in the main entrance, I saw about a dozen cars parked across from this building. Whose cars are those?"

"All the managers," said Marlene, "have special parking spaces within the company ground."

"Does George have a space there also?" asked Tom.

"Yes said Marlene as she looked into her note book. "He is in parking space number seven."

"Thank you so much for letting us do this investigation," said Tom.

"Have a great day," said Vicki. Tom and Vicki then left Marlene's office. They walked to where the Manager's cars were parked. Tom went to parking space number seven. It was the black car that the neighbor and Andy had seen. He took out his tools he carried in his pocket and opened the car door. Fortunately inside was a button that opened the trunk. He looked in the trunk. There he found a rifle.

"I'll bet this is the gun that shot Colene," said Tom. "I will take you to your car and then take this gun to the lab." Tom then drove Vicki to her car.

"I will go to the apartment building complex that Dr. Wilson told me about," said Vicki. "I will probably be busy the rest of the day. I will call you tomorrow and tell you how I made out with getting an apartment. Have a good night."

"I hope to see you soon," said Tom as he left for the lab. At the lab Tom turned in the rifle.

"I hope that you have the bullets that were taken from the victim Colene Rineli," said Tom to Mike the lab manager at the front desk.

"Yes we do and fortunately the lab is currently available. Mike then took the rifle into the lab. He then came back and he and Tom talked about politics. About thirty miutes later the lab attendant came out and informed them that the rifle was the weapon that shot Mrs. Rineli. Tom then got three police officers that were available and went to the Aerospace building. It was only a little past four o'clock. Tom was hoping that they could arrest George before he left the building. He got there just in time. George was just leaving and was at his car. Tom and two of the police officers walked up to George.

"George Medelsen," said Tom. "You are under arrest for the shooting of Colene Rineli." Two of the officers grabbed George and put handcuffs on him. They then brought him to Tom's car. The other officer got George's car keys and drove George's car to the police station. At the police station Tom took George to the interrogation room. Tom and Bill, Tom's old friend, and an attorney that they appointed for George, went into the room to interrogated

George. It didn't take long when Tom and Bill's questions set George off yelling.

"I didn't mean to shoot Andy's wife. I was trying to get even with Andy. The dirty rat in some unethical way stole the job from me. He had only been there one year and all the accomplishment he did he stole from me. I have been with them five years and have had great success in all that I did and they gave the promotion to that idiot." When he finally calmed down, the Captain, who was listening through the glass wall on the side of the integration room, came into the room.

"I think we have everything we need Tom," said the captain. You can leave any time you wish. We will not need you anymore. Thank you for your help. I think that a judge will complete the job." Tom left with a good feeling due to his success in the job. He went home wondering what the future would bring him.

CHAPTER EIGHT

A New Beginning

Vicki, after recovering her car, drove down Bancroft Road to Elgin road. There she turned right and drove down to the light on Cleveland Massillon road. When the light turned green, she crossed Cleveland road to Rosemount Boulevard. She drove down Rosemount keeping her eye on the right side of the road. Soon she saw the apartment building. She pulled into the drive way and pulled into a spot where she saw the sign that said 'Rosemount Apartments Manager' She parked her car and walked up to the door to the building. Before she entered she stopped to think about the building. She realized that it was a very beautiful building in a very nice neighborhood. She decided that she had better put in an offer on Dr. Wilson's apartment before it got taken by someone else.

"Hi, my name is victoria Graton. Are you the apartment manager?"

"Yes I am," said the elder woman that answered the door I'm Donna Greer. What can I do for you?"

"I was wondering," if I could rent the apartment of Dr. Wilson. I understand they are moving out this week end."

"How many are there in your family that would be moving in with you?" asked Donna.

"I will be the only one," said Vicki. "I am single and I have no children."

"Then I have a better deal for you," said Donna. "It actually is a better apartment. It is on the bottom floor and is at the end of the building. The inter apartments only have windows on two places, the front and back. This has windows on three sides. It is a little smaller but for just one person it is perfect. It became available a week ago. We have up dated it and cleaned it so it looks like it is new. I like to rent it to a single person especially a young woman because you keep it in good condition and very clean. Come let me show it to you." After getting the key she brought Vicki to the far end of the building. She opened the front door and they went inside. Donna took Vicki through the complete apartment. Vicki was very impressed. She loved it.

"What will it cost me?" said Vicki.

"You will have to pay one month in advance," said Donna. If you are interested, let's go into my office and we will get the paper work done and decide on the rental fee that is dependent on how long you will sign up for." In the office Vicki signed up for a year which made the rental fee a lot lower. After Vicki signed a check for the month, she then asked Donna the number one question on her mind.

"How soon can I move in?" asked Vicki.

"Here is the key," said Donna. "You can move in anytime you want."

"I would like to move in right now," said Vicki.

"You have the key," said Donna. "Welcome to Rosemount apartments." Vicki then got into her car and parked backwards in front of her apartment. She opened the car trunk and brought in the two suitcases and all the other things she had brought from Columbus. It took her a couple of hours to get her clothes hung in the closet and all the other things settled in place. The special dishes fit perfectly in the kitchen shelf. She then got her note book and wrote down all that she would need. The first Item was food. The refrigerator was empty. The next item was living room and family room furniture. All that the apartment had was the refrigerator, the kitchen table with six chairs and the Family room cabinet where a TV could be placed. It also had master bedroom furniture. Donna had assured her that the mattress was new and the bed sheets were all recently washed. Vicki was all most finished with all that she could do without going out shopping when her cell phone rang. It was Tom.

"Hi Tom," said Vicki. "How did everything go with your shooter case?"

"We got George to confess, so my job is complete," said Tom. "How about you, where are you and what are you doing?"

"Oh Tom," said Vicki. "I got myself an apartment. I am now in the process in putting everything away that I brought from Columbus.

"It's close to dinner time," said Tom. "Why don't you come over to my house and have dinner with me?"

I would love to Tom," said Vicki, "but I have too much to do. I have to go to the grocery to buy some food. My freezer and refrigerator are empty. I also need to see what furniture I will need to buy. I only have furniture in the master bedroom and the kitchen. By the way, will it be alright if I get a truck and come and get the stuff I stored in your barn after I sold my house?"

"I don't know if I will be home," said Tom. "This wedding that is coming up is taking a lot of my time. I'm the sub for a mother. However I will unlock the barn tomorrow morning and you can come and get your stuff. By the way, there is some furniture that Ellie and Chris didn't want. Instead of giving it to a charity I though since it was yours in the first place that you may want it. Basically it is the front room and dining room furniture."

"I would love that," said Vicki. "It is most of what I need. I hope to see you tomorrow. If you are not home I will see you Sunday at church"

"That is fine," said Tom, "however I would like you to have lunch with us after church service. I will not take no for an answer."

"How can I argue with that," said Vicki. "I will than see you tomorrow or Sunday." With that they hung up and Vicki quickly left for Giant Eagle Grocery store to get some food for the next few days.

The next day at about one in the afternoon, Vicki rented a truck and went to Tom's house. Fortunately Tom was home.

"Hi Tom," said Vicki. "I'm so glad you are home."

"I was to meet Alex at the flower shop," said Tom, "But I couldn't let you load the truck by yourself. The furniture is much too heavy for one person. I don't think I could have done it myself. I postponed my meeting with Alex. We could go later."

"That is so sweet of you," said Vicki. "Will you come to my apartment and help me put the furniture in place?"

"I have no choice," said Tom. "You could not do it yourself. Anyway, I would like to see your apartment."

"That is great," said Vicki. "Let's go." A few minutes later they entered Vicki's apartment. Vicki took him through all the rooms.

"This is the nicest apartment that I have ever seen," said Tom. "How did they keep it so nice? It looks like it was just built. Look, I would like to spend more time with you, but Alex is waiting for me. So, let's bring all of you furniture in side." Slowly they carried everything inside each into the room Vicki wanted each item. Soon they had emptied the truck.

"I know you have to leave," said Vicki. "Why don't you go? I can rearrange everything now that we have everything inside I can't thank you enough. I could never have done this by myself. Thank you so much." Tom said good bye and left. Vicki immediately closed the apartment and brought the truck back. She got into her car which she had left there when she rented the truck and headed directly to the Giant Eagle Grocery store. She bought enough food to last her a complete month. When she got back home she rearranged the food, some in the freezer and some in the refrigerator. She then spent the rest of the night rearranging her furniture. She only stopped long enough to have a sandwich for dinner. The next morning she got up early and drove to several furniture stores looking for the furniture she still needed. Most of what she bought she was able to bring home in the car. The rest of the day she rested.

The next day Vicki went to church where she met Tom, Alex and Liana.

"Hi Tom," said Vicki as she sat next to Tom. She then looked at the seats in front of her and Tom. Alex and Liana turned around when they heard Vicki's voice.

"Hi Vicki," said Alex and Liana together. "It is so good to see you. We have missed you so much."

"Hi there you guys," said Vicki. "I have missed you all too. However, tomorrow, I will start working and we will be all together again. Thank the Lord."

"You are coming home and have lunch with us aren't you?" asked Alex.

"Your father said he would not take no for an answer when he asked me yesterday," said Vicki. "I don't want to find out what he would do if I didn't come. By the way, where are Ellie and Chris? I hope they are alright."

"They went to Cleveland to be with Chris's parents," said Tom. "They will be with them the rest of the day." After the service they went to Tom's house and had a very good Lunch. Tom had prepared it earlier and set the oven timer so that the food would be ready when they got home. After lunch Alex turned to Tom.

"Dad if you remember we have some where to go. I don't want us to be late."

"Yes you are right," said Tom. Then turning to Liana and Vicki he said goodbye and started to leave with Alex.

"Couldn't you go some time during the week?" asked Vicki.

"I have to work during the week. They close at four. I would have to wait until next Saturday. That would be too late." They purposely didn't mention where they were going because they didn't want Liana to know.

"If you are going then I will leave also," said Vicki. "I have a million things to do."

"Why don't you stay and keep me company," said Liana. "I hate to be alone especially on Sunday.

"Alright,' said Vicki. "I can stay for a little while." That little while lasted until a little after five in the evening. They enjoyed each other's company. Liana told Vicki the history of her life. Vicki did the same thing. Vickie then got up and got ready to leave.

"Thank you for staying and keeping me company," said Liana. "I enjoyed the time with you.

I enjoyed it too," said Vicki. "Tom and Alex should be home soon so you will have company. As you know I just moved in an apartment. I have so much settling work to do. I feel like I am starting a new life. See you at work." With that said Vicki left. It was only about fifteen minutes later when Tom and Alex came home. Liana asked no questions and they told Liana nothing.

It was Wednesday when Vicki got a call from Tom.

"Hi Vicki,' said Tom, "How are you doing?"

"I'm up to my ears trying to organize my apartment," said Vicki. "I love it though. I feel like I am starting a new life."

"I'm sorry that I haven't called you sooner," said Tom. "But you can't believe all that is required to set up a wedding. I was hoping to ask you out this week end but you know most of the work is done on the week end because they all work during the week days."

"Oh Tom," said Vicki. "I understand perfectly. You not only have one wedding to worry about but two months later you will have another. Please don't worry. We will get together more often after both weddings are over. You will get tired of seeing me that often."

"I will never get tired of seeing you," said Tom. "I am sure that after Ellie and Chris get married I will have more time. After all the second wedding will just be a repeat of the first one."

"I will see you every once in a while," said Vicki. "You will not get rid of me that easily." They both said good bye and hung up.

The days seemed to go by very slowly. Soon it was the Friday before the wedding. That evening they all met for the Rehearsal dinner. Tom got to sit next to Chris's family. He enjoyed the conversation he had with them. He was very pleased to get to know them. Tom's parents were also sitting across the table from him. He had a very nice evening with them also. The evening went by too soon.

The next day, they all went to church for Ellie and Chris's

wedding. The look in Chris's eyes, that Tom saw as he walked Ellie down the church isle, told Tom how delighted and surprised Chris was at seeing how beautiful Ellie was in her wedding dress. The rituals were soon over and they all drove to the wedding hall. Ellie and Chris were delayed because they went with the photographer to take the wedding picture. Tom sat with Vicki and his parents. Alex being Chris's best man sat next to him at the wedding table. Liana, being Ellie's maid of honor sat next to her at the wedding table. After they had a very satisfying meal, Liana got up and gave a beautiful speech on how much in love Ellie and Chris were.

"I never met two people that are so much in love," said Liana. "They are also a very sweet and loving to all their friends. They are like brother and sister to me. I love them both very muck. I wish them all the happiness in the world. Let us drink a toast to their happiness." After Liana raised her glass, everyone in the room raised their glass and toasted to their happiness. After Liana finisher her speech the musicians started to play dancing music. After the bride and groom danced their first dance Tom asked Vicki to dance. Tom and Vicki danced most of the night except for a few times when they were asked by one of the other guests. The time went by to quickly Ellie and Chris left at twelve on the dot after going around to all the tables to thank everyone for coming and the gifts they received from each. Tom didn't know what they needed and he didn't have time anyway. Tom gave them a congratulation card with a five thousand dollar check inside. After Ellie and Chris left Tom said goodbye to everyone and left for home. He was delighted that all went so well. He had enjoyed it very much. However somewhere hidden in a corner of his heart there was a small piece that was happy that it was over.

The next two weeks were very delightful for Tom. Allie's wedding was over. He only had to work on Alex's wedding. He dated Vicki at least twice a week. However his weekends were never free. He had to work on Alex's wedding details. He had week days free since the Bride and the Groom had to work. When Ellie and Chris returned from the honeymoon, Tom had to help them move into their new home. They need help with getting all the new furniture they needed. Ellie and Chris also wanted to refurbish the rooms. That required some painting. It was on Monday the next week that Tom got a call from Captain Richard.

"Hi Tom," said the captain. "How are you?"

"Hi captain," said Tom. "I'm fine. What's up?"

"I know that you are retired and you have a wedding to plan but I need your help. I think it will be a short one, but I don't have any one with the skill you have."

"What is the problem?" asked Tom being surprised at the captain's voice which sounded like he was begging.

"A woman's car was hit on the driver's side by a young man who went through a stop sign and hit her. He was under the influence of a drug or alcohol. The woman was badly hurt. She had a swelling on the left side of her head, a bad swelling on her shoulder, a broken arm and a broken leg. I think she also had a broken rib."

"So what is the problem?" asked Tom being confused as to why he was calling.

"The problem is that she is unconscious. We check the license plate and found that it was an Indiana plate. The plate was under the name Ron Holland. We checked the complete car. We got two suit cases from the trunk. We took all the items in the glove compartment. We didn't find a purse. We could not find out who she is. We cannot call any relatives."

"So what do you want from me?" asked Tom.

"I would like you to go to the hospital and find out who she is," said the captain.

"If she is unconscious with head injury and has no memory," said Tom. "How am I to find out who she is?"

"I think you can do it," said the captain. "If anyone can, you can. So please, go to the hospital and see what you can do."

"I will go right now," said Tom. "I cannot promise you anything." Tom had not finished his breakfast but left anyway for the hospital.

When he got there he went directly to the room where the lady was brought. A man was standing over her.

"Hi," said Tom. "I am Detective Thomas Corey. Who are you?"

"I am Doctor Braner," said the man. "I am the one that has done the surgery on the young lady. She had a severe hit on her head. I cannot cure that. I have operated on her ribs and fixed them. I also put casts on her arm and leg. The shoulder is very badly swollen but I could not find any other damage.

"What are her chances of survival," said Tom.

"Her body has a fifty percent chance of going back to normal," said the doctor. "However, I don't know how badly her brain has been hurt. The good news is that the ex-ray and the other tests don't show any permanent damage"

"How come you have done the surgery?" asked Tom. "Doesn't Dr. Wilson do most of the surgery here in this department?"

"Yes that is correct," said DR. Braner. "Dr. Wilson is on second shift and we just decided we could not wait." The doctor then left. Tom went directly to his daughter Ellie's office

"Hi Ellie," said Tom as he entered Ellie's office.

"Hi dad," said Ellie. "What are you doing here?"

"I hear that Dr. Wilson is now on second shift," said Tom.

"Why has that happened?"

"He had some kind of school he as to teach or attend. I don't know which."

"Is Vicki now on second shift also?' asked Tom.

"Yes. It started to day," said Allie.

"Why didn't you tell me yesterday?" asked Tom.

"I didn't know until this morning," said Ellie. "I didn't believe that the Board of Directors would approve it."

"Thanks honey," said Tom and left. He then went back down to the lady's bedroom. When he got there he decided to look closer to the patient. Earlier he had been more interested in what the doctor had to say then look at the patient. When he looked down on her he was surprised. He felt like he knew her. He could only see her closed eyes and forehead due to the air unit she had over her mouth that covered most of her face. The black and blue on the left side of her face didn't help. He stood there for several minutes trying to figure out where he has seen her before. Tom waited around until noon. He wanted to wait to see Vicki when she came to work. At twelve he went down to lunch. When he came back from lunch he found Vicki in the unknown woman's room.

"Hi Tom," said Vicki when Tom walked into the room. "What are you doing here?"

`"Hi Vicki," answered Tom. "I am here to see if I can find out who this woman is."

"I just came in to see if she is any better," said Vicki. "I was not here when the surgery was done."

"That is my question," said Tom. "How come you are on second shift?"

"I am as surprised as you are," said Vicki. "Dr. Wilson asked that I go into the second sift with him. He had some kind of school he had to go to in the mornings. I came here before I go to work to see how our patient is doing."

"She is still alive," said Tom. "They think that she will recover from the surgery and all her broken bones, but they are not sure of the condition of her mind."

"Well I will keep in touch," said Vicki. "I have to go now. I don't want to be late." That said she left for Dr. Wilson's office. Tom stayed a little while longer then decided to go home. He had too many things about the wedding to think about.

The next morning Tom was at the hospital at eleven. Nothing had changed. The patient looked like she had not even moved. A few minutes later the floor nurse came in.

"Hi Caroline," said Tom. "What can you tell me about the patient?"

"Hi Detective Tom," said Carol. "The doctor checked her this morning. He said that her heart and lungs are back to normal. He also said that her brain shows a little more activity. He said if things don't change I can remove the air tub from her mouth."

"Sounds great," said Tom. "I will be back this afternoon."

Tom then went to lunch. He sat there reading the newspaper that someone had left on an adjacent table. It was after two when he went back to the hospital room. The nurse and Vicki were both there. The nurse had checked her heart and breathing and was about to remove the air tube. After the nurse remover the air tube and backed off, Tom bent over the patient to look closely to her wondering why he felt that he knew her to look at her.

"Dear Lord," said Tom out loud. "I do know her. I recognize her like she was part of my family."

"Who is she?" asked the nurse.

"I," said Tom delaying further comments. Then after a minute he continued. "Her name is," then he hesitated. "Just give me a few miutes. I will think about it." After a few minutes later he confessed. "I can't remember her name. I feel that I know it like I know my own name."

"Well you think about it and let us know when you remember it," said the nurse and left the room. Vicki however stayed with Tom. She knew that Tom was confused and frustrated and not thinking strait.

"Have you checked her possessions," asked Vicki, "to see if there is anything there that will help you remember."

"No I have not," said Tom. "That is a good idea." He then went into the closet and checked all her possessions. All he found were dirty and torn cloths."

"I'm sure she has no purse here," said Vicki, "because we have a problem as to how she is going to pay for her stay here."

"That is a great Idea," said Tom. "I'm sure she had a purse I think I will go and double check her damaged car."

"I'm sure the police who investigated the accident would have found the purse if it was in the car," said Vicki.

"I will check anyway," said Tom. "I can't believe a woman will travel without her purse."

"Good luck," said Vicki as she left the room. Tom called the captain to get permission to check the Car. He needed permission so that the junk yard manager will let him in. Tom then went directly to the junk yard

"Hello," said a young man who came out to meet Tom. "How can I help you?"

"I am Detective Thomas Corely," said Tom. "I came to inspect the car that was in the auto accident a couple of days ago."

"Yes," said the attendant. "Captain Richards called and told me you were coming. That's the car over in that corner. Help yourself." Tom walked over to the car. He checked the truck first since it was open. He then checked the front seat and the rear seat. He was about to leave when he noticed the tow truck. It had a crane that was ten feet high. Tom realized that the crane must have pulled the wrecked car to the junk yard. It would have hooked up the car from the front and lifted it up so that it would be at a forty five degree angle. If the purse had been knocked down on the floor during the accident then the purse would have slid to the floor of the passenger side of the car. If the crane lifted it up, the purse could have slid under the front seat. Tom then went to the passenger side of the car. The door was stuck due to the accident. He had to pry it open with a tool the attendant lent him. He then reached under to passenger front seat. He felt something there. He pulled it out. It was a purse. With joy Tom took it to his car. There he opened the purse. He found her driver's license, a credit card and her Aetna health card. The name on all of the cards was 'Gina Holland'. All of a sudden his memory came to life. He remembered who she was. He quickly drove to the hospital. When he walked into the room Vicki was there.

"Hi Vicki,' said Tom as he walked into the room. "I remember who she is. I went to the car and found her purse. Her name is Gina Holland. However she has a stage name. I will think of it any minute. She is a singing star. She has the most beautiful voice. She was part of the Benny Ray's Band. It was broadcast from eight to nine every Saturday. She also dances. Remember, Benny Ray's Band had a great orchestra, several singers, and two fantastic dancers. Benny had a delightful exciting show. Gina had a stage name like Gina lane or Gina Ray, no it was Gina Lee. Yes, that was her name. It is her stage name. Holland must be her married name.

"Wow," said Vicki. "You must have a great affection for Gina.

"She would sing by herself, sing with other singer's and even dance with Benny's other show girls." Just then they heard a moaning sound coming from Gina. Tom went and bent over the bed to look at Gina's face. Suddenly her eyes opened. However they stared straight up to the celling. It looked like the brain was not connected to her eyes.

"I hope she doesn't end up blind from the hit on the head she got," said Vicki. "I have seen that as the results of a head injury many times." Tom did not answer. Suddenly Gina closed her eyes and started to mourn again.

"Does her moaning indicate that she has a lot of pain?" asked Tom. "Or is this the way they wake up?"

It could be a little of both," said Vicki. "However I don't think it is from pain. She is not conscious enough to feel pain." After about five minutes the moaning stopped. Tom went to see if she had died. He looked down on her face ready to feel her neck for a pulse and was surprised to see that her eyes were open and she was looking at him. Shocked he just stood there.

"Hi," said Gina.

"Hi' said Tom still in shock. Vicki just stood there waiting for Tom to comment. "How do you feel?"

Hi," she repeated. Then a moment later as if she just realized what Tom had said, she spoke. "Ok" is all she said.

"My name is Detective Thomas Corely. I'm here to see that you are alright and to contact your relatives." She didn't answer. What is your name?" asked Tom finally to see if there was any damage to her brain. Gina becoming more awake, hesitated for a while, and then answered.

"My name," she said. Then after hesitating for a while she repeated. "My name? I don't remember my name." Then hesitating a while longer she said, "I think it was like lees or Gee."

"Was it Gina?" said Tom feeling sorry for her problem.

"Yes it is Gina," said Gina beginning to remember things. I think my full name is Gina Holland. I remember now. Where am I and why can't I move my arms?"

"You in the Hospital," said Vicki taking over. You were in an automobile accident. You had a severe blow to your left shoulder, a broken rib which was fixed by surgery; you have a broken arm and a broken leg. The good news is that you will survive and be back to normal in a few days."

"Wow," said Gina now fully awake.

"Listen Tom," said Vicki. "You stay here and get all the information you need. I have a surgery to assist. I will check on you later Gina." Vicki then left.

"I'm sorry that Vicki was so cold in telling you your problem," said Tom. "She usually is a very sweet and gentle person. She was in a hurry. Do you feel like answering my questions or do you need some rest."

"I don't know if I can answer all your questions," said Gina. Let me rest and think of who I am."

"Alright," said Tom, "I will be back tomorrow morning. Tom then left.

The next morning Tom got busy with wedding problem so he showed up at eleven.

"Hi Detective Corely," said Gina as Tom walked in. "I now know who I am,"

"I know who you are," said Tom. "Perhaps what I know will help you remember better. But before I start I want you to know that I am retired and I also want you to call Me Tom."

"I'm listening," said Gina.

"Your name is Gina Holland," began Tom. "However you have a stage name of Gina Lee. You were a member of Benny Ray's band. You are a singer with a beautiful voice. And you are a great dancer. You live in South Bend Indiana. Your married name or your birthday name is Holland. Did I leave anything out?"

"How in the world do you know all this?" asked Gina.

"Many of your shows were broadcast on TV," said Tom. "I

watched it every Saturday. You were my most admired star. I loved the facial expressions you made when you sang, especial to another member of the show. The one I remember the most was when you sang, 'You must have been a beautiful baby, cause baby look at you now' to the fellow who was sitting in a chair with you in his lap."

"Holland is my married name," said Gina. My birth name is Gina Vista. My father was Italian."

"I don't see a ring on your finger," said Tom.

"My husband and I are separated," said Gina with a sad look on her face. "He left me."

"Are you divorced?" asked Tom.

"No," said Gina. "I'm a Born-again-Christian. I will not give him a divorce."

"That is fantastic," said Tom. "I am a Born-again-Christian also. There are not too many of us. Tell me your story. Where do you come from and where were you going?"

"Let me start from the beginning," said Gina. "I am telling you this because your admiration is appreciated. I graduated with a degree in finance. I worked at a clothing store in the local mall. I got a singing job in a local restaurant that had a band and a dance floor. I was heard by a member of the Benny Ray band. He set up a meeting with Benny and the rest is history. I traveled from town to town with the band. One of the places we performed was in South Bend Indiana. That is where I met Ron. We immediately fell in love. He was an architect who design and built different structures. He mostly designed and built office or storage buildings. I resigned from Benny's Band and got a job there in South Bend in the sales department. We were very happy for a couple of years. Then Ron got transferred to the design and building of Product Storage Buildings. That job required that he travel all over the country and even in Europe. I was tired of traveling all over America and now even Europe. However, Ron demanded that I go with him since most jobs were three months or longer. Finally he got a job in New York. It was a six months job. I also found a job singing in several theaters in New York. I was hoping that as big as New York and the vicinity was that Ron would get an architectural job there in New York. When the six months were completed Ron was directed to build a Storage Building in Europe. I begged him to look for a job in the New York area. He declined. He liked what he was doing. I told him that I was not going with him. I told him that I was tired of traveling to different cities every three months or more. I would wait for him in South Bend. He got very angry. He said that as his wife I had to do what he said and that I was going to travel were ever he went. When I declined he left. The next day I got a letter telling me that if I didn't show up at the New york Airport at eight O'clock on the next day that the separation paper that he included in the letter would become effective, till he got back to sued for a divorce. I will never give him a divorce. I am a Christian. I believe what God has put together that no man put asunder. I have not heard from him since. When my last singing contract was up I decided to go home to South Bend Indiana. The rest is history."

"Well," said Tom, "your life will make a fantastic novel. Anyway, I'm so glad you told me because it tells me two things. First where you were going and second that your brain was not damaged in the accident."

"At least one of those is good news," said Gina with a smile on her face. "Where do I go from here?"

"First you get well," said Tom. "Next I will see if we can get you a car to take you home. The next thing I want to know is if you have any relatives near here that could come and visit you and maybe stay with you until you get well, perhaps you had a good friend in South Bend?"

"My closest relatives are in California," said Gina. "They are all busy working. I don't think they would come even if they were close. We were too busy in South Bend to make friend during the short time we were there."

"I'm going now to get something for lunch. After that I will see about getting you a car," said Tom as he was ready to leave.

"Will you come back soon," asked Gina. "It gets very lonely here without someone talk to."

"So you need company," said Tom. "I will at least come back to tell you about your car."

"I can't even move so my life here is very boring. I hear one of your nurses say that you are an author with several books published. I hear also that you read one of your novels to one of their other patient. Would you consider reading one of you novel to me?"

"Would you like that?" asked Tom.

"I would love that and also I would love your company," said Gina.

"All right then," said Tom, "I will be back. What type of story do you like?"

"I like romantic stories," said Gina.

"See you later," said Tom as he left. Tom then contacted Captain Richard.

"Hi Captain, said Tom. "I think you may know all this but here is what I have found out about the accident victim. Her name is Gina Holland. She is a singer that was with Benny Ray's band. Her stage name is Gina Lee. She lives in South Bend Indiana. What I would like to know is what progress have you made with getting her a car."

"Thank you for all the information, said Captain Richard. I didn't have it all. Blood test showed that the other driver that hit Mrs. Holland was high on drugs. Our lawyer has obtained the required funds from the other drivers insurance Company to purchase a car for Gina as you call her. Her old car was only one year old. We will try to get one similar to the one that was hit. It may take a little time to find one with the same amount of mileage."

"Thank you Captain," said Tom and hung up. Tom then went home for lunch where he picked up one of his most romantic novels. He then went to the hospital.

"Hi Gina," said Tom as he walked into her hospital room. "I have some good news."

"Where have you been?" said Gina trying to be funny. "I missed you. Don't stay away so long."

"Very funny," said Tom. "The one who hit you was found to be high in drugs. He was found guilty and his insurance has agreed to pay for your car. They are now looking to find a car that matched the one you had."

"Very good," said Gina. "By the way, your daughter came down to see me. She was very excited to meet me. She was very nice. She told me that you showed her a video of one of our TV shows that you taped on a DVD. You are very lucky to have such a lovely daughter. I see that you have a book in your hand. Why don't you tell me about it? I wish I could move my hand so that I could look at it." Tom then put the book right in front of her so that she could see the cover closely.

"That is all there is to see," said Tom. He then opened the cover and started to read from it. It was about an hour later that Vicki came in.

"Hi Gina," said Vicki. "What are you doing here Tom?"

"That is the nicest hello I have had for a long time," said Tom, with a grin on his face, "nice to see you too."

"Hi Tom," said Vicki. "I was surprised to see you here. I thought that you investigation was complete."

"My investigation is over," said Tom. "However, I am keeping Gina company. It isn't often that I can spend time with a television Star."

"Are you so attracted to her," said Vicki showing her jealousy

"Look Vicki," said Tom getting slightly angry with Vicki for not understanding. "She has no one she can even talk to. She is all alone here. I don't have anything to do since the wedding party members are both working. This keeps us both entertained."

"Well, have fun," said Vicki and left.

Tom spent about three hours every afternoon for the next three days He finished reading the book he was reading to her. She enjoyed it very much. It was on the fourth day while Tom was describing his next book when Dr. Braner walked in.

"Hello Detective Corley," said the doctor. I am glad you are here because I have something to tell Miss Holland.

"Hi doctor Braner," said Gina. "I hope it is good news."

"I have two things to tell you. First you are healing slowly and are doing fine. The other news is that the hospital is releasing you. Tomorrow you will be released from the hospital."

"I thought that she could stay for a week or more," said Tom.

"If she still needed medical attention," said the doctor, "that would be the case. Her insurance would pay up to three weeks. However Gina does not need continuing attention. I check with the Board of Directors and they would not extend her stay here. I do want to see her in about three weeks from the surgery. I hope that at that time I can remove the casts from her leg and arm. I also can check the healing of the chest rib. The one rib was separated and we had to try and push it together. It will take longer to heal then the leg and the arm." Just as he finished talking Vicki came into the room.

"We will see that she checks out of the hospital early tomorrow morning," said Vicki. Then turning to Tom she spoke directly to him. "Ellie and I tried to get permission for her to stay longer but we could not get permission. She will have to leave early tomorrow morning."

"That may be fine with you two, but where will I go if I am released from the hospital," said Gina with a worried look on her face. "With these casts on my body I can't even walk let alone take care of myself.

"We will find a place for you to stay," said Vicki. "Perhaps at a nursing home or perhaps a hotel room and we can see that you hire a nurse to take care of you."

"I am not going to a nursing home," said Gina, "and I am not going to a hotel. Is a nurse going to see that I get fed at a restaurant?"

"No, you not going to a nursing home or a hotel," said Tom. "You are coming home with me. I have two empty bed rooms and nothing to do during the week days. At night time Liana will help you with whatever you need."

"Are you sure Tom?" asked Gina. "I don't want to be a burden to you."

"Actually it will help me," said Tom. "I can read you one of my books and I don't have to travel to the hospital every day."

"I don't think that is a good Idea," said Vicki looking upset. "You have a lot of work to do for your son's wedding."

"They all work during the day and for the short time I have to go someplace, I'm sure Gina could just lie around and wait for me."

"I absolutely am against this." said Vicki seeming very upset. "Can you imagine what this will do to your reputation? You will be spending all day alone with beautiful young super star."

"I don't give a darn what other people think, said Tom. "I am a Born-again-Christian. People who know me know that I would never dishonor her or anyone." In discus Vicki left. After spending a while with Gina, Tom excused himself and left for home. However, before he went home he stopped at the police station. He explained to the captain what he was doing. He then took the two suitcases and the small package that had all the glove compartment items and other items the police had found in the car and went home. There he set up all the items in the bed room across from his bed room. Tom figured that Liana would not mind giving up the room. After all she was only going to be there for around another month. That evening when Liana and Alex got home Tom, when they were all at the dinner table Tom turned to Liana.

"Liana," said Tom. "Will you mind if Gina takes your bed room. I would like her to be across from me so that I can keep an eye on her. You can move to one of the back rooms."

Nonsense," said Liana. "Let her take the other bed in the room. I can stay there and help her if she has a problem during the night. I would love to share a room with her. After seeing that video of her I feel closeness to her."

"You presently have the bed next to the window," said Tom. I will put her on the inside bed. That will put her closer to the TV room. That will make it easier, for her to go and watch TV when I am not home, like on Saturdays and Sundays." Tom then grabbed the suitcases and the box of items that he had set in the hallway and brought then into the bed room. He got everything ready for him to go and pick up Gina the next morning. Tom had no idea of all the problems that decision would make in his life.

CHAPTER NINE

The Bad Days and the Good Days

Early in the morning Tom picked up Gina at the hospital front door. The nurse wheeled her down in the hospital wheel chair. Tom had to position the back of the front seat so that it was at about a forty-five degree angle. Because of Gina's rib problem she could not sit straight up. Tom asked Gina to put her good arm around Tom's neck. Tom then lifted Gina out of the wheel chair and gently seated her on the front seat. Fifteen miutes later, Tom arrived at his house. He pressed the button above his rear view mirror that opened the garage door. He then drove into the garage.

"Well we are here," said Tom. "I will have to open the door to the family room to bring you into the house. We have to do this three times. First I have to get you up four steps into the family room. Then I have to get you up eight steps to the kitchen area and next I have to get you up eight steps to the bed room area. So take a deep breath and let's go."

"I am tired from just listening to you," said Gina with a smile on her face, "But I'm ready."

"We may have to rest between them," said Tom. "To start, put you good arm around my neck as you did at the hospital." Gina did as Tom asked her to do. Tom lifted her up and slowly carried her into the family room. He felt good enough to take her up to the kitchen.

On the top of the stairs on the left of the kitchen was a door way into the living room. Tom continued to carry Gina into the living room and then set her on the living room couch. "I think I have to rest for a minute said Tom. I'm not as young as I used to be."

"I think you are doing a fantastic job," said Gina. "I didn't think you would carry me this far. Let's stay here a few miutes. I am enjoying what I see of your house. I loved your family room. That was a large screen TV you have down there. I hope I will get well soon so that we can watch some nice movies there."

"Well when we go upstairs I will show you one of the bed rooms that was made into a TV room. It's TV is as large as the one in the family room."

"Wow," said Gina. "You have a beautiful house. I will enjoy getting well here." After about fifteen miutes Tom picked up Gina again and took her up to the bed room area. At the first door on the right, Tom stopped to show Gina the room.

"This is the room I was talking about," said Tom. "You can see there on the left is a couch. Across from it is the large TV I told you about. When you are able to walk you can come and relax in this room. If you notice at the other end of the room by the window is a folding table. When you get better you will be eating on that table. I unfold it and the feet slid under the couch and it will be right over your lap."

"Wow said Gina. "This is a hundred times better than the hospital. I will never be able to thank you for doing this for me." Then Tom brought her to the next bedroom.

"This is your bedroom," said Tom. "Liana has the bed next to the window. You will have the bed here next to the door. That will make easier for you to go to the TV room when you are able to move." Tom then set her down on Liana's bed to sit while he pulled the bed spread down so he could place Gina there. He then laid Gina in the bed and pulled the bed spread over her. Fortunately she was wearing hospital cloths. Tom figured if she needs to be changed or washed Liana could do it when she gets home.

"This is a very confortable bed," said Gina. "It is so much better than the hospital bed."

"Now you get some sleep," said Tom. "I know that you must be very tired from the trip here and all the effort to get you up here to a bed. I will make some lunch around noon and bring it up to you. Are you ready to eat regular food?"

"I think so," said Gina. "The hospital did not hold back any food from me. I could order what ever there was on the menu" Tom then went down to his office to answer some of his E-mail and work on his book. At about noon he went to the kitchen and made some Chicken soap. He felt he should give her a light meal for now. After he had made the soap he went upstairs to give it to Gina. When he got there he found that she was fast asleep. He didn't want to wake her up yet. He decided to wait about an hour and come up again. At one o'clock he warmed up the soup and took it back to Gina's bed room. She was still asleep. He decided to wake her.

"Hay sleep head," said Tom. Gina woke up immediately. Apparently she was ready to wake up.

"What time is it?" asked Gina.

"It is one o'clock and you need some lunch," said Tom. "I make you some chicken soap. I thought that I will start you lightly."

"I am hungry," said Gina. Tom put a pillow behind her back so that she could eat. Gina then ate the food using her good hand while Tom held the dish near her lap. She enjoyed the food. After that she went back to sleep. That afternoon when Tom saw that Gina was awake he took her into the TV room. She enjoyed the film that Tom set up for her. After the film, Tom took her back to her bed. That evening Tom made some fish. After Alex and Liana got home they all ate and Liana took some fish up to Gina. Gina was awake.

"Hi Gina," said Liana. "I have some food for you. Do you want me to feed you?"

"If you will put a pillow behind me so that I will sit up a little, and hold the dish I can eat with my good hand. It worked fine this noon with Tom holding the dish. And I also want to thank you for help. I'm sorry to put you through this."

"It's no problem at all," said Liana. "I'm glad I could help. You are one of my favorite stars. Tom showed us some videos of Benny's Ray shows that you were in. You were wonderful. You have a marvelous voice. I feel like I should thank you for letting me help you. I feel it is an honor to help you."

"Thank you so much," said Gina. "You and all of Tom's family are special" The routine that was done that day was repeated for the next week. It was the beginning of the next week when Tom went up to serve Gina breakfast that he found her in the TV room.

"Gina," said Tom with a surprised look on his face. "How did you get here?"

"I felt a little stronger, especially my bad foot, so I got up and using the crutches I got here."

"Well since you are here you may as well eat here," said Tom. He then got the folding table and opening it he slid its feet under the couch where Gina was siting. The table then was right over her lap. Tom set the food on the table and handed her the spoon. "Enjoy," he said and left. This went on for a few days until Gina's appointment with Dr. Braner.

"Gina," said Tom "It is time to go see Dr. Brandon. But before I take you there I want to tell you something that I have done."

"I noticed that the last week you have been very busy," said Gina. "I hardly saw you during the day. I only saw you when you feed me."

"Well I will tell you now what I have been up to," started Tom. "I have been trying to locate your husband. It took a lot of checking around and by using my police advantage I final found him. I told him about your accident and explained all the injuries and broken bones that you got and about the severe hit that you got on your head that left you unconscious and hardly knowing who you were. I exaggerated a little. When I told him about your head injury, I could hear him crying on the phone. He said that he was leaving for the US as soon as he could get a flight. So you see. You are going to have company all day long. Gina didn't say anything she was crying too hard to speak. Tom then took her to the hospital emergency entrance where Dr. Brander asked to meet him. Tom carried Gina into the waiting room and sat her in a wheel chair that was there. Five miutes later Dr. Braner walked in.

"Hi," said the doctor. "Tom, you can go home and I will call you when she is ready or you can wait here in my office I don't know how long this will take. I have to take her into the lab and have several tests done."

"I will wait here," said Tom. "I don't have anything to do."

"As you wish," said the doctor. He then wheeled Gina into the hall way and at the end of the hallway was the lab. The doctor wheeled her into the lab waiting room. The doctor handed the girl at the desk the form that had a list of the test he required. He then left her there. It was about a half hour later that Gina was wheeled into the lab for the required test. After the tests were completed the nurse at the desk called the doctor's office. A nurse came down and took Gina up to the doctor's office. About ten miutes later the doctor walked into his office.

"I have good news and bad news," said the doctor. "Your arm and leg are both healed. However one of your ribs is still not together close enough to heal. We are going to put a tight band over your body to bring the rib parts together. The nurses call it a breast corset. If that doesn't work we will have do surgery.

"How long with the rib healing take?" asked Gina. "I am being taken care of by a friend. I don't want to impose on them any more than necessary."

"We will know in about two weeks," said the doctor. "For now let's get rid of the heavy casts on your arm and leg." The doctor then started to remove the casts. It wasn't long before it was complete. Just as it was completed Vicki walked into the office.

"Hi Gina," said Vicki. "I see you have your casts removed."

"Yes but I have to stay another two weeks before I am completely healed. It seems like one of my ribs still needs healing." While they were talking two nurses came in with what they called a breast corset. They applied it around Gina as tight as they could.

"I'm sure you will enjoy the time with Tom," said Vicki trying to find what was going on with them.

"Oh Tom has been like an angel," said Gina. "He has a heart make of pure gold. He is the nicest person I have ever met. He is kind, generous and so much fun to be with."

"You have strong feelings for him don't you," asked Vicki.

"Feelings don't cover it," said Gina. "I have a strong affection for him. I adore him for all that he has done for me. Let me tell you what he has spent a week doing for me."

"Do you love him?" asked Vicki.

"Yes in a way, you can say that," said Gina. "But let me tell you the greatest thing he has done for me. He spent several days and several hours to accomplish it." Just then the doctor came in.

"I'm sorry to interrupt you but I need to take her for a final check to see if that breast device has pulled the rib together." After that he took her down to the lab. Gina never got to tell Vicki what the wonderful thing Tom did for her was. Vicki then went down to the waiting room where Tom had gone to wait for Gina.

"Hello Tom," said Vicki when she got there, "waiting for the love of your life?"

"Very funny," said Tom thinking that Vicki was kidding. "I hope they find that she is back to normal. I want her to be back to normal so that she will be able to enjoy the wonderful gift I am giving her."

"So you two have a thing going on between you," said Vick. "You have strong feelings for her."

"I have strong feeling toward her," said Tom. "She was one of my most honored stars."

"Do you love her?" asked Vicki.

"I have a very deep admiration for her," said Tom wondering what Vicki was getting at. "I have affection for her. She is a very beautiful and extremely talented woman."

"You have not answered my question," Said Vicky "Please just answer the question. Are you in love with her?"

"In a way, yes," said Tom becoming a little angry at her

questioning. "One can love more than one person. I love her like a very good friend."

"What are your plans with her?" asked Vicki. Before Tom could answer Gina came in walking gently using a cane.

"Gina," said Tom, "are you back to normal. I see that you are walking. Are you ready to travel?"

"My leg and arm are fine," said Gina. "The doctor said that I should take it easy for a couple of days, because my legs are still weak. However, one of my ribs didn't heal right. He put a corset on my ribs to push the rib together. He believes that this will do the job and it will not be necessary to operate. He wants me to come back in two weeks. I don't think we are going to do any traveling. We will have to spend the next two weeks together in your house." Gina was talking about her husband who was on his way to Tom's house. When Vicki heard the "we" she assumed she meant Tom and her. That caused Vicki to go wild.

"When were you going to tell me?" asked Vicki. "Are you feeling so bad as a betrayer that you can't get up the nerve to tell me?"

"What are you talking about?" said Tom. "What do you want me to tell you?"

"I never dreamt that you were such a coward," said Vicki now very upset.

"You have me now completely out in left field," said Tom being puzzled in what Vicki was talking about."

"Were you just going to disappear?" said Vicki. "Then you would not have to face me or anyone."

"What have I done that has upset you so much?" asked Tom. Gina not being aware that they were talking about her went to the checkout window. She did not hear the rest of the argument

"You are still denying it," said Vicki. "You betray me and you act like you don't even know it. I take it you were never going to tell me. You figured that I would find out by myself. That is why I haven't seen you in over a week."

"That is a stupid remark," said Tom. "You are working the second shift. You come to work at one and after taking a 30 minute dinner brake you work until nine thirty and get home about ten. There is no time to see you."

"I had mornings free," said Vicki. Tom ignored her statement

"Are you referring to my relationship with Gina?" asked Tom. "There is no romantic relationship between Gina and I. You are just imagining it."

"I talked to Gina before she came down here and she told me that she loved you and that you loved her too. Gina is my witness. So you don't really love me"

"You talk about my not loving you," said Tom getting irritated with Vicki. "You are the one who came up with so many excuses to not having a romantic relationship. First it was because you husband had died too recently. Next you had to go to Columbus to bury your husband. Then you used the excuse that you had to take care of your mother in law. You have put off any relation with us for over one year. You haven't even let me kiss you."

That is a very poor excuse," said Vicki. "You are in love with Gina."

"I do love her like a sister," said Tom. "And you don't believe me because you don't really love me. If you really loved me you would have known that I would never have betrayed you. You would have trusted me. You would have delighted in the care that I gave Gina. You are right in your thinking. We are not compatible. We do not have a solid relationship. Without trust there is no relationship. Therefore I'm telling you what you want to hear. We have no relationship so goodbye and have a good life. I hope you will find someone that you can really love and trust." In a state of anger and discuss Vicki left the area and disappeared down the hall.

"I'm sorry," said Gina. "I had no intention of getting involved in your trouble with Vicki. That is why I walked away. I think and hope she will get over it. I know without a doubt that she loved you very much. It is because of this great love that I know that she will get over what you both are arguing about."

"She is just angry that I have not dated her for a while. How can I date her when she works from one in the afternoon to nine-thirty at night? Weekends, I have the wedding plus I am helping Alex with his new house. He has purchased a house not too far from the house Ellie and Chris have. He wants it to be ready when they get back from their honeymoon. Vicki said that I could date her in the morning. Sure I said. I could take her to breakfast. I told her that my daughter could set her back to regular hours if she asked. She likes to be a nurse for Dr. Williams. Anyway let's change the subject. While I was waiting for you I got a phone call from your husband Ron. He was very distressed. The only flight to this country was to Canada. The flights were canceled due to bad weather. He won't be able to get here until next week."

"That may be a good thing," said Gina. "You have a wedding to go to this Saturday. This will make things a little less complicated."

"You and me, we have a wedding to go to," said Tom. "I want you to go with me. I want to have a last dance with you." With a smile on Gina's face they got into Tom's car and left for home.

The wedding rehearsal dinner on Friday came up faster that Tom expected. At the rehearsal dinner Tom was in a trance. He felt like he was up in a cloud. The next day he couldn't remember who was at the dinner. He remembered being there saying hello to everyone, but not who was there with him. The next day Tom was still in a trance. It was four in the afternoon when the wedding took place. Tom and Gina were there on time. Chris was Alex's best man and Ellie was Liana's maid of honor. What Tom remembered most was the joy he felt taking Liana down the aisle to get married to Alex. After the pastor married them they all left for Todaro's for the wedding celebration. Alex and Liana came later. They stayed in the church for wedding pictures and after they took the picture they needed inside they took pictures outside. After Alex and Liana arrived at Todaro's, the dinner was served. Tom sat with his parents, Gina, and two nurses he knew well. Ellie being the maid of honor sat at the wedding table next to Liana. Chris sat there also on the side of Alex. Tom was surprised to see Vicki there. She was sitting with Chris's parents and friends of Chris from both the hospital and friends from Cleveland. When everyone just about finished eating, Ellie stood up.

"Let's have a toast for the happy couple," started Ellie. "Before we drink the toast let me tell you about the two Love Birds. They are two that have true love in all its glory. Alex is my brother. No woman has a more loving and affectionate brother. He is a fantastic doctor and yet you will not find any one as humble as Alex is. Liana is also a very intelligent woman. She controls all the finances of the place she works. But I don't think I could have a more loving sister. I love them both with all of my heart. I also believe that my father loves them as much as I do. Let us raise our glass to Alex and Liana." Every one raised there glass to toast Alex and Liana. After that the orchestra started the music. Alex and Liana danced first. When the next song was played many people broke in the couple to have a dance with them. Tom got a chance about the third song. After he danced with Liana he turned to Gina.

"How do you feel?" asked Tom. "May I have this dance?"

"I feel much better," said Gina. "I think we could try one dance and see how much strenght I have." They walked to the dance floor. Tom was amassed on how well Gina danced. Then he remembered that singing was only one of her talents. He remembered that dancing was also one of the things he saw her perform on TV. From that moment on he was thrilled to be dancing with her. He felt everyone was watch him and were jealous of him. A Couple of men tried to cut in on them but Tom saw them coming and using large strides eluded them by dancing to the other side of the dance floor. After the song was over they went and sat down at the table they had sat before. A few men came and asked Gina to dance but she declined.

"I'm sorry," said Gina. "I just got out of the hospital and am too tired to dance again. Sorry." They soon stopped coming. Tom saw Vicki sitting with some nurses and a couple of doctors that she worked with. Tom noticed that Vicki was dancing every song. She danced with the doctors she was sitting with. There were other men that would ask her to dance who she did not refuse. Tom suddenly felt a jealous streak in his heart. At about midnight Alex and Liana walked around to all the tables to say goodbye. After they left Tom turned to Gina.

"What do you say we go home," said Tom. "I'm sure you are tired as I am."

"Yes," said Gina. "I had a very nice time. I am so glad you brought me here, but yes I am tired. Let's go home."

"It has been a very enjoyable day," said Tom. "Most of my joy was when I danced with you."

"The only thing flattery will get you is a smile," said Gina with a big smile on her face. When they got home they went directly to bed.

The next morning Tom got up about eight and went to the kitchen to cook breakfast. He make Mother's Oats for two. He knew that Gina liked mother's Oats. When he was finished he yelled up the stair way.

"Gina," he yelled. "Breakfast is ready"

"I'll be right down," yelled Gina. After breakfast they sat down and talked about their future.

"What do think you will do when you get back to South bend?" asked Tom.

"I don't really know," said Gina. "Before I was hired by Benny Ray's band I was a financial director for a Clothing company in South Bend Indiana. I hope to get that job back. If not I will get a job as sales clerk. My college degree is in finance." "I don't see why you should not get your job back," said Tom. "If not, I don't see that in a large city like South Bend there would not be a place that could use you."

"Don't worry. I will find something to do. Maybe I will just spend my time raising children," said Gina with a smile on her face

"How about your husband?" asked Tom. "What will he do. I think he will have to resign from his present job if he wants to stop traveling. However in a large city he should be able to find some kind of construction work."

"I'm sure we will be able to get by," said Gina. "How about you, what will you be doing? Both of your kids now have homes and lives of their own. What will you do?"

First of all I have a new novel to write," said Tom. "And I am sure that Captain Richard will have a new case to ask me to take on."

"I don't understand," said Gina. "I thought when you retire; you no longer have to go to work."

"I am retired," said Tom, "but the Captain wanted to place me on the list of part time police. He wanted me to be a part time police that was on special call when there was a mission he could not cover with all the other things he and his full time police could not handle. So I accepted the position."

"And I think you would like a break once in a while," said Gina. Before Tom could answer her, the doorbell rang.

"I wonder who that could be this early in the day," said Tom as he got up to answer the door. "How may I help you," said Tom as he opened the door and faced a good looking you man.

"Are you Tom Corely?" said the young man.

"Yes that is me," said Tom. "And who are you?"

"My name is Ronald Holland," said Ron. Before he could say any more Tom grabbed him by the hand and pulled him inside.

"I am so happy to see you," said Tom. "We have been waiting for you. Come on in. Gina is sitting in the family room. She will go wild when she sees you. Just come straight in. Follow me. The family room is just at the end of this entrance hall." When they entered the family room Gina looked up and saw Ron. She quickly got up and threw herself into his open arms. Soon their lips found each other and they remained kissing for over a minute. When they final parted Gina turned to Tom.

"Tom," said Gina. "This is Ron, the love of my life." Then looking into Ron's eyes she continued," I will never let him out of my sight for the rest of my life. Ron this is Detective Tom. He has been like a father to me. I am going to need several days to tell you how much kindness he has shone to me. Not just him, but his family also. His daughters took care of me in the hospital.

"I don't know how I could ever thank you," said Ron. "I will be grateful forever."

"You are so kind," said Tom. "But it is our job. I am a detective that helps people that are in trouble no matter what that trouble is. My daughters work in the hospital. That is what a hospital is created for."

"See how humble he is," said Gina. "I will tell you later what they have done which are not part of their job."

"However," said Tom, "before I let you two alone, I would like to know one thing. I had a very hard time finding you. When I called your company they could not tell be where you were and how to contact you. What is going on with that company?"

"I didn't know until I got home to get my car to come and get Gina," said Ron. "When I got to the company office to resign they would not let me resign. They said that my boss had a heart attack and passed away. They could not fine his folder with all the jobs and who was where. That is why you couldn't find me. They offered me the job my boss had as manager of the design and building of the product storage buildings. I will have to either find the job folder or start one of my own. I took the job because with that job I will not have to travel. I could stay home with my wife."

"That is enough talking for now," said Gina. "Right now I want to spend some time alone with Ron"

"You two sit and spend greatly needed time with each other," said Tom. "I am going into my office to do work I have neglected to long. I will be out about twelve thirty to prepare lunch for the three of us." Why don't you take Ron into your private bedroom where you two will spend the next two weeks or until the doctor releases Gina?" With that said Tom left them alone and went into his office.

"Ron," said Gina. "Tell me where have you been and how did you get off your job to come here. And why it took you so long?"

"When I got the call from Tom," started Ron, "I was shocked with the thought that I could lose you."

"I know," said Gina. "Tom told me that you started to cry on the phone."

"I decided to get the next flight to the US," said Ron. "The only flight I could fine was a flight to Canada. In Canada a major storm held up the flight. Then the only flight I could get was to Chicago. From there I took a bus to our home to get my car. After stopping at my company as I told you I came right here."

"Come with me upstairs and I will show you my bedroom."

"Is it your bedroom or our bedroom?" asked Ron.

"I don't know," said Gina. "What are the limits for two who are officially separated?"

"I am sorry," said Ron. "I never submitted the separation papers. It was a fake. We are still married. Remember I said that if you loved me as much as I love you, you will be at the airport tomorrow morning and you will go with me. I felt that if you loved me a lot you would meet me at the airport. It broke my heart when you didn't show up."

"It is almost funny," said Gina. "I felt that if you loved me as much as I loved you, you would not leave and you would come back and get a job in New York or better yet take me home and get a job in South Bend. You broke my heart also."

"We are such idiots," said Ron. "From now on I will spend the rest of my life trying to making you happy."

"And I will be the best loving and obedient wife like the Bible says a wife should be."

"How about you," said Ron. "tell me what have you been doing since we parted?"

"I finished my singing contact with The Sandia restaurant, checked out of the hotel, and headed home in South Bend. I was going to try and get my job back at the clothing shop and live in the house we both loved so much. That is when I got into the accident and spent most of the time in the hospital."

"Sweet heart," said Ron, "I will never let you out of my sight and I promise never to do anything that offends you." Gina took Ron to her bedroom which Tom had her change it for her privacy. It was the last one down the hall. She showed him the closet and the queen size bed.

"What do you think?" asked Gina. "Are you willing to spend the next two weeks here?"

"I could spend the rest of my live here," said Ron being impressed with the whole house.

"Now follow me to the first bed room we past," said Gina. "This is where I spent most of my time here. This bedroom has been converted into a TV room." She led him into the room and sat on the couch which was on the side of the room opposite a large TV.

"Let's sit here in each other's arms and rest," said Ron. "I don't know about you but I am very tired from the trip here."

"I'd love that," said Gina. She then placed her head on Ron's shoulder with her forehead against his neck. It only took a few minutes and they both went to sleep

Tom spent the morning writing a new chapter in his novel. At twelve noon he went upstairs to see if Gina and Ron were hungry for lunch. He found them both asleep. Realizing how they both would be tired, he didn't want to wake them so he went back down to his office. It was about one when he started Lunch. He decided to just have a sandwich. He set out the bread and some cheese, turkey balcony and some sliced tomatoes. He then started to go upstairs. He only got half way when he heard them talking.

"Do you guys want some lunch," yelled Tom from the stair way.

"We will be right down" yelled Ron back. Two miutes later Ron and Gina came down to the kitchen.

"I'm sorry but I only have sandwiches for lunch. I will prepare a great supper for tonight," said Tom.

"Wow," said Gina. "It is after one o'clock. I didn't know it as so late."

"I came up at twelve but you guys were asleep and so romantically in each other's arms. I just couldn't wake you up." Gina and Ron both smiled and sat down to eat. After they ate the three just sat down and talked about what had happened since the accident. At about five thirty Ron and Gina went down to the family room to watch a Game show they both liked. Tom stayed in the kitchen to prepare dinner. He made four large pieces of Tilapia fish. Tom knew that Gina loved it. He hoped that Ron would like it also.

"That was the best fish dinner I have ever had," said Ron after they had finished eating. "You will have to give Gina the recipe."

"I don't know if I could cook that good," said Gina. "Tom has had a lot of experience." Tom then wrote down the recipe, recording every little thing he added to the sauce, and everything he had to do and the timing of each action. He then gave it to Gina.

"I think you will not have any trouble cooking the fish," said Tom. "By the way you can cook Salman exactly the same way. It will taste just as good. It is the sauce that gives the fish the good taste." The rest of the evening they spent watching two videos of the Benny Ray band where Gina was performing in the video. Rob was impressed. He had never seen some of shows that Gina was in. After the movies they all went to bed.

The next morning Tom got up early to make breakfast. He decided to cook Mother's Oats. He had cooked it for Gina before and she loved it.

"Wow," said Ron after eating breakfast. "I don't thing I want to leave here. We will miss all of this when we get home."

"I admit it is something to follow," said Gina. "I will do my best. Tom has taught me most of the things he cooks."

"I'm sorry honey," said Ron. "I didn't mean to down grade you. I just want to tell Tom how much I appreciate what he is doing for us." Just then the telephone rang. Tom picked up the phone.

"Hello," said Tom.

"Hi Tom. This is Captain Richard. I need you for a case that Bill is covering. However Bill needs your help in solving it. He has two more cases that he is working on at the same time. The one I want you to do has him baffled. Now that both of your children are married and moved into their own home I'm hoping you will have time to help us as a Part Time Police Detective."

"Well," said Tom. "I would like a couple of weeks to rest. What is this all about?"

"This is about the Crown Hardware Store," started the Captain.

"The owner and store operator Mr. Walter Crown was killed. He was shot in the chest. Bill has checked every aspect he could but has made no progress. He needs your help."

"I will go right now," said Tom.

"Do you need the address or anything?" asked the Captain.

"No I know where it is," said Tom. "I will let you know what I find out." Tom then hung up and turned to Ron and Gina.

"I'm sorry Ron and Gina," said Tom. "I have been assigned a Murder case. I have to go right now. You guys help yourself to anything that is in the refrigerator. I will try to get back by supper time. If I am not here, just go and cook your own dinner. Don't wait for me. I may eat out near where I am investigating the case. Make believe this is your home. I will try to solve this case as soon as I can. Have a good day." Then Tom left to go to the Crown Hardware Store.

At the store he found that Bill had the two sons and all workers in the store assembled at the rear of the store. Also Tom found that the store was closed.

Tom," said Bill. "This is Mr. Crown's oldest son Richard." Tom shock hands with him. "And this is his youngest son Jimmy." Tom shock hands with him. "And this is the purchasing agent, Georgia Baden, and this is the Sales Manager, Corinne Barina, and these are," continued Bill, "Katrina Lonti and Sophia White, the sales ladies." Tom bowed his head toward the ladies and said,

"Glad to meet you all," said Tom."I am Detective Thomas Corely" Then he turned to Bill. "Is there a reason that the store is closed? I think the store may need the business."

"I just wanted to get everyone together," said Bill. "However if you think it is OK then lets open the store."

"All I ask is that no one leaves the building," said Tom. "I would like to speak to each one individually in the office. First Bill will you come with me in the office. I would like to know what you have found out so far. No sense getting the others from their jobs. Georgia please go and do what has to be done to open the store.

Rickard and Jimmy I will want to see you one at a time next so don't go away." Tom and Bill then went into the office.

"I am at a loss to figure out who had a motive to shoot Mr. Crown," said Bill. "I can't find a reason."

"Well," said Tom. "Tell me all that you know."

All I know is that the oldest son and his father didn't get along," said Bill. "You will have to find out why. "The other thing I heard was that Georgia was unhappy with her job. That is all I know."

"Well send in the oldest son," said Tom. Bill went out and came back with Richard.

"Hi Richard," said Tom. "Please sit down. I have a few questions to ask you. I know that you and your brother would like to go back to work. First I understand that you and your father had a problem. Can you tell me what that was?"

"My father was a very stubborn man," started Richard. "He said that since I was born he raised me to take over the store. However when my mother was sick I noticed that the nurses left out so much they could have done for her. From that time on, after my mother past away, that I decided to go into the medical perfection. I wanted to be a doctor but dad would not give me the funds I needed. So I became a nurse. Dad has never forgiven me."

"That is all I need to know," said Tom. "You may go back to work. Please don't leave town. Please be available if we need you again. On your way out please send in your brother."

"I don't see that he has a motive unless he needs money to become a doctor," said "Bill. "But I don't see that as a strong enough motive to kill him." Just then Jimmy walked in.

"Hi Jim," said Tom. "Please come in a sit down. I am wondering how you got along with your father and why you are not working in the store?"

"My father and I got along just fine," said Jimmy. "I called him at least once a week to see how he was. By the way everyone calls me Jimmy. I am used to the name. Please call me jimmy."

"Alright Jimmy," said Tom. "Why are you not working for you dad?"

"I went to college and graduated with a degree in financing," said Jimmy. "I would have loved to work in dad's store but he had Georgia who did all the finances for the company. She has been doing that job for around ten years. Dad would not replace her. The only job that was available was assistant manager. That was not what I wanted to do. I then was offered a job at the mall clothing shop. I've been there ever since I graduated from college."

"I think that there is no other course then for you to take over the store," said Tom. "You can take over the finances and make Georgia your assistant."

"I think that Georgia would probably resign if I did that," said Jimmy.

"Then you can take over the complete job that you would prefer anyway," said Tom.

"We will see what will happen," said jimmy. "I don't think I have an option except to take over as the store manager. I will think about it."

"Well that is all I wanted to know," said Tom. "You are free to go back to your job. Thank you for your time."

"I don't see that he has a motive," said Bill. "I think he will make a fine store manager."

"Go out and bring in Georgia," Tom asked Bill. Bill went out into the store to get Georgia.

"Hi," said Georgia when she came in the office. "I hope that you find the rat that shoot Walter. He should be hanged. Walter was the nicest man you could ever meet."

"Hi Georgia," said Tom. "Have a seat. I will not keep you long. "I hear that you were unhappy when you heard that Mr. Crown was retiring. What was that about?"

"First of all I was very dismayed that he retired. We worked so well together. At first I was also disappointed that he insisted that one of his sons take over the business. I felt that for ten years I had run the business for him and I expected that when he retired that he would name me to run the store for him. However after thinking about it, it made sense, since he would leave the store to his sons that he would ask one of them to run it. I also realized that neither of the boys want the job so, I would probably be running it for the sons anyway."

"Can you think of anyone who would want to hurt Mr. Crown? Do you know of anyone that would gain from his death?"

No," said Georgia with a sad look on her face. "He was very strict with us all but you will never find any one more kind. We all loved him. The only one that I could think of that could want to harm him is an unhappy costumer. But I don't know of any one that has complained and even if one did, it seems very unlikely that they would kill Mr. Crown. I'm sorry I can't help you."

"Thank you so much for your time," said Tom. "Have a great day."

"You have a great day too," said Georgia as she got up to leave. "I pray that you find the murderer." After she left Tom asked Bill to get Corinne the sales manager. Bill had no trouble bring in Corinne.

"Hello Corinne," said Tom. "Please take a seat. I will not keep you long. I need to know if you have any idea as to who would harm your boss."

"I have no idea," said Corinne. "I have had very little contact with Mr. Crown. He pretty much kept himself in his office. I only provide sales information to Georgia."

"Do you have anything that is in your mine even if it is a small insignificant thing? Is there anything that you have wondering about? Perhaps some problem with a customer or if there is something that is missing that you can't find that would suggest a theft?"

"I cannot think of anything that is different from our every day time in the store." After a short pause she added, "Now that I think about it there is one thing that has me confused. I understand that the business has a financial problem, however the sales is the same and even greater."

"Thank you very much for you time," said Tom. "You may go back to your job."

"I guess the sales ladies are the next ones you want to see," said Bill. "I suspect you want to see both at the same time. I will go get them."

"Hi Girls," said Tom. "You are Katrina and Sophia I believe. I wonder if either of you have any idea as to who or why someone wanted to kill Mr. Crown?"

"I believe I could speak for both of us," said Katrina. "We hardly recognize any of the upper management. We sell hardware and report to Corinne. That is all we know."

"Do either of you have any little thing that has bothered you about your job," asked Tom.

"The only thing I can tell you," said Katrina, "is that Corinne mentioned the other day that she wondered why the company had a money problem because the sales have been greater than ever"

"I agree with them. The sales have been great," said Sophia wanting to get her voice in the discussion.

"Well thank you girls very much for your time," said Tom. "Let me know if you think of anything else." With that statement the girls understood that their meeting was over so they left the office

"Well what do you think?" asked Bill. "Did you get anything from all this?"

"Well we are sure that it is not for inheritance," said Tom, "because the boys will inherit the store whether their father is dead or alive. The thing that bothers me the most is that the sales people don't see a slowing of customers. Then why is the company just surviving? That is the next thing we should have to look into."

"So where do we go from here?" asked Bill.

"First we have to get a court order to get the bank to co-operate and give us all the information we need from them."

"Let's go to the court house," said Bill. "I know the judge that is on duty right now."

"Let's go to lunch first," said Tom. "It is almost one O'clock. The judge may be out to lunch. We can sit and talk about the case." They then said goodbye to the staff at the store and drove to the nearest restaurant. After ordering their lunch they sat and talked.

"Have you any idea," said Bill, "who is guilty of this crime?"

"It looks like, if the bank backs up what I think," said Tom, "that the problem is that someone is stealing money from the stores income. The only one I could think of is Georgia the purchasing agent."

"How," asked Bill, "will the bank be able to help?"

We will see," said Tom. "Maybe they will not be able to help. However, if they are a good bank they will have good records of the stores financial history." After eating their lunch they went directly to the court house. It took about fifteen minutes to get to see the judge. They explained to the judge all that they knew and what they suspected. The judge gave them a court order to get information from the bank. Tom and Bill left the court house feeling like they were getting close to solving the case.

"Look Tom," said Bill. "I think you have a good handle on this case. I think you can take it from here. I have two cases that I'm working on. You don't need me."

"I think I can handle it from here," said Tom. "You go on your other cases. Thank you for sticking with me. If you need help I will be available."

"Thank you Tom," said Bill as he left. Tom then went to the bank. Tom walked directly to the mangers office.

"Hello" said Tom to the woman sitting at the desk. "I'm Detective Thomas Corely. I would like to speak to the bank clerk who handles the finances for the Crown Hardware store." He then handed her the court order. "This will assure you that I have the right to the required information"

"That is fine," said the woman. "I am Martha Hartford. I am the branch manager. Deborah Evens is the clerk that handles all of Crown Hardware finances. Wait just a minute and I will set up a meeting with her." She then got on the phone "Debbie," she said, There is detective here that needs some information from you about Crown Hardware store finances. He has a proper authority from the court, so answer all his questions. Hold nothing back from him." She then turned to Tom "She is in the second office by the windows. She is standing by her office entrance. Good luck in getting all the information you need." Tom then walked out her office and notice a young lady stand at the entrance of her office. Tom then walked up to her.

"Hi," said Tom. "I am Detective Tom Corley."

"Come on in," said the young lady. "My name is Deborah Evens. Have a seat here across my desk. How can I help you?"

"As you have heard the owner of the Crown Hardware store has been shot. I am investigation the case. I would like to get all the information I can on the finances of the Crown Hardware store to see if there is any connect to the murder," started Tom. "First Deborah, has there been any difference in the income that you have received from the store? I understand that Georgia Baden brings the checks and the cash from all the sales that the store has made."

"Yes that is correct," said Debbie, "and please call me Debbie. There has been very little money coming as cash. It has all been by customer checks." Debbie then went into her computer to take out all the information she had on the store income. "About five minutes later she turned to Tom. "Detective Corely, I have checked the average income for the last year and I find that it has been about ten percent larger than average the past several months.

"Please call me Tom. Are you saying that business has been better the last few months then it was earlier in the year?"

"Yes about ten percent," said Debbie repeating what she had said before. Why does that surprise you?" asked Debbie.

"It surprises me because the information I got was that the store was in financial trouble," said Tom. "Can you tell me if the amount of checks that are written for the purchasing of Hardware items has increased in number or in monetary value?" Debbie then went back to her computer. After a few minutes she turned to Tom.

"It looks like for the whole year it has been the same," said Debbie. "The amount that is put into the checking account and the amount taken out are about the same."

"Do you see anything," said Tom," in the store account that is different?" Debbie went into the computer.

"There is one thing that is different Tent," said Debbie. "The amount of the money that went into the stores money market account is much less. It used to be in the hundred thousand dollar class, but in the last year it is less than one hundred dollars."

"Can you explain what happen to the rest of the money?" asked Tom.

"Yes," said Debbie. "I remember now. Georgia said that a lot of new dealers gave a ten percent discount if they were paid by cash. Therefore Georgia took out most of the earned money, which did not go into the checking account, in cash."

"Thank you so much Debbie," said Tom as he got up to leave. "You can't imagine how great a help you have been in solving this case. You have a great day" Tom then left and went directly to the court house. Tom explained to the judge what he had learned about the shooting of Walter Crown. He had no trouble in getting a court order to search Georgia's apartment and her car. Since it was late in the afternoon he decided to do the searching the next day. He didn't want Georgia to come home a find him there. So he went home thinking he could cook a nice dinner for Gina and Ron. He was shocked when he got home.

"Hi Tom," said Ron who met him at the door. "You are a little earlier than we thought. However all will be completed in less than an hour."

"What are you talking about?" asked Tom. "What is going on?"

"Gina is going to show you what a great cook she is," said Ron with a proud look on his face. "She is cooking you a very special Italian dinner."

"What have I done to deserve this?" asked Tom.

"We can never describe in words how much we appreciate what you have done for us," said Ron.

"You have to understand that I have enjoyed this more than I could describe," said Tom. "Without you two I would be all alone.

"I'm afraid that as much as we would like to stay here with you," said Ron, "we will be going home in a couple of days. We will leave as soon as the doctor releases Gina.

"So," asked Tom, "what is Gina cooking?"

"She wants to leave you with something to remember us by,"

said Ron. "She got up very early this morning and started to cook you dinner. She is cooking you Cavatelli with pork bones and meat balls."

"Wow," said Tom. "Known what that could be like. "My wife Rita; God rest her sole, used to cook the tomato sauce the day before. That evening we would eat the neck bones for dinner. Then we would have the Cavatelli and meat balls the next day." When Gina finished cooking the Cavatelli she called them up to the kitchen. They ate like it was a gift from heaven. Tom was so full that he could hardly move.

"What do you want to do now?" asked Ron.

"I can hardly move," said Tom. "I think that I would like to just sit and watch TV."

"When do you want your desert?" asked Gina. "I made your favorite Coconut pie."

"Dear lord," said Tom, "when did you have time to make that?"

"I made it yesterday," said Gina. "I hid it in the down stairs refrigerator."

"I don't know if I have room for anything else tonight," said Tom. "Why don't you save it for tomorrow? What do you think Ron?"

"I agree with you," said Ron. "I can hardly finish my coffee." They then went down to the family room to watch a TV movie. Tom and Ron never saw the end of the movie. They both fell asleep in the family room couch. It was around ten when Gina woke them up. The movie had ended and Gina shut off the TV.

"Why don't you guys get up and go to bed?" suggested Gina. They did not have to be asked twice.

The next morning Tom got up at eight. He took his shower got dressed and headed down to the kitchen. He was surprised that Gina was there. They were never up before Tom.

"I though since I couldn't sleep, that I will come down and cook you a special breakfast."

"I see that you have made Scrambled Eggs with Bacon," said Tom. "I better not eat too much or I will not be able to do my investigating job." Just as Tom finish eating his eggs Ron came down.

"Honey," said Gina, "what are you doing down this early?"

"I could smell all the food and got hungry," said Ron.

"Well you came just in time. I am cooking some scrambled eggs for you and me. After Tom finished his coffee he left for Georgia's house. He was sure that by now she would be at work. Tom asked for a police officer to meet him there. It was Brian Coffman that met him there. Using the tool he always had with him he opened the front door.

"Listen Brian," instructed Tom. "I am going to check the main bedroom. You check the other two bed rooms. You know what to look for. Check all the furniture drawers and the closets."

"Yes," said Brian. "I know what to look for. I have done this before." They each then went in a bedroom. In the bed room that Tom went into he found that it had a desk at one end of the room. Tom went directly to the desk. Inside the top drawer he found a pistol. He placed it into a plastic bag he always carried with him when he is investigating. He was sure that it was the gun that shot Mr. Crown. He kept looking into the other drawers. On the right hand bottom drawer he found two check books. The one was the one from the same bank that the Hardware store dealt with. The other one however was from another bank. He checked and it only had ten dollars in that account. However the interesting point was that the name on the check book was not Georgia Baden, but Georgia Brown. He checked further and found a bank statement for Georgia Brown. It showed that it had eight hundred thousand dollars in the saving account. Brian then walked into the bedroom where Tom was.

Tom," said Brian. "All the furniture drawers were empty. The closets only had hundreds of dresses and shoes. She must have spent hundreds of dollars for all those clothes. Have you found anything interesting?

"Yes," said Tom "I found that Georgia has an account in another bank under a different name. I think she has been stealing from the store."

"That is a very good possibility," said Brian. "Can I help you in here?"

Yes," said Tom. "Why don't you look into the closet in this room? I have not had a chance to check it." Brain then went into the closet. He was checking all the dresses in there and was about to leave when he noticed something different.

Tom," said Brian. "Look at this. She has a picture hanging here at rear of the closet. I moved it and it looks like there is a safe behind it."

"That is something I have never seen," said Tom. "Can you open it?" asked Tom.

"No it has a combination lock. "I pulled on it and it did not open. We need the locks combination."

"You know," said Tom. "One of the things that is becoming popular is to hide the combination under a drawer. People have gotten to think that is it an unknown and rare thing to do." Tom then started to look under all the drawers in the desk. Under the lowest drawer on the left he found the combination. It was taped on the underside of the drawer. He quickly used it to open the safe. He was not really surprised to find stacks of one hundred dollar Bills. After checking it out it turned out to be over one hundred thousand dollars that was in the safe. They put the money in a plastic bag.

"How in the world has she gotten away with this crime," said Brian.

"I don't think she has gotten away with it," said Tom. "I think we have more than we need. Let's get out of here." From there they went directly to the police station. Tom turned over everything he had to Captain Richard. The money including the bank account under Georgia Brown amounted to around nine hundred thousand dollars.

"I think we should check this gun to see if it is the gun that killed Mr. Crown," said the Captain. He then called the lab asking them to send a lab assistant to pick up the pistol. A few miutes later an assistant came and picked up the pistol.

"How long will it take to check out the pistol?" asked Tom. "I believe they already have the bullets that were removed from Mr. Crown.

"Yes," said the captain. "It should only take a few miutes to find out if the bullets came from that pistol. Why don't you sit and wait. Brian, you can go back to you normal job." Brian then left. They sat there for a few miutes. Tom told him all that occurred that day. Soon the lab technician came in.

"Captain Sir," said the technician, "the tests show that the bullets came from the pistol we tested." He then gave the captain the lab report and left. The captain then called Police Sargent Jeffrey Denizen and instructed him to take two Police officers and go to the Crown Hardware store and arrest Georgia Baden.

"Tom," said the captain. "I think we have all we need for now. Thank you for accepting this case. You did a very great job. I will call you if we need your testimony. Have a great day I promise that I will not bother you again unless it is a very special emergence. Goodbye."

"Goodbye Captain," said Tom and left. As he drove home he said to himself. "With the Captain it is always a very special emergency."

CHAPTER TEN

The Long Road To Destiny

When Tom got home he decided that since he was home earlier than usual he would start making dinner for Ron and Gina. He decided to cook Pork Chops. It was a tedious job. It would take more than an hour. It would be ready by six that evening. When he started to pound on the chops Ron and Gina heard the noise and came down stairs. They had been upstairs in the TV room. The TV there was larger than the one in the family room. It also was a smaller room so that the couch in that room was closer to the TV.

"Tom," said Ron. "What are you doing that makes that much noise?"

"I am making dinner," said Tom. "You have been making dinner for the past several days, so it is my turn now."

"I'm glad that you are home," said Ron. "We have to talk."

"What do you want to talk about?" asked Tom.

"Are you still working on a case for the police force?" asked Ron.

"I think we have the culprit. I may still have to go to the court to testify. Why are you asking?"

"Well," said Ron. "This Friday Gina is going to the hospital to have her final tests. I called the doctor and he assured me that Gina would have a ninety- five percent chance of being released to go home. That is four days away. We decided since we had two cars here that I would leave the day before to fix our home so it was livable. Gina then after her examination would leave to come home to Indian from there."

"The time has gone to fast," said Tom. "I am going to miss you guys so much. I am going to be alone for the first time in my live."

"We will miss you too," said Gina, "more than you know. You however should go and make up with Vicki. She is crazy about you and I know that you are crazy about her. Go and fight for her. Then you would not be alone."

"I don't think she wants to talk with me," said Tom. "Anyway Ron, was there another reason you brought this up?"

"Besides letting you know of our plans," said Ron. "We only have two days left that we could be together. We would like to spend that time with you."

"Sounds like something I would love to do," said Tom. "What would you think of the idea of having a picnic at the Fairlawn amusement park? It is for children but it has a covered patio behind the main building that faces the park. It has tables for the public to use. We can be together and see kids enjoy the small but nice children rides. Or we could go deeper in the park and have a picnic on the grass under a tree. What do you guys think?"

"Sounds fantastic," said Gina. "I love children. I am hoping to have a few of my own. What do you think honey?" She said turning to her husband.

"I think it will be something to remember," said Ron. "I am all for it."

"Let's do it tomorrow," said Tom. "We will have an early breakfast, pack a lunch basket that I have used with my kids when they were small. We can then go early and spent the time there and eat the lunch there at about twelve. We can then stay there until supper time if it is pleasing to the three of us." The next morning they did as Tom had suggested. They had a very enjoyable time. They enjoyed watching the children happily sliding down the slides that were on the right side of the swings. They enjoyed eating lunch outside, spending the time together and watching the children. Before they realized it, it was seven O'clock. It was too late to go home and cook dinner so they decided to go to Olive Garden for dinner.

The next day was Wednesday. Gina made breakfast. After eating Tom turned to Ron and Gina.

"Well, what do you want to do today?"

"Yesterday," said Ron. "I notice that east of the park was a wooded area. I also noticed a path going into it. I would like to go down the path and when we find a nice clear area we could lay a blanket on the ground and have lunch there. What do you think Gina? Do you feel like a nice walk in the woods?"

"I noticed that two," said Gina. "I was wondering what it lead to. I think it is a good idea. I can't think of a better way for us to be together. What do you think Tom? I suspect that you have been down that path."

Yes I have," said Tom. "I even had lunch there a couple of times. Just a few feet down that path is a small river. I had lunch in a clearing down besides the river. It is a very beautiful area along the river. I have a large back pack that I can take with us to carry the blanket and food."

"Do you have a small pack?" asked Ron. "Then I could help you carry some of the stuff."

"I have two small back packs," said Tom. "If you want to take some of the load we could take them both, one for you and one for me."

"Let's do it," said Gina. "I love the idea. We will not have a chance like this. The area around our house in Indiana is rather flat and open. I don't remember ever seeing a wooded area like this. Let's go for it." It took them about an hour to get everything ready. At ten-thirty they left for the Fairlawn Park. They walked down the path. The scenery along the river was fantastic. They all loved it. At about noon they came to the area that Tom had told them about. There was a large area on the edge of the river where they could lay the blanket to eat lunch.

"I don't understand," said Ron. "All the clear area we passed and especially this one has beautiful grass."

"Remember this is part of the Fairlawn Park. The city takes care of it all. They even have someone come every so often to feed and cut the grass"

"I wish that we could live here," said Gina, "Maybe we should look for work around here."

"Honey this is a small town," said Ron. "I have a manager job waiting for me in South Bend."

"Honey," said Gina. "I was just day dreaming. We have a very beautiful house in Indiana. And I'm sure that I could find a great job waiting for me there." They laid out the blanket and had a delicious lunch. Somehow it tasted better in the open country air. After lunch they gather up everything and continued walking down the path enjoying the scenery. At about six they decided to go home.

"You know guys," said Gina. "I am too tired after enjoying this beautiful day to do any cooking. I also think you both are also very tired. What I would like to suggest that we go back to Olive Garden and have supper there. We had a very wonderful dinner there yesterday. They have a few dinners that I would like to try."

"I think it is a great idea," said Ron and Tom at the same time. They enjoyed a great diner at Olive garden and finally went home. Gina wanted to watch TV. They all were too tired to do anything else. They never saw more than a third of the movie because all three fell asleep.

The next morning Tom got up early to make breakfast for Ron since he was leaving that morning. However Gina also got up. She wanted to spend more time with him before she say had to say goodbye to her husband. All three ate breakfast and after they ate Ron was ready to leave. Ron loaded his suit case in the car trunk and then turned to Tom.

"Tom, I can't thank you enough for all that you have done for us. I would like it if we try to have our vacations at the same time each year. One year you will come and visit us, and one year we will come to visit you."

"And I hope when you do," added Gina, "you will bring your wife to be Vicki."

"For now I need to say goodbye to our best friend," said Ron as he hugged Tom. Then he turned to Gina who followed him to the car door. "And you take care and drive carefully when you come home tomorrow." Gina then wrapped her arms around him and kissed him passionately.

"And you drive careful too," said Gina, "goodbye" Ron was soon out of sight. Tom and Gina then went inside.

"Tomorrow will seem like it was a year away," said Gina sadly. I am going to pack my suitcase and be ready to leave after I am released by the doctor," said Gina.

"What time is your appointment with the doctor?"

"M appointment is at eleven," said Gina. "That is why I will leave right after I see the doctor. I don't want to drive in the dark. Besides, the freeway is just beyond the hospital. I will be more than half way there."

The next morning while they were eating breakfast Tom got a telephone call. It was from the Captain.

"Hi Captain," said Tom knowing that it was the captain from the number that showed on his phone.

Hi Tom," said the captain. "They have moved up the court hearing to nine o'clock this morning. "So please hurry and be there."

"I'm leaving right now," said Tom and hung up.

"Did something important come up?" asked Gina.

"Yes," said Tom. "They have moved up the court hearing to nine this morning. So I have to be there to testify what I know."

"So you will not be here when I leave," said Gina. "I guess this is good bye. I love you like a brother. Thank you so much for opening up your home for me and Ron. Please keep in touch like Ron suggested."

"I will," said Tom. "I have to leave now if I want to be there in time. So I love you guys also and God Bless you and keep you safe on your way home and always." He then hugged Gina passionately and quickly left before ether one showed their tears.

It was about ten-thirty when Gina packed all her belongings, put them in the trunk of her car, and left for the hospital. At the hospital she went to the doctor's office. The doctor's secretary said that the doctor was on a phone call and asked her to sit and wait for the doctor. It was about fifteen minutes later when the doctor told the secretary to send Gina in. The doctor asked her a few question about how she felt around the area of her rib problem, and a few other questions. When he got through, he called the lab. He gave a sheet of paper that Gina realized was the order for the tests. She went to the lab and went through several tests. They had her turn on her side for one, the other side for the other and on her back for the last. After the tests she went back to the doctor's office. It was now almost noon. A few minutes after she sat in the doctor's office he came out.

"Well Mrs. Holland," said the doctor with a smile on his face. "We have been successful in taking care of your problem. Everything is great. You are well enough to leave the hospital and are not required to come back. Gina felt relieved. She was ready to travel to Indian. However since it was close to noon she decided to have lunch in the hospital cafeteria. As she walked in the cafeteria she saw Vicky sitting in one of the tables. She walked up to her.

"Hi Vicki," she said. "May I join you?"

"Are you trying to rub it in?" said Vicki. "Sure, sit across from me."

"I just got released from the hospital," aid Gina. "I am going to be with the love of my heart. I am leaving right from here." The waitress came and Gina ordered her lunch. It was a hamburger. She didn't want too much food in her stomach while driving.

"Why isn't he here with you?" asked Vicki. "I thought that he would be here with you."

"He left yesterday," said Gina. "He has gone to our house in South Bend Indiana. He is going to fix up the house so that is livable. It has been empty for over a year."

"You love Tom very much don't you?" asked Vicki.

"Of course," said Gina. "He is the nicest person I have ever met. Who could not love him? He is humble, kind, generous, considerate and most of all very affectionate." The waitress then brought Gina the hamburger. Vicki had finisher her lunch and was ready to leave. Gina finished her lunch before another word was spoken.

"What is Tom going to do with his house here in Ohio" asked Vicky. "Is he going to sell it?"

"He never talked about selling his house," said Gina. "Why would he want to sell it?"

"What would he do with it?" said Vicki, "now that he has no one to live in it."

"Are you referring to the fact?" said Gina, "that his kids are all married and have houses of their own."

"That is a good point," said Vicki. "I guess he could leave it too his children."

"I don't understand," said Gina. "Why are you so worried about his house?"

Well if Tom is with you," said Vicki, "why would he want to keep a house here in Ohio?"

"I am confused." said Gina. "What are you talking about? Why are you talking about Tom?"

"You say that you love Tom and He loves you," said Vicki. What else should I think?"

"You lost me," said Gina. "I don't know what you are talking about. I do love Tom. But what has that to do with me and the love of my life, my husband?"

"What does your husband have to do with this?" said Vicki. "I thought that you were separated."

"I see the problem," said Gina suddenly realizing what Vicki was talking about. "The separation was a fake. My husband's job caused him to travel constantly all over the world. I told my husband that I was tired to travel. I wanted to stay in one place and raise kids. My husband thought that if he gave me a fake separation, that I loved him so much that I would give up my requirement to stay in one place and go with him. I however felt that if he loved me as much as he said that he would not leave. We were both wrong. I didn't meet him at the airport as he expected and he did take off to his next job as I hoped he wouldn't."

"So it is your husband that you are talking about," said Vicki.

"Yes," said Gina, "Oh Vicki, didn't you hear of the most wonderful thing that Tom did for me. He tried to call the company where my husband Ron worked to find out where he was. However, Ron's supervisor had died. They looked for his record of where he had sent the workers, but they could not fine it. So Tom with all the power he had as a police detective, spent a whole week on the phone to find him. He finally found out where Ron was. He was in France. Tom finally contacted him and told him of my accident. I think he exaggerated because Tom said that he heard Ron crying on the phone. Ron then took the first plane he could get to the US and landed in Chicago. From there he came here. He spent the last week with Tom and me at Tom's house."

"That is a fantastic romantic story," said Vicki. "You should write a book on your life. So where is Tom?"

"I said goodbye to Tom this morning before I came to the hospital," said Gina. "He had to leave to handle a police case. So the fight you and Tom had was that you thought that Tom and I were having an affair"

"Well you said that you loved him very much," said Vicki, "and he said that he loved you. What was I to think?"

"Oh Vicki," said Gina, "with all that he did for me how could I not love him. I do love him very much. But I am not in-love with him. Do you see the difference? I love him like a big brother. He loves me like I was his little sister. "Dear Vicki, He is so in love with you. It is destiny. No matter what you do I know that you will end up together. It is destined to be that way. So relax and let God bring you two together."

"Thank you so much for all that you have told me," said Vicki. I have to go to work. At the end of the month I am going back to the first shift so I will have time to find out if Tom still loves me after all the stupid things I said to him. You have a wonderful life and a safe trip home."

"Goodbye Vicki," said Gina as she got up to leave. "God bless you." Gina then left. A few minutes later Gina was on her way home.

Tom got to the court ten miutes before nine. He was ten miutes early. There he met Captain Richards.

"Hi Captain," said Tom. "How come the court session got moved up?"

"The actual court session was dismissed," said Captain Richards. "It is only going to be a hearing because Georgia's attorney talked her into confessing. So we only going to hear her confection and what the court attorney feels are chargeable information. The judge then will take all the evidence and decide the time in jail" Right at nine o'clock the judge came into the court room.

"Let's hear the confession of the woman that is charged with the crime." Georgia then came forward and sat on the chair on the right of the judge.

"I have worked at the Crown Hardware Store for over ten years. I have been the purchasing and financial director. When Walter said that he was planning on retiring, I felt that since nether of his sons wanted the position that I would be given the job. I then got the stupid idea that if I held up the money and slowly replace it, that it would look like I was doing a good job so that the son's would not replace me. When he told me that he was going to have one of his sons replace him, I became very angry. I pulled out my gun from my rear belt area, where I kept it hidden. I always carried one because every day I carried a lot of case to the bank. I was only trying to show him that I was very good at protecting myself with the money I carried. I pointed it at his stomach hoping only to scare him. Unfortunately he wasn't scared and suddenly grabbed the gun trying to take it away from me and it went off. I did not want him to die. I had a better chance at a good job with him alive. I was the one that called 911 to get help for him. I then left feeling guilty to what happened. That is the truth, I swear it."

"Does anyone have anything to add to her statement?" asked the judge.

"I have," said the court attorney. "In her defense, I had the lab check Mr. Crown's hand and his cloths to see if there was any gun powder marks. There was very heavy gun powder in both his hand and cloths. It indicates that the gun was in his hand and up close to his chest. The only other evidence against her is, why she had eight hundred Dollars in her safe."

"Is there any other comments that anyone wants to make?" asked the judge. When no one answered he got up. "I will take all the information and evidence and look it over and determine the jail sentence I will set for Mrs. Baden. The case is over and you are all dismissed."

"Before you leave," said Captain Richard to Tom. "I would like to talk with you."

"Do you have another case you want me to solve?" said Tom. You promised me that you would only ask me to help if it was an absolute emergency."

"I am keeping my promise," said the captain. "It is not a case I am asking you to solve. However it is a case that requires solving."

"I don't understand," said Tom.

"I got a call from a police officer from the Cleveland area," started The Captain. "It was from a fellow named John Anderson. If you remember you worked with him on that Nicky Lane case. They were very impressed with you and would like you to help them. You would be working for them not me. They wanted your phone number but I declined. He gave me his number so that you can call him if you are interested in helping him. If you are not interested just forget it." Tom couldn't forget it he was too interested in what it was all about. After all he could refuse to help if he wanted to after talking with John. When he got to his car he phoned the phone number he was given. A woman's voice answered the phone

"How may I help you?"

"I would like to talk to Detective John Anderson." Tom heard a click on the phone and then a man answered.

"Hi," said the man. "This is Detective Anderson. Who am I talking to?"

"This is Tom Corely," said Tom. "I heard that you needed help with a case you are on."

"Oh Tom," said John. "I need you so badly. I have been working on this case for over a week and have gotten nowhere. I need your help badly. Listen instead of discussing this over the phone, why don't you go home pack a suit case and drive down here. You will be hired by my police department. We will pay you the same salary you got in your home town police department. We will get you a room near the scene of the crime so that you will not have to drive back and forth from you house. We will pay for your room and board."

"How long do you think I will have to stay there?" asked Tom.

I thing you should prepare for about a week," said John. "It is still early. Why don't you go home pack your suit case and drive out her now. That will save you some time."

"I'm on my way," said Tom. "Wait for me at you police office. I know how to get there." Tom then hung up and drove home. It was almost two, so he decided to eat lunch first. When he finished lunch he started to pack his suitcase. He then drove to Cleveland. He arrived at the Cleveland police station at about six in the afternoon.

"Hi John," said Tom as he entered John's office. "I'm here so where do we go from here?"

"Hi Tom," said John. "I think we should go get you a room to sleep in tonight and then go to my favorite restaurant for dinner. Dinners are on me. There I could fill you in on all the details of the case." John drove Tom to the hotel nearest to the police station, got him a room, and then drove to the restaurant. After they ordered their meals John started to inform Tom of the case they were investigating.

"The case is about a family that got shot," started John. "It was the husband Leon Harris, his wife Lois, and their daughter Gina that were shot. The first question I had was why would they kill all three? At first I thought that two were witnesses but then why would he kill one when the other two were witness? Anyway a neighbor, Brigitte Adkins was coming home late and saw a young man running out of the house. He got into his car and hurriedly drove away. The neighbor noticed that he left the door open. Being concern she went into the house and found the three of them dead. That is when she called us."

"So what have you investigated up to now?" asked Tom.

"The first thing I did was checked the companies that each worked in. Leon worked in a factory building furniture. His boss and all the ones that worked with him said that he was the nicest fellow they knew. He was the best of the bunch but was very humble. His wife was a sales lady at a woman's clothing shop. They all loved her. No one could imagine who or why anyone would want to kill her. I got the same from the workers in John's company. So what do you think I missed so far?"

"I think the most probable cause for the killing of all three is inheritance. Someone either wants their money or they want them out of the way so that they could inherit what they would have inherited."

"Sounds logical," said John. "So let's go down that path. Lois's family have all past away. Her grandparents and all her other relatives live in Germany. So there is no one that could inherit through her. As for the husband his parents were killed in an automobile accident. He had no brothers or sisters and the only relative I could find was his uncle Fred who lives in California. I checked him out and he was at work during the time of the murder. His wife died of cancer and they had no children."

"Well it looks like you have everything covered," said Tom. "I see why you are so desperate. I think some where there is an answer. I know where I have to look. Tomorrow morning I would like to check an area that I think could give me some clues. I will use all the avenues that I have developed during my time as a detective. I will have to use your computer and your office. I will keep you informed with all that I find. For now I am very tired and I would like to go get my car and then go to the hotel and get some sleep." John did as Tom asked and Tom was soon in bed asleep.

The next morning Tom went to the police station and got to John's office at nine o'clock.

"Hi John," said Tom. "How are you today?"

"I'm fine," said John. "Listen Tom, we set you up in the last office which is empty. We set you up with a phone and computer. I have some other things that I have to take care of. If you need my help I'll be in my office all day."

"That is great," said Tom. "This way I'll not be disturbed. I also brought my lunch so I will have all day for my search" Tom then went into the office and started his research. Tom ate his lunch at twelve and went back to his investigation. That evening John walked into Tom's temporary office.

"I think it is time for dinner," said John. "Come, it is on me. They went to the same restaurant. After they ate John asked Tom what he had found so far.

"I found that Leon's grandfather had a brother," started Tom. "Although he died, he did leave a wife who is very ill and in a hospital in Jeannette Pennsylvania. She has Cancer and needs surgery. I found her searching the name Harris. You can imagine, with a common a name that, it was quite a search."

"I can imagine," said John.

"I will search out her life tomorrow," said Tom. After they ate they went home.

The next day Tom went back to the computer. He searched all morning but could not find anything. After lunch Tom went into John's office.

John," he said, "I could not find any new evidence. We will have to visit her in Pennsylvania."

"I will take care of it this afternoon," said John. "We will travel tomorrow. I will also get us a room in a hotel in case we have to stay there. You can contact the police depart there to get their approval." Tom did just that. The next day they found them self at the hospital talking to Martha. They told Martha of the death of Leon and his family. She was very sorry to hear of their death. However, she couldn't think of anyone that would want to harm them. She then made a phone call.

"Steve," she said. "Please come to the hospital I need you."

"Who was that you called if I may ask?" asked Tom.

"That was my lawyer Steve Walters," said Martha. "I have to change my will before I go into surgery."

"That was fine," said Tom. "I was going to ask you about you attorney. I will see him when he gets here." About an hour later Steve came in. After a short introduction Steve turned to Martha.

"What is it that you want me to do?" he asked of Martha.

"My family in Ohio were all killed, so I have to change my will. I would like to leave all my possessions to the three charities that I was leaving fifty thousand before"

"Do you still want to leave the twenty thousand to Ryan Harris?" asked Steve.

"Yes," said Martha. "Even though he is not worth it he is family.

"Who is Ryan?" asked Tom.

"He is Martha's grandson. After Martha's son and his wife died in an auto accident, Martha was the only one left to take care of Ryan. Ryan was very evil. He tried to rob Martha by forging her checks. He got away with several thousand dollars. When Martha caught him he tried to kill her. He stabbed her three times with a kitchen knife and left her to die. Thank goodness she stayed awake long enough to call for help. Ryan spent three years in jail"

"How much are we talking about?" asked John.

"I think the total including the value of her house is about one million six hundred thousand dollars," said Steve. Tom then pulled Steve and John out into the hall.

"I think we found our criminal," said Tom. "Please keep the death of Martha's family a secret. I think he killed Martha's family so being the only relative he could claim her possessions. We have to catch him in the act. I have a plan that may work." Tom and John got all the information they need to find Ryan. They got a court order to search his apartment and his car. They spent all day searching his apartment while Ryan was out working at his job. He worked for a company that cut the grass for clients. They found nothing that they could use to convict him. They had to wait until he was fast asleep that night to check his car. The go nothing there either. The next day they waited until it got dark when Ryan got home. After he had time to settle in they rang his door bell. Ryan answered the door.

"What do you want?" He said in a very unfriendly voice.

"We are looking for Ryan Harris," said Tom. "We have bad news and good news."

"What is this all about?" asked Ryan.

"We will make this short," said John. "We are from Ohio. We traced to find Leon's relatives. We only found you and your grandmother. Since she is in the hospital we thought we would not bother her. You can tell her if she survives the surgery. So you are the only relative besides her that we could find."

"So what are you trying to tell me?" asked Ryan.

"Well we are here to tell you that your aunt Lois and her daughter Gina where shot and killed by a robber who broke into their house and tried to rob them. He must have thought that they were not home.

"How about my Uncle Leon," asked Ryan with a strange look on his face.

"He was shot also. The bullet went into his chest side wise and just missed his heart," said Tom. "The woman next door saw someone running out of the house leaving the front door open. So she went in and found the victims. Your uncle Leon survived. He just got home from the hospital where he had surgery that saved his life. He just got home yesterday. He is physically well but he is hurting very much from the loss of his wife and daughter." While Tom was talking, John pretending that he was texting took a picture of Ryan.

"Well we have done our job," said John, "We have to go now, so Ryan, have a nice life." They then went to their hotel rooms.

The next morning they headed for Ohio. When they got there John pulled up next to Tom's car.

"I think that we have all the information that we can get, so why don't you go to your hotel room. I am going to print the picture I took of Ryan and see if one of hotels recognizes him. Even if they don't recognize him I can give them a copy of Ryan and have them call me if he registeres in their hotel. I will call you tomorrow or if anything comes up. You can spend the day watching TV. Tom agreed and left for his hotel room. John then made four copies of Ryan and went to each hotel in the area. Of the four he visited, it was the last hotel that recognized him. However he left a picture to each of the hotels. To John's amazement he got a call from the last hotel that afternoon about four.

"Hello," said John when he answered the phone.

"Hello Detective Johnson," said the hotel manager. "The fellow whose picture you gave us has just registered for a room. He registered as Robert Brown."

"Thank you so much," said John who then quickly called Tom.

"Tom," he said after Tom answered the phone. "Ryan has just registered in one of the hotels. He is not wasting time. Please come over to the victim's house." John then gave Tom the address. John also got a Police officer name Sam Bruster to go with him to the victim's house. He brought two motion detectors and a mop that had dark washing fibers to the house. John set it in the bed with three pillows. He lined them up so it looked like the shape of a person and placed the mop with the fiber ends on top side of the bed. He covered then with the bed blanket. A small part of the mop stuck out under the blanket so that it looked like the hair of a person sleeping in the bed. He then set up the motion detects, one at the entrance, and the another in the main bed room. The motion detector displayers he brought to the bedroom that was nearest to the main bedroom. It now was near midnight. The three sat quietly in the extras bedroom. It was about two o'clock when they heard a noise at the front door. Tom then went into the main bedroom and got into the clothes closet. John and Sam stayed just by the door of the bedroom they were in. It took about ten miutes before the gadget Ryan had unlocked the door. As soon as he entered the Motion monitor display in the extra bedroom started to flash. Soon the monitor that was in the main bedroom started to flash. John and the Sam then walked up to the main bedroom door. They hear Ryan speaking.

"So you think you were going to get away from me," said Ryan and lifted his gun to shot what he thought was Leon. John and Sam then entered the room turning on the bedroom light as they entered. Tom who had left the door partly open came out with is gun pointing at Ryan. Ryan was completely surprised. He turned around and faced John and Sam.

"You have three seconds to drop your gun," said John, three two." Before John could say one Ryan dropped his gun.

"Ryan Harris," said John. "You are under arrest for the murder of Leon and his family. Officer Bruster, please handcuff and take Ryan to prison." John then using a plastic bag he always carried place the gun in it. Sam then went around the corner where he had parked his car out of sight. He drove to pick up Ryan. He then left to take Ryan to jail. John then turned to Tom.

"Listen Tom," said John. "I think I have all I need to put him in jail for life. If I need you during the trial I will call you. I am very grateful for all your help. I would not have done it without you. I never even dreamed of the aunt's grandson. Anyway I don't think you need to stay here any longer. Go get a good night's sleep and before you drive home don't forget to stop at the station and get you pay. If you ever need me, I will be available. I hope if I have another problem that you will be available." Tom then left, had a good night sleep, and got his pay check the next morning before going home to Fairlawn. He was surprised that he was given a thousand dollar extra as a bonus.

Tom got home in the afternoon. He felt good for the success he had for John. After dinner he went into his office to work on his book. He barely got started when he heard the Doorbell ring.

"Who could that be?" he said out loud. He answered the door.

"Vicki," said Tom. "What are you doing here? I thought you worked second shift until nine."

"I am on the regular shift now," said Vicki. "It changed at the end of the month."

"So what are you doing here?" repeated Tom.

"I think we have to talk," said Vicki.

"I don't think we have anything to talk about," said Tom.

"Oh Tom," said Vicki with a soft tone in her voice. "Please forgive me. Try to understand my position. Here is a very very beautiful television star. She is not only beautiful but very talented and intelligent. If you were in my position you would be just as jealousy. I'm sorry. I let jealousy blind my brain. It wasn't that I didn't trust you, it was that I didn't trust her. I was afraid that she would use everything she had to win you over. I love you so much that it shut down my brain. It wasn't that I didn't love you enough; the problem was that I loved you too much. I couldn't stand the thought that I might have lost you."

"I thought that if you really loved me you would have fought for me,' said Tom.

"I am fighting for you right now," said Vicki. "If you really loved me you would have fought for me. Where were you?"

"I was here waiting for you to omit that you were wrong," said Tom. "I want to hear that you will always trust me."

"I promise that I will trust you till I die," said Vicki. "I also remember something that I think you have forgotten. Do you know that you have never kissed me?"

""Before I consider doing that I have something that I have to get done that I have been putting off. I got to do it now. Just sit here. I will only be a minute." Tom then left and went upstairs to his bedroom. Soon he came down and walked up to Vicki. He went down on his knee. "Vicki," said Tom. "Will you marry me?" Vicki full of tears threw her arms around him.

Yes," she said hardly get it out with the lump in her throat. She had not expected this. Suddenly Tom kissed her. Their toughs found each other. They felt a joy they had never felt before. After a few miutes Tom pulled his lips from her lips.

"Is that a strong enough fight?" asked Tom.

"A few more kisses would do the job," said Vicki. Tom did as she asked.

"Is that enough?" asked Tom.

"It will never be enough," said Vicki. "However we could save some for later. May I ask you, when did you get the ring? Were you so sure that I would come to you to ask forgiveness?"

"I got the ring just before you went to Columbus. I was going to ask you during the holidays.

"So when do you want to get married," asked Vicki.

"As soon as we can get a venue," said Tom.

The days that followed had both Tom and Vicki up in a cloud. They went by faster than they expected. Soon the wedding day came. Alex, Liana, Ellie, and Chris were all in the wedding party. Alex was the best man and Ellie was the maid of honor. Tom was in a haze the whole day. All he could remember was how beautiful Vicki was when she walked down the Aisle. The only other thing he remembered was the pastor saying "I now pronounce you husband a wife. He also remembered the kiss that made him feel like he was back in his family room kissing Vicki for the first time. The next thing he realized was that he was on the high way on the trip to Niagara Falls on his honeymoon. Vicki had never been to Niagara Falls. He extended his hand and grabbed hers. He suddenly remembered what Gina had told him. She said that it was destiny for Tom and Vicki together. She was so right. It was all God's plan. It was destiny.

The End

9 781961 017146